SHORT LINES

SHORT LINES

A Collection of Classic American Railroad Stories

EDITED BY ROB JOHNSON

ILLUSTRATED BY DON HAZLITT

BARNES & NOBLE BOOKS
NEW YORK

Illustrations by Don Hazlitt

This edition published by Barnes & Noble, Inc., by arrangement with Rob Johnson

2000 Barnes & Noble Books

ISBN 0-7607-2044-4

Printed and bound in the United States of America

00 01 02 03 04 MC 9 8 7 6 5 4 3 2 1

FG

CONTENTS

Contents

INTRODUCTION: THE GOLDEN AGE OF RAILROAD FICTION

FROM 1895 TO 1920, the influence of the railroad on the lives of Americans was at its height, and Americans not only rode the rails in unparalleled numbers, they were also eager to read stories about the mode of transportation which had changed their lives. The "railroad story" was a distinct, popular genre during these years. Railway fiction crowded the pages of magazines such as *McClure's*, *Scribner's*, and the *Saturday Evening Post*, and novels and short-story collections about the railroads were best-sellers with both adult and juvenile audiences. The genre was so popular around the turn of the century that the author of *The Virginian*, Owen Wister, felt the need to parody railroad fiction in a 1904 short story. Railroad historian Frank P. Donovan, Jr., has called this period the "golden age" of railroad fiction, but even as late as 1941 the editors of the *Saturday Evening Post* still reported a "clamor" by their readers for more railroad stories.

During these years, dozens of writers, mostly railroad men themselves, published exciting stories on all aspects of the rails—disasters, strikes, romances, Indian attacks, train robberies. The best of these writers included Frank Hamilton Spearman, Cy Warman, Frank Lucius Packard, A. W. Somerville, and Harry Bedwell, and although their names are now little-known even by literary historians, their work remains timeless reading for those interested in the heyday of rail travel and the development of the American West, or for those who enjoy first-class examples of American literary realism. As historian Donovan describes the railroad stories and their writers: "Railroad yarns are especially adaptable to the basic requirements of a short story. Because of their reliance on action—action plus characterization above everything else—the compact, swift-moving, down-to-business style of a brief story is desirable. Railroad men are essentially blunt, practical, frank, and honest; railroad stories are usually succinct, realistic, direct, and sincere."

The stories in this collection date from 1897 to 1941, and they feature some of the best work of the best railroad writers, as well as stories by their better-known contemporaries such as Frank Norris, Owen Wister, Jack London, O. Henry, Christopher Morley, and Thomas Wolfe. In Frank Spearman's classic story "The Nerve of Foley," an engineer breaks rank in a strike and drives his engine in the face of all threats. O. Henry relates a train robber's account of his exploits in "Holding Up a Train." In "Mrs. Union Station," Doug Welch shows how a man's obsession with model trains nearly ruins his marriage. An excerpt from Frank Norris's great railroad novel, *The Octopus*, dramatizes the turn-of-the-century conflict between railroad magnates and wheat farmers in California's Central Valley. Several stories recount rail disasters and disasters averted; other stories—of railroad eccentrics, railroad heroes, and railroad mysteries (based, of course, on "fact")—add to the body of railroad folklore.

They are particularly American stories in many respects. The American literary theme of man in conflict with nature underlies many stories: trains race through forest fires, round a bend to find a flash flood, and plow through deep snow. Road engineers challenge mountains and ravines with their track designs, defying nature's obstructions by laying down parallel lines across a resistant, chaotic landscape. The characteristic American faith in technology is evident in stories where, for example, "boomer" telegraph operators heroically avert disasters by sending their precise orders from lonely stations out hundreds of miles into the darkness. At the heart of many of the best of these stories is also a sense of mystery, ingrained in American literature since the first European settlers confronted America's vastness: The awesome landscape can trick and change from run to run; trains mysteriously disappear. And there is the implied mystery behind the motivation of these rootless men, who are most at home flying down the rails, the mystery of a settled nation whose desire is freedom and mobility, of always going farther and faster—but to where?

Railroad historian George H. Douglas recently wrote that "the railroad, more than any other form of transportation in this country, has left us a rich legacy of cultural artifacts." Almost all of the "artifacts" collected here are long out-of-print; but a unique quality of railroad fiction is that stylistically it has dated very little. Something about the discipline and precision of machinery found its way into the prose of this particular genre. Railroads and railroad stories are an excellent example of all things old becoming new again. As the American fascination with rail travel has returned, so, too, should these stories return—to their place in our literature.

Rob Johnson
The University of Texas–Pan American

ACKNOWLEDGMENTS

For their encouragement and help, the author would like to thank the following: Ronald Gottesman, Jay Martin, Steve Badrich, Bob and Sondra Johnson, Maurice and Charlene Carson, Diana and Dave Heath, Dominique Brousseau, Gavin Schulz, Eric and Melissa Williamson, Jake Elwell, L. H. Packard, Jed Clauss, Donna Johnson, Dashiell Johnson, and the staff of the Harry Ransom Research Center at the University of Texas, Austin. This book is dedicated to Frank P. Donovan, Jr., railroad literature's greatest fan.

SMART BOOMER

HARRY BEDWELL

EDDIE SAND, slightly battered, came into the chief dispatcher's office at Little Grande, moving like a cat in a strange backyard, on the prowl, cautiously belligerent. Passenger conductors on the west end of the Anaconda Short Line hadn't been obliging with free rides on the cushions, and freight skippers and their enginemen had threatened him with violence when asked for a lift in cab or caboose. This lack of tact was a rare and humiliating experience to a young veteran of the iron highway on tour. A rambler was entitled to the courtesies of the rail when a crew was all hitched up and going his way. He had covertly ridden anyhow, but it hadn't been clean or comfortable. He was therefore resentful and punitive, and he had paused to retaliate.

Updike, the chief, looked at him once, a quick, sardonic flick of shrewd eyes. There was considerable slim length to Eddie, and the glint of red in his hair might mean something. Updike placed him at once as a boomer telegraph operator, that restless breed of railroaders that is always going someplace else. Lately, the drifters hadn't strayed to the High Desert Division. The crews had discouraged that emphatically. They hadn't succeeded with this one, but his disheveled appearance showed that he'd come the hard way.

Updike considered craftily. He needed another operator of just the right sort, but it wasn't likely this boomer would do. The west end was at the time involved in too much grief to add to it an equivocal, benighted casual. Yet that long string bean might be the answer to his impious prayers. His nod invited Eddie to wait.

The low sun thrust bars of hard light into the long room. A dozen telegraph instruments chanted a frantic cadence. Preoccupied operators sprawled before typewriters, swiftly punching out messages with indolent indifference. The trick dispatcher brooded over his train sheet at his narrow table. Train and enginemen of a freight crew wrangled morbidly over their report of a mishap that had befallen them on the run just completed. The yardmaster shambled in to verify the makeup of an impending hotshot.

Eddie Sand took a tattered book from his pocket and sat down on the bench by the railing. He started in reading with grim tranquillity.

Conover, the engineer of the freight crew, disengaged his stubborn mind from a deliberate study of their accident report, written by the conductor and contributed to by the glib observations of the other four, and scowled to himself.

"Seems to me we had only one mischance," he grumbled, "but this account of it sounds like there'd been a dozen." He breathed heavily. "I hope it sticks."

His baffled glance fell on Eddie and frosted. His large face puckered under the stress of vinegarish reflections. These produced an expression the cross between an impending sneeze and a cordial distaste of something he'd eaten. He seized his conductor by the arm and pointed. Inarticulate sounds became plaintive words.

"Ain't that the brass pounder what caused us this grief?" he pleaded.

Conductor Allen stared, then scrutinized. "Yes," he said, and wheeled on his two brakemen. "Did you let that smart boomer ride with us, after all?" he demanded.

The two shacks denied it with hot indignation. "We left that guy at Felicity," the hind man declared. "I saw him when we pulled out."

"Yeah," stormed Allen, "but he couldn't have come in with anybody else and be here now."

"Listen, Chief," Conover implored, "this is the tramp lightning slinger what caused our accident. We turned him down when he asked us for a ride. Then he sneaked aboard anyhow. But the joke was on him," the hogger brightened, "because we set out the car he was ridin' in at Felicity, and when I saw him unload there I heaved coal at him. I let the engine drift while I was so engaged. Which is when it cornered the boxcar what hadn't cleared on the house track."

"What joke was on who?" Updike inquired acidly.

The crews were dubious and resentful of smart boomers. The brittle and hard-bitten drifters knew train-operation rules and were obstinate about applying them. During a protracted period of disorganization, these mountain men had tossed the book away. Like spirited horses given a slack line, they'd run off with this outfit if not checked and disciplined. Now that a new set of officials rode the swivel chairs, they wanted no intruder on the line who might throw in with the brass hats.

Updike knew the answer. The men should have their ears bent forward. But not knocked down. You couldn't blast that organization without destroying it. These men were rough and tough, but competent. There hadn't yet been any definite adjustments between them and Stewart, the new division superintendent sent from the East, but a decisive understanding was rapidly approaching. When it came it would be abrupt. Stewart was the kind of official who would likely dynamite. Updike, bushy and gray and wily, was trying to contrive a balance. He studied Eddie Sand covertly.

Conover muttered, "It's funny what rubble the chief allows to clutter up his office." He glared at the boomer.

The hogger bulged from his straining overalls, but Updike knew he was as hard as nails. Conover couldn't endure a day without eight meals and snacks. Usually he boiled with energy. But he was inclined to relax heavily after a bulk of victuals. From the way certain incidents had occurred out on the line, Updike suspected that the engineer napped in his cab while running. Authority had been that badly shot.

Billy Lomax, the fireman, chanted, "Run him through the wringer and see what comes out."

Updike wasn't amused. Billy waggled with delight at anything these old railbenders did. Just a dumb kid come down out of the mountains to put on his first pair of shoes and go to work for the railroad.

The chief gave the studious boomer a cautious glance. Eddie was apparently absorbed in his book, oblivious of the ribbing. But the raucous tones were meant to be overheard, and he couldn't have missed the remarks. His lack of resentment was disappointing.

A breathless switchman thrust his head in at the doorway and his roving eye speared the yardmaster.

"Hey," he sputtered, "what do we do with that car of hogs Seventy-six brought in?"

The yardmaster ruminated. "Hogs?" he said.

A quiet, penetrating voice interrupted his cogitations. It slithered through the room above the chatter of the sounders. "I'd say to switch 'em down to the yard office and have somebody take the hogs' brains out," the voice remarked. "That way they make good enginemen and fair conductors. Better than most."

It sounded ventriloquial, coming from the boomer's impassive lips. He didn't raise his head from his book. Everybody stared about for the origin of the observation. Then vindictive eyes began to center on Eddie. He read on placidly.

The silence thickened. A locomotive hooted derisively down in the yard.

Updike spun in his swivel chair. "Did you want to see me?" he asked Eddie abruptly.

Eddie marked his book with a burnt match. Updike liked the way he got his feet under him. The tinge of red in his hair seemed charged with hostile voltage. The set of his head was slightly arrogant. You got that way when you'd mastered your craft.

"Need a good telegraph operator?" Eddie inquired briefly.

Durban, the trick dispatcher, snickered. Updike quelled him with a sharp look. Durban wasn't certain how he might come out of the impending shake-up. Meanwhile, he was trying to throw in with the crews.

Eddie lifted an eyebrow. "Does it sound funny to you when a good operator asks to go to work for this outfit?" he asked.

The trick man turned pink.

"I've got a job for you," said the chief, "if you're used to obeying rules and orders."

"That's what they're made for," Eddie said.

Updike flicked him another glance and slid a ten-dollar bill across the counter. "Till payday," he remarked.

Eddie's eyes became bleak. "I'll get by," he said.

Conover moaned. "If he takes that tenspot, Chief," he protested, "he'll spend it on a bender, and you'll never see him again."

Eddie smiled at the hogger. "Mebby not," he decided, and picked up the money.

That didn't create any fraternal feeling for Eddie on the west end. The division was immediately assured that he was a brass-hats man, and the crews were as subtle as a sledge in showing him that they thought so. They tried ways to break him down, but they found at once that he knew the book and was intolerant of operating frauds within his jurisdiction.

Conover encountered this first at Sulphur, where Updike sent Eddie as relief night operator.

Conover was coming west that night on Extra 3814, and Eddie had an order for him, giving him more time on Nine. Just before reaching Sulphur, the engineer absorbed four thick sandwiches within a mile and an eighth, and was relaxing as he approached the station.

When the headlight showed, Eddie got out on the platform with his lantern and copies of the order clipped to hoops, ready to hand them up to the engine and the caboose as they went by. His order board was red, and as the extra approached he swung his lantern in a highball, notice to the engineer that he had an order that would clear the board.

But Conover didn't reply to his sign, and he didn't check his speed. Eddie considered he was being hardmouthed, just to show him he didn't have to go through the routine of signals the book prescribed. But the engineer should have eased up a little. It was slightly dangerous to stand close to a speeding engine and deliver an order on the fly.

When the locomotive blasted down on him, Eddie stepped in and held up the order hoop with his lantern alongside to mark it. There was a sucking breath of hot oil and steam, and cinder dust whipped into his face. The engine slammed past. But no one snatched the hoop.

Eddie glimpsed Conover leaning on the armrest at the window, his head bobbing on his chest, oblivious of the proffered hoop. The head end had missed the order.

Boomers get about, and he knew the answer to that one. He began to swing his lantern in a washout as the taillight on the caboose swam toward him.

The brakeman was on the rear step ready to snatch the order, but Eddie didn't offer it.

The trainman yelled profanity as he whiffed by. Then he darted up the steps and pulled the air on his engineer. The brakes went on with a wham, and the line of wheels sparked as the shoes grabbed.

The train stopped a half mile out of town, then backed into the station to pick up the order.

Conover and Allen conferred outside, then stormed into the office.

"Listen, smart boomer!" Conover yelled. "Don't you know enough to deliver the order to the caboose when we miss it on the head end?"

"It don't say so in my book," Eddie said softly. "Mebby, when there's an attempt to grab it from the engine, and it's not an order full of dynamite. But when nobody even tries to get it from the cab, then something's haywire, and I pass."

"My dumb fireman didn't wake up that we was coming to the station," Conover raved, "and he wasn't out on the step to snare it. You want to get the kid in trouble?"

"If you'd whistle for the board," Eddie suggested, "and answer lantern signals, your fireman'd know where he was at."

Conover stamped back to his engine and hooted out of town.

Eddied OSed Extra 3814 to the dispatcher, in and out, and Durban shot back at him: "How come he had to stop there?"

"The head end missed the order, and he had to come back and get it," Eddie told him.

"I'll bet you were asleep and didn't get out in time to catch the head end," Durban made the sounder snap.

"You turn it in any way you think you ought to," Eddie gave him cheerful permission.

Durban did report it as a possibility. And Conover raised his voice at headquarters and said more than he intended.

Neff, the new trainmaster, got a confused notion of the incident, and had them all into his office for questioning. Nobody was much concerned about Fussy Neff. Conover could talk louder and more glibly than the trainmaster. Billy Lomax, the fireman, in confusion and juvenile loyalty, got the blame and ten brownies. Eddie answered only what he was asked and got twenty brownies and ominous words of warning from Neff.

Updike, who had sat in as an observer, caught Eddie in the hall after it was over.

"I guess Neff forgot to ask you, did Conover pass you any signals as he approached your station?" The chief made it an interrogation.

Eddie considered. "He didn't ask about that, did he?" he remarked.

Updike eyed him sharply. "Durban turned you in as being asleep on duty," the chief warned.

"Yeah," said Eddie; "he told me he was going to."

Updike was slightly exasperated. He had a suspicion of what had actually occurred and he wanted the truth brought out. But he decided he'd better not crowd the boomer. "You are through at Sulphur tomorrow," he said, "and then I'm sending you to Pyramid."

"Okay," said Eddie.

He might have taken that as a rebuke and a punishment. Pyramid consisted of a station, a semaphore, and a passing track, overhung on the east by lonely Pyramid Peak, and threatened by drifting sand dunes from the west. The remainder was flat and vacant desert. Not a thing else, save when a train roared by. None of them stopped, except to take siding to let an opposing schedule by. A one-man day job, with a call bell which the dispatcher could ring with selectors if he wanted the operator when off duty at night. You'd get to talking to yourself in time.

But Eddie could get along with himself. He read a good deal in the office at night, the telegraph instruments on the long table beside him babbling of the traffic on the high iron; and even as he read, the telegrapher's part of his mind absorbed from the chatter what was moving on the division.

That night, he knew that Conover was coming west on a banana special, thirty refrigerator cars, a light hotshot that would be rambling fast.

On the other side, Ninety-two was slogging up the grade, a doubleheader with a hundred loads. The helper engine would be cut off at Highpoint. It was mostly downhill from there, and one engine could handle her, with luck.

Then Conover ran some hot journal boxes, because he was wheeling them too fast, and he was badly delayed. Durban was raving at him and at all the other crews out on the division, when Eddie blew out the lamp and went to bed.

At 10:50 he was torn from sleep by the dispatcher ringing his call bell. That mad sound clamored through the dead quiet of the desert like an alarm. Eddie fell out of bed and stumbled blindly through the kitchen into the office. He shut off the bell and lit the lamp and answered the wire. Durban was in a tearing hurry.

"Is the banana special in sight?" He made the sounder storm.

Eddie made a sleepy "No."

"Take an order for him," Durban snapped, and began to send it.

Eddie stopped him by opening the key. This was coming too fast when you'd just been jarred out of sound sleep. You don't take chances when the trains are rambling. The close ones have made you cautious.

"Wait a minute while I listen for him," he sent back.

Durban made the sounder yell. "I've got Ninety-two at Highpoint all set to go. You're holding him up."

But Eddie went out into the crisp starlight. There wasn't even a breeze, and the silence was so clear it tingled. The thin air bit through his pajamas like acid. A faint glow spilled over a shoulder of Pyramid Peak. The sibilant far whisper of an exhaust crawled along the mountainside. You got a feeling of unleashed, thundering power from that creeping purr. He went back to his key.

"Yeah," he sent, "he's coming."

Durban rushed into the order, but Eddie checked him again.

"Wait till I get a light in my order board," he said.

Durban boiled over. "You're holding up Ninety-two," he chattered. "You railroad like an old hen. You can put up your light after you repeat the order. He's not that near."

"It don't read like that in my book," Eddie answered him.

"Smart boomer!" Durban raved. "You'll tell the chief about this delay."

But when Conover was riding the line, you had to get all set for him. Eddie put up the semaphore and lit the light. He fired his lantern and got out a fusee and two track torpedoes and laid them on the table. Then he told Durban to go ahead with the order.

The dispatcher tore it off like ripping a rag. It changed the meeting point between Ninety-two and the hotshot from Highpoint to Pyramid, and when the two operators had repeated it, Durban told Highpoint to tell Ninety-two that he'd have the special in the clear for him at Pyramid so he wouldn't have to slow for the short grade beyond the station. Then he instructed Eddie to head the hotshot into the passing track.

Eddie considered the whole setup as slightly slippery. Durban had somehow overlooked his hand in not changing the meeting point of the two trains farther down the line, when it wouldn't have delayed either of them. That had in turn caused him to go out on a limb now, telling Ninety-two that the main line through Pyramid would be clear for him. The engineer would take Durban's word for it, but a dispatcher can't always make things come to pass a hundred miles from headquarters.

Presently the concussions of Conover's blaring stack climbed high on the Pyramid. Eddie took up his lantern and the fusee, dropped the two track guns into his pajama pocket and went out onto the platform.

The headlight of the banana special moved along the mountain wall beyond the last ridge. The roll of her exhaust beat against the stars. Conover had her latched out. Then the headlight moved into sight.

The hogger didn't shut off when he tipped the rise and swung down the grade toward the station. And he didn't give any sign that he saw the red light in the semaphore against him as he approached. He wouldn't be expecting Pyramid to be open at this time of night, but he should be alert to everything ahead. Eddie began to swing his lantern. Conover didn't check or answer.

Eddie got a chill in the back of his neck that didn't come from the atmosphere. He tore off the cap of the fusee and scratched it alight. He stuck the wire point into a tie as the red light inflated into a misty balloon. But the engineer didn't acknowledge it, and the exhaust didn't ease.

Then Eddie caught the low moan of a whistle to the west, and

Ninety-two's headlight flourished in a bright halo over the dunes. He could tell by the way it swept the arc of a curve that the engineer was pouring it on so as to make the short grade the hotshot was now descending. The chill in the back of his neck slid down the length of his back. This was going to be tight.

He squinted in the stab of light from the hotshot. Conover might have loosely thought, at sight of the board against him and the lantern on the platform, that Eddie had an order for him that would clear the signal. But he couldn't miss the peremptory fusee if he had half an eye ahead. It bloomed like a bonfire.

Ninety-two's whistle shrieked in again above the roar of the hotshot. The yell of it ruffled the air under his ears and made them stand out. He fumbled the track torpedoes from his pocket as he stretched out in a long-legged gallop to meet the plunging special. He lost a bedroom slipper at the second jump. But that call from the freight train behind him was like a typhoon that caught his extended ears and shoved him forward as if they'd been sails. He didn't pause to recover his footgear. The other slipper slid about on his foot and hampered him. He kicked it off as he ran. He dug his bare feet into the cinders and held his breath and stepped up his speed.

You can't judge accurately the speed and distance of an approaching train when you are sprinting to meet it with the headlight in your eyes. He cut it fine. He was near to a collision with her when he stopped in a skid. He stooped and clamped one of the track torpedoes to the rail. He'd barely ducked clear of the main line when the locomotive whiffed past him. The torpedo went off with an explosion that tore across the flats and dunes like a banshee.

Time got lost somewhere in the high desert while the refrigerator cars clattered by, and Eddie, strangling on thin dust, stood and waited for the blast of the torpedo to jar Conover out of his heedlessness. Then compressed air sizzled. The brake shoes grabbed, and the line of rolling wheels was ringed with fire. The cars locked and bucked like wild steers.

He crammed air into his lungs and watched the taillight soar at him. He ran with the convulsing cars and snatched at the rear-end grab iron when it arrived in the dark. The iron scorched his hands as they slid up the curve of the grab, and his bare feet stung as they slapped on the bottom step of the caboose. The brakeman had

"You can't judge accurately the speed and distance of an approaching train when you are sprinting to meet it with the headlight in your eyes."

slammed out the rear door. He goggled at the spectacle in pajamas that was cast up from the smoking dust.

"Get your train in the clear!" Eddie yelled. "Ninety-two's coming close and expects to find you on the siding!"

The station platform swam under him and he dropped off. The special grumbled on, slowing to the stubborn clamp of shoes. The brakeman swung down at the passing-track switch, and the green light on the stand flared red as he pushed the handle over. His lantern cut streaks in the dark as he signaled his engineer to back up. He'd seen the flow of Ninety-two's headlight over the near dunes.

The hotshot grunted to a stop. The desert silence throbbed at the temples. Then the air pump hammered as it fought for pressure to release the clamped shoes. Air sneezed at last and the reluctant brakes slackened. Draw-heads mumbled as the engine stamped hard in reverse. The taillights on the caboose bobbed and crawled back toward the siding.

Ninety-two's headlight blinked into sight like a damp moon. Above the slow blasts of the hotshot's stack you could hear the churn of the long freight's exhaust. The engineer was wheeling those hundred cars to make the short grade out of the station.

With the hotshot's headlight stabbing him in the face, Ninety-two's engineer should by the rules have brought his train under control immediately. But they'd thrown the book away on the west end. Time got lost in the solitude again while Eddie waited for a sign that he'd checked. He knew why the hogger didn't, what he was considering. The dispatcher had told him the special would be in the clear. If events disproved what Durban had prophesied, that would be up to him to explain. The hotshot had for some reason come up the main line to back into the passing track, instead of heading in. She was still showing her headlight, so she hadn't cleared. But, on the word of Durban, she certainly would before he got to her. If he checked all those hundred trailing cars too much, he'd have to double the hump. The sound of her exhaust eased, but he didn't touch the brake-valve handle.

Conover worked his engine with a sure, hard hand. He didn't fumble. He didn't slip a driver as he picked up his short train and shoved it back through the open switch. He knew the exact ounce of power she'd take. The engine didn't falter as Ninety-two snaked at them. The bark of the stack multiplied and deepened to a savage roar.

You couldn't stop the rolling string of a hundred loads on that grade by wishing. But Eddie tried, standing on the platform shivering in pajamas and bare feet. He didn't realize exactly when Conover had begun to screech his whistle. The racket of it was just an added note to the rest of the clamor. But immediately thin spurts of fire flickered for the length of Ninety-two as the engineer at last gently touched the brake-valve handle. He had come in close before he realized it, with the hotshot's headlight blinding him, and now he had to fight to keep off the special's head end.

Time didn't register, but Ninety-two had suddenly eaten up the gap between the two trains. The hundred freight cars crowded and jostled the engine, nudging her jovially, whining at the tightening restraint of brake shoes. The engineer couldn't give the lunging line a full emergency application without risk of throwing his train all over the desert. He had to juggle it, to check and check again with fingertip precision, hold them back and keep them on the rails.

The hotshot choked and stumbled once as Conover's exacting hand urged her too hard. Then the engine took up her smooth thunder again as she scrambled to avoid the lumbering avalanche at her pilot. She fought valiantly to be clear of the high iron. The beams of the two headlights dilated around the locomotives. Ninety-two inched up.

The brakeman was stooped over the switch stand, the handle in both hands, ready to flip the points over and separate the nuzzling pilots if the hotshot cleared. If she didn't, he'd be included among the resultant splinters.

The mountain men were rough and tough and headstrong, but they could handle their trains in an emergency, and they took the hazards as an item of the job. When they had to, they split the seconds to cram all the incidents into the fraction of time allowed to clear.

Eddie caught a shadowy movement at the switch stand. Ninety-two's headlight detached itself and stared at him as the engines broke apart. The engineer cracked his throttle at once. The big jack took up her deep belly laugh as the blast of the hotshot died. Draw-bars grunted and strained as the hogger shook out the slack. The whistle yelled once in high derision. Ninety-two roared past the station, storming for the grade. The hotshot subsided on the passing track.

Eddie uncurled his cold toes and grinned. "A very good performance," he decided, "but they'll throw the book at you for it."

UPDIKE REALIZED, with Stewart's abrupt summons next morning, that the superintendent was prepared to dynamite the participants in the affair at Pyramid. The Old Man was going to hold a hearing himself, and he was at last all set for a cleanup.

The chief had to do most of the listening at that ominous interview, but he managed a crafty suggestion. "That boomer operator," he offered. "He thinks fast on his feet, and he plays them close."

Stewart growled. "If he hadn't, we'd still be picking up the pieces. He's in the clear." Then he caught the allusive spark in the chief's eye, and he demanded suspiciously, "So what?"

"Smart boomers get around," the chief considered, "and they're hard to fool. He's in the clear, all right, but he could enlighten us a good deal on what actually happened, if you'd ask him. He won't lie, but he won't give you any more than you ask for."

Stewart said, "Yes?"

The hearing was as frigid and as noncommittal as the crews could make it. They realized that this was at last a showdown, and they held to a blind faith that they could cover up. Stewart had to chisel fragments of evidence from them with cold and biting steel.

There was a chance that the worst hadn't been proved when Eddie was called. The men studied him sullenly. He could line up with their tactics and likely save several jobs. But they'd always said he was a brass-hats man. They hoped now that they'd been wrong about that.

But Eddie began at once to show how right they'd been. For the first time that day Stewart got brisk and prompt replies to his volleyed questions. The operator neither hedged nor expanded. He stated. And his statements were damning to all concerned.

A thickening cloud of hopeless and resentful silence gathered among the men as the examination buzzed on endlessly.

The boomer was laying it all out there before the Old Man exactly as it had happened, without mitigation. He fitted the items together into a convincing picture that condemned them all. They'd known he'd do it, but they'd hoped to the last that he wouldn't.

Stewart dismissed him at last with an abrupt, "That's all."

The stunned quiet was stirred by the shifting of feet and the low mutter of sullen voices.

"Not quite."

The tranquil voice slithered through the grim murmurs. It sounded ventriloquial coming from the boomer's impassive lips. Eddie hadn't moved from his chair.

Stewart's clipped mustache bristled. "What's that?" he snapped.

"You haven't got it all yet," Eddie said. "Not like I saw it."

It didn't seem possible that silence could become more dense than it had been. It shut in like a vacuum. Stewart's metallic tone when he broke it made men flinch.

"There's something else?" he inquired ominously.

"Yeah," said Eddie. "There's a little more. I've been around, and I've seen men handle trains. Right now I'd say you'll seldom find a bunch on any man's railroad with the nerve to stick it through with sudden death and violent destruction only about six inches away. And I mean sudden death. Any one of them could have stepped back, or unloaded, and there'd have been a smash. They didn't do that. They all stuck and played up to each other and pulled it out without a scratch. Mebby you haven't been around much. Mebby you don't think that's extraordinary. But wait till the next time, with crews that don't know the mountains. If I hadn't known they'd stand by and pull it out of the fire, I'd be running yet, because I was close enough to be included in the pieces if Ninety-two had kissed the hotshot. That's all."

Eddie got down.

Stewart hesitated, and encountered Updike's bland eye. He knew now what the wily chief had been trying to show him. He had sensed hard faiths and alliances among these men that he hadn't encountered in operations on the prairies. Now he could credit their obstinate convictions and their loyalties for associates with whom they faced the daily hazards of mountain traffic. He was beginning to appreciate their mettle. He studied them briefly across his desk.

"I think," he said, "that we have now gone through the initial period of our association. From now on we are going to understand one another. Everything that has happened up to this moment is cleared from the record. It's all behind and forgotten. We start from scratch. Which is going to make it harder on anyone who so much as nicks the rules from here out. You will find I mean that literally. That's all."

The congestion at the doorway developed into a mild stampede to be out of that room.

Conover stopped Eddie in the hall by getting in his way.

"Look, boomer," he gulped. "If you think it took nerve to stick to the cab in the face of Ninety-two, I'll say it took a lot more to stand up to the Old Man the way you just now did."

Eddie grinned. "Take it easy, hogger," he advised.

Updike fell in beside him and steered him toward the dispatcher's office.

"Had enough of Pyramid?" the chief asked.

"Nearly," said Eddie.

"I've got a job for you in my office next," Updike suggested.

"I guess not," Eddie decided. "I just paused here to hand out some retribution to your crews for refusing to give me free transportation. I might come this way again, and I'd not want to have to sneak my rides. Pretty quick now I'll be shoving off."

"I was afraid of that," Updike sighed. "Boomers always move on or they wouldn't be boomers. But anytime you have some more of that rankling spirit, bring it back to the High Desert Division."

"Okay," said Eddie.

—1941

HOLDING UP A TRAIN

O. HENRY

NOTE: *The man who told me these things was for several years an outlaw in the Southwest and a follower of the pursuit he so frankly describes. His description of the* modus operandi *should prove interesting, his counsel of value to the potential passenger in some future "holdup," while his estimate of the pleasures of train robbing will hardly induce anyone to adopt it as a profession. I give the story in almost exactly his own words.*

O. H.

MOST PEOPLE WOULD SAY, if their opinion was asked for, that holding up a train would be a hard job. Well, it isn't; it's easy. I have contributed some to the uneasiness of railroads and the insomnia of express companies, and the most trouble I ever had about a holdup was in being swindled by unscrupulous people while spending the money I got. The danger wasn't anything to speak of, and we didn't mind the trouble.

One man has come pretty near robbing a train by himself; two have succeeded a few times; three can do it if they are hustlers; but five is about the right number. The time to do it and the place depend upon several things.

The first "stickup" I was ever in happened in 1890. Maybe the way I got into it will explain how most train robbers start in the business. Five out of six Western outlaws are just cowboys out of a job and gone wrong. The sixth is a tough from the East who dresses up like a bad man and plays some low-down trick that gives the boys a bad name. Wire fences and "nesters" made five of them; a bad heart made the sixth.

Jim S—— and I were working on the 101 Ranch in Colorado. The nesters had the cowman on the go. They had taken up the land and elected officers who were hard to get along with. Jim and I rode into La Junta one day, going south from a roundup. We were having a little fun without malice toward anybody when a farmer administration cut in and tried to harvest us. Jim shot a deputy marshal, and I kind of corroborated his side of the argument. We skirmished up and down the main street, the boomers having bad luck all the time. After a while we leaned forward and shoved for the ranch down on the Ceriso. We were riding a couple of horses that couldn't fly, but they could catch birds.

A few days after that, a gang of the La Junta boomers came to the ranch and wanted us to go back with them. Naturally, we declined. We had the house on them, and before we were done refusing, that old 'dobe was plumb full of lead. When dark came we fagged 'em a batch of bullets and shoved out the back door for the rocks. They sure smoked us as we went. We had to drift, which we did, and rounded up down in Oklahoma.

Well, there wasn't anything we could get there, and, being mighty hard up, we decided to transact a little business with the railroads. Jim and I joined forces with Tom and Ike Moore—two brothers who had plenty of sand they were willing to convert into dust. I can call their names, for both of them are dead. Tom was shot while robbing a bank in Arkansas; Ike was killed during the more dangerous pastime of attending a dance in the Creek Nation.

We selected a place on the Santa Fe where there was a bridge across a deep creek surrounded by heavy timber. All passenger trains took water at the tank close to one end of the bridge. It was a quiet place, the nearest house being five miles away. The day before it happened, we rested our horses and "made medicine" as to how we should get about it. Our plans were not at all elaborate, as none of us had ever engaged in a holdup before.

The Santa Fe flyer was due at the tank at 11:15 P.M. At eleven, Tom and I lay down on one side of the track, and Jim and Ike took the other. As the train rolled up, the headlight flashing far down the track and the steam hissing from the engine, I turned weak all over. I would have worked a whole year on the ranch for nothing to have been out of that affair right then. Some of the nerviest men in the business have told me that they felt the same way the first time.

The engine had hardly stopped when I jumped on the running board on one side, while Jim mounted the other. As soon as the engineer and fireman saw our guns they threw up their hands without being told, and begged us not to shoot, saying they would do anything we wanted them to.

"Hit the ground," I ordered, and they both jumped off. We drove them before us down the side of the train. While this was happening, Tom and Ike had been blazing away, one on each side of the train, yelling like Apaches, so as to keep the passengers herded in the cars. Some fellow stuck a little .22-caliber out one of the coach windows and fired it straight up in the air. I let drive and smashed the glass just over his head. That settled everything like resistance from that direction.

By this time all my nervousness was gone. I felt a kind of pleasant excitement as if I were at a dance or a frolic of some sort. The lights were all out in the coaches, and, as Tom and Ike gradually quit firing and yelling, it got to be almost as still as a graveyard. I remember hearing a little bird chirping in a bush at the side of the track, as if it were complaining at being waked up.

I made the fireman get a lantern, and then I went to the express car and yelled to the messenger to open up or get perforated. He slid the door back and stood in it with his hands up. "Jump overboard, son," I said, and he hit the dirt like a lump of lead. There were two safes in the car—a big one and a little one. By the way, I first located the messenger's arsenal—a double-barreled shotgun with buckshot cartridges and a .38 in a drawer. I drew the cartridges from the shotgun, pocketed the pistol, and called the messenger inside. I shoved my gun against his nose and put him to work. He couldn't open the big safe, but he did the little one. There was only nine hundred dollars in it. That was mighty small winnings for our trouble, so we decided to go through the passengers. We took our prisoners to the smoking car, and from there sent the engineer through the train to light up the coaches. Beginning with the first one, we placed a man at each door and ordered the passengers to stand between the seats with their hands up.

If you want to find out what cowards the majority of men are, all you have to do is rob a passenger train. I don't mean because they don't resist—I'll tell you later on why they can't do that—but it makes a man feel sorry for them the way they lose their heads. Big, burly drummers and farmers and ex-soldiers and high-collared dudes and sports that, a few moments before, were filling the car with noise and bragging, get so scared that their ears flop.

There were very few people in the day coaches at that time of night, so we made a slim haul until we got to the sleeper. The Pullman conductor met me at one door while Jim was going round to the other one. He very politely informed me that I could not go into that car, as it did not belong to the railroad company, and besides, the passengers had already been greatly disturbed by the shouting and firing. Never in all my life have I met a finer instance of official dignity and reliance upon the power of Mr. Pullman's great name. I jabbed my six-shooter so hard against Mr. Conductor's front that I afterward found one of his vest buttons so firmly wedged in the end of the barrel that I had to shoot it out. He just shut up like a weak-springed knife and rolled down the car steps.

I opened the door of the sleeper and stepped inside. A big, fat old man came wobbling up to me, puffing and blowing. He had one coat sleeve on and was trying to put his vest on over that. I don't know who he thought I was.

"Young man, young man," says he, "you must keep cool and not get excited. Above everything, keep cool."

"I can't," says I. "Excitement's just eating me up." And then I let out a yell and turned loose my .45 through the skylight.

That old man tried to dive into one of the lower berths, but a screech came out of it, and a bare foot that took him in the bread-basket and landed him on the floor. I saw Jim coming in the other door, and I hollered for everybody to climb out and line up.

They commenced to scramble down, and for a while we had a three-ringed circus. The men looked as frightened and tame as a lot of rabbits in a deep snow. They had on, on an average, about a quarter of a suit of clothes and one shoe apiece. One chap was sitting on the floor of the aisle, looking as if he were working a hard sum in arithmetic. He was trying, very solemn, to pull a lady's number-two shoe on his number-nine foot.

The ladies didn't stop to dress. They were so curious to see a real, live train robber, bless 'em, that they just wrapped blankets and sheets around themselves and came out, squeaky and fidgety-looking. They always show more curiosity and sand than the men do.

We got them all lined up and pretty quiet, and I went through the bunch. I found very little on them—I mean in the way of valuables. One man in the line was a sight. He was one of those big, overgrown, solemn snoozers that sits on the platform at lectures and looks wise. Before crawling out he had managed to put on his long, frock-tailed coat and his high silk hat. The rest of him was nothing but pajamas and bunions. When I dug into that Prince Albert, I expected to drag out at least a block of gold-mine stock or an armful of government bonds, but all I found was a little boy's French harp about four inches long. What it was there for, I don't know. I felt a little mad because he had fooled me so. I stuck the harp up against his mouth.

"If you can't pay—play," I says.

"I can't play," says he.

"Then learn right off quick," says I, letting him smell the end of my gun barrel.

He caught hold of the harp, turned red as a beet, and commenced to blow. He blew a dinky little tune I remembered hearing when I was a kid:

Prettiest little gal in the country—oh!
Mammy and Daddy told me so.

I made him keep on playing it all the time we were in the car. Now and then he'd get weak and off the key, and I'd turn my gun on him and ask what was the matter with that little gal, and whether he had any intention of going back on her, which would make him start up again like sixty. I think that old boy standing there in his silk hat and bare feet, playing his little French harp, was the funniest sight I ever saw. One little redheaded woman in the line broke out laughing at him. You could have heard her in the next car.

Then Jim held them steady while I searched the berths. I grappled around in those beds and filled a pillowcase with the strangest assortment of stuff you ever saw. Now and then I'd come across a little popgun pistol, just about right for plugging teeth with, which I'd throw out the window. When I finished with the collection, I dumped the pillowcase load in the middle of the aisle. There were a good many watches, bracelets, rings, and pocketbooks, with a sprinkling of false teeth, whiskey flasks, face-powder boxes, chocolate caramels, and heads of hair of various colors and lengths. There were also about a dozen ladies' stockings into which jewelry, watches, and rolls of bills had been stuffed and then wadded up tight and stuck under the mattresses. I offered to return what I called the "scalps," saying that we were not Indians on the warpath, but none of the ladies seemed to know to whom the hair belonged.

One of the women—and a good-looker she was—wrapped in a striped blanket, saw me pick up one of the stockings that was pretty chunky and heavy about the toe, and she snapped out: "That's mine, sir. You're not in the business of robbing women, are you?"

Now as this was our first holdup, we hadn't agreed upon any code of ethics, so I hardly knew what to answer. But anyway, I replied: "Well, not as a specialty. If this contains your personal property you can have it back."

"It just does," she declared eagerly, and reached out her hand for it.

"You'll excuse my taking a look at the contents," I said, holding the stocking up by the toe. Out dumped a big gent's gold watch, worth two hundred, a gent's leather pocketbook that we afterward found to contain six hundred dollars, a .32-caliber revolver; and the only thing of the lot that could have been a lady's personal property was a silver bracelet worth about fifty cents.

I said: "Madam, here's your property," and handed her the bracelet. "Now," I went on, "how can you expect us to act square with you when you try to deceive us in this manner? I'm surprised at such conduct."

The young woman flushed up as if she had been caught doing something dishonest. Some other woman down the line called out: "The mean thing!" I never knew whether she meant the other lady or me.

When we finished our job we ordered everybody back to bed, told 'em good night very politely at the door, and left. We rode forty miles before daylight and then divided the stuff. Each one of us got $1,752.85 in money. We lumped the jewelry around. Then we scattered, each man for himself.

That was my first train robbery, and it was about as easily done as any of the ones that followed. But that was the last and only time I ever went through the passengers. I don't like that part of the business. Afterward I stuck strictly to the express car. During the next eight years I handled a good deal of money.

The best haul I made was just seven years after the first one. We found out about a train that was going to bring out a lot of money to pay off the soldiers at a government post. We stuck that train up in broad daylight. Five of us lay in the sand hills near a little station. Ten soldiers were guarding the money on the train, but they might just as well have been at home on a furlough. We didn't even allow them to stick their heads out the windows to see the fun. We had no trouble at all in getting the money, which was all in gold.

Of course, a big howl was raised at the time about the robbery. It was government stuff, and the government got sarcastic and wanted to know what the convoy of soldiers went along for. The only excuse given was that nobody was expecting an attack among those bare sand hills in daytime. I don't know what the government thought about the excuse, but I know that it was a good one. The surprise—that is the keynote of the train-robbing business. The papers published all kinds of stories about the loss, finally agreeing that it was between nine thousand and ten thousand dollars. The government sawed wood. Here are the correct figures, printed for the first time: forty-eight thousand dollars. If anybody will take the trouble to look over Uncle Sam's private accounts for that little debit to profit and loss, he will find that I am right to a cent.

By that time we were expert enough to know what to do. We rode due west twenty miles, making a trail that a Broadway policeman could have followed, and then we doubled back, hiding our tracks. On the second night after the holdup, while posses were scouring the country in every direction, Jim and I were eating supper in the second story of a friend's house in the town where the alarm started from. Our friend pointed out to us, in an office across the street, a printing press at work striking off handbills offering a reward for our capture.

I have been asked what we do with the money we get. Well, I never could account for a tenth part of it after it was spent. It goes fast and freely. An outlaw has to have a good many friends. A highly respected citizen may, and often does, get along with very few, but a man on the dodge has got to have "sidekickers." With angry posses and reward-hungry officers cutting out a hot trail for him, he must have a few places scattered about the country where he can stop and feed himself and his horse and get a few hours' sleep without having to keep both eyes open. When he makes a haul he feels like dropping some of the coin with these friends, and he does it liberally. Sometimes I have, at the end of a hasty visit at one of these havens of refuge, flung a handful of gold and bills into the laps of the kids playing on the floor, without knowing whether my contribution was a hundred dollars or a thousand.

When old-timers make a big haul they generally go far away to one of the big cities to spend their money. Green hands, however successful a holdup they make, nearly always give themselves away by showing too much money near the place where they got it.

I was in a job in '94 where we got twenty thousand dollars. We followed our favorite plan for a getaway—that is, doubled back on our trail—and lay low for a time near the scene of the train's bad luck. One morning I picked up a newspaper and read an article with big headlines stating that the marshal, with eight deputies and a posse of thirty armed citizens, had the train robbers surrounded in a mesquite thicket on the Cimarron, and that it was a question of only a few hours when they would be dead men or prisoners. While I was reading that article I was sitting at breakfast in one of the most elegant private residences in Washington City, with a flunky in knee-pants standing behind my chair. Jim was sitting across the table talking to his half uncle, a retired naval officer, whose name you have often seen in the accounts of doings in the capital. We had gone there and bought rattling outfits of good clothes, and were resting from our labors among the nabobs. We must have been killed in that mesquite thicket, for I can make an affidavit that we didn't surrender.

Now I propose to tell why it is easy to hold up a train, and then, why no one should ever do it.

In the first place, the attacking party has all the advantage. That is, of course, supposing that they are old-timers with the necessary experience and courage. They have the outside and are protected by the darkness, while the others are in the light, hemmed in to a small space, and exposed, the moment they show a head at a window or door, to the aim of a man who is a dead shot and who won't hesitate to shoot.

But, in my opinion, the main condition that makes train robbing easy is the element of *surprise* in connection with the imagination of the passengers. If you have ever seen a horse that has eaten locoweed you will understand what I mean when I say that the passengers get locoed. That horse gets the awfullest imagination on him in the world. You can't coax him to cross a little branch stream two feet wide. It looks as big to him as the Mississippi River. That's just the way with the passenger. He thinks there are a hundred men yelling and shooting outside, when maybe there are only two or three. And the muzzle of a .45 looks like the entrance to a tunnel. The passenger is all right, although he may do mean little tricks, like hiding a wad of money in his shoe and forgetting to dig up until you jostle his ribs some with the end of your six-shooter; but there's no harm in him.

As to the train crew, we never had any more trouble with them than if they had been so many sheep. I don't mean that they are cowards; I mean that they have got sense. They know they're not up against a bluff. It's the same way with the officers. I've seen Secret Service men, marshals, and railroad detectives fork over their change as meek as Moses. I saw one of the bravest marshals I ever knew hide his gun under his seat and dig up along with the rest while I was taking toll. He wasn't afraid; he simply knew that we had the drop on the whole outfit. Besides, many of those officers have families and they feel that they oughtn't to take chances; whereas death has no terrors for the man who holds up a train. He expects to get killed someday, and he generally does. My advice to you, if you should ever be in a holdup, is to line up with the cowards and save your bravery for an occasion when it may be of some benefit to you.

Another reason why officers are backward about mixing things with a train robber is a financial one. Every time there is a scrimmage and somebody gets killed, the officers lose money. If the train robber gets away they swear out a warrant against John Doe *et al.* and travel hundreds of miles and sign vouchers for thousands on the trail of the fugitives, and the government foots the bills. So, with them, it is a question of mileage rather than courage.

I will give one instance to support my statement that the surprise is the best card in playing for a holdup.

Along in '92 the Daltons were cutting out a hot trail for the officers down in the Cherokee Nation. Those were their lucky days, and they got so reckless and sandy, that they used to announce beforehand what job they were going to undertake. Once they gave it out that they were going to hold up the M. K. & T. flyer on a certain night at the station of Pryor Creek, in Indian Territory.

That night the railroad company got fifteen deputy marshals in Muscogee and put them on the train. Beside them they had fifty armed men, hid in the depot at Pryor Creek.

When the Katy Flyer pulled in, not a Dalton showed up. The next station was Adair, six miles away. When the train reached there, and the deputies were having a good time explaining what they would have done to the Dalton gang if they had turned up, all at once it sounded like an army firing outside. The conductor and brakeman came running into the car yelling, "Train robbers!"

Some of those deputies lit out of the door, hit the ground, and kept on running. Some of them hid their Winchesters under the seats. Two of them made a fight and were both killed.

It took the Daltons just ten minutes to capture the train and whip the escort. In twenty minutes more they robbed the express car of twenty-seven thousand dollars and made a clean getaway.

My opinion is that those deputies would have put up a stiff fight at Pryor Creek, where they were expecting trouble, but they were taken by surprise and "locoed" at Adair, just as the Daltons, who knew their business, expected they would.

I don't think I ought to close without giving some deductions from my experience of eight years "on the dodge." It doesn't pay to rob trains. Leaving out the question of right and morals, which I don't think I ought to tackle, there is very little to envy in the life of an outlaw. After a while money ceases to have any value in his eyes. He gets to looking upon the railroads and express companies as his bankers, and his six-shooter as a checkbook good for any amount. He throws away money right and left. Most of the time he is on the jump, riding day and night, and he lives so hard between times that he doesn't enjoy the taste of high life when he gets it. He knows that his time is bound to come to lose his life or liberty, and that the accuracy of his aim, the speed of his horse, and the fidelity of his "sider," are all that postpone the inevitable.

It isn't that he loses any sleep over danger from the officers of the law. In all my experience I never knew officers to attack a band of outlaws unless they outnumbered them at least three to one.

But the outlaw carries one thought constantly in his mind—and that is what makes him so sore against life, more than anything else—he knows where the marshals get their recruits of deputies. He knows that the majority of these upholders of the law were once lawbreakers, horse thieves, rustlers, highwaymen, and outlaws like himself, and that they gained their positions and immunity by turning state's evidence, by turning traitor and delivering up their comrades to imprisonment and death. He knows that someday—unless he is shot first—his Judas will set to work, the trap will be laid, and he will be the surprised instead of a surpriser at a stickup.

That is why the man who holds up trains picks his company with a thousand times the care with which a careful girl chooses a sweetheart. That is why he raises himself from his blanket of nights and listens to the tread of every horse's hoofs on the distant road. That is why he broods suspiciously for days upon a jesting remark or an unusual movement of a tried comrade, or the broken mutterings of his closest friend, sleeping by his side.

And it is one of the reasons why the train-robbing profession is not so pleasant a one as either of its collateral branches—politics or cornering the market.

—1916

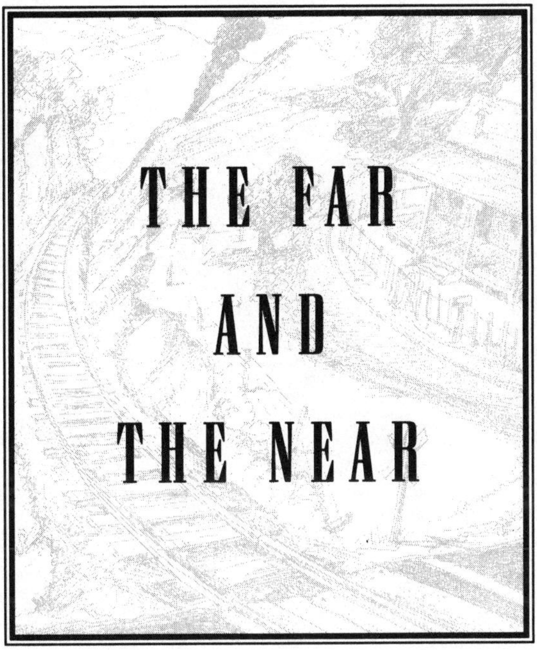

THE FAR AND THE NEAR

THOMAS WOLFE

ON THE OUTSKIRTS of a little town upon a rise of land that swept back from the railway there was a tidy little cottage of white boards, trimmed vividly with green blinds. To one side of the house there was a garden neatly patterned with plots of growing vegetables, and an arbor for the grapes which ripened late in August. Before the house there were three mighty oaks which sheltered it in their clean and massive shade in summer, and to the other side there was a border of gay flowers. The whole place had an air of tidiness, thrift, and modest comfort.

Every day, a few minutes after two o'clock in the afternoon, the limited express between two cities passed this spot. At that moment the great train, having halted for a breathing space at the town nearby, was beginning to lengthen evenly into its stroke, but it had not yet reached the full drive of its terrific speed. It swung into view deliberately, swept past with a powerful swaying motion of the engine, a low smooth rumble of its heavy cars upon pressed steel, and then it vanished in the cut. For a moment the progress of the engine could be marked by heavy bellowing puffs of smoke that burst at spaced intervals above the edges of the meadow grass, and finally nothing could be heard but the solid clacking tempo of the wheels receding into the drowsy stillness of the afternoon.

Every day for more than twenty years, as the train had approached this house, the engineer had blown on the whistle, and

“For a moment the progress of the engine could be marked by heavy bellowing puffs of smoke that burst at the spaced intervals above the edges of the meadow grass, and finally nothing could be heard but the solid clacking tempo of the wheels receding in the drowsy stillness of the afternoon.”

every day, as soon as she heard this signal, a woman had appeared on the back porch of the little house and waved to him. At first she had a small child clinging to her skirts, and now this child had grown to full womanhood, and every day she, too, came with her mother to the porch and waved.

The engineer had grown old and gray in service. He had driven his great train, loaded with its weight of lives, across the land ten thousand times. His own children had grown up and married, and four times he had seen before him on the tracks the ghastly dot of tragedy converging like a cannonball to its eclipse of horror at the boiler head—a light spring wagon filled with children, with its clustered row of small stunned faces; a cheap automobile stalled upon the tracks, set with the wooden figures of people paralyzed with fear; a battered hobo walking by the rail, too deaf and old to hear the whistle's warning; and a form flung past his window with a scream—all this the man had seen and known. He had known all the grief, the joy, the peril, and the labor such a man could know; he had grown seamed and weathered in his loyal service, and now, schooled by the qualities of faith and courage and humbleness that attended his labor, he had grown old, and had the grandeur and the wisdom these men have.

But no matter what peril or tragedy he had known, the vision of the little house and the women waving to him with a brave free motion of the arm had become fixed in the mind of the engineer as something beautiful and enduring, something beyond all change and ruin, and something that would always be the same, no matter what mishap, grief, or error might break the iron schedule of his days.

The sight of the little house and of these two women gave him the most extraordinary happiness he had ever known. He had seen them in a thousand lights, a hundred weathers. He had seen them through the harsh bare light of wintry gray across the brown and frosted stubble of the earth, and he had seen them again in the green luring sorcery of April.

He felt for them, and for the little house in which they lived, such tenderness as a man might feel for his own children, and at length the picture of their lives was carved so sharply in his heart that he felt that he knew their lives completely, to every hour and moment of the day, and he resolved that one day, when his years of service should be ended, he would go and find these people and speak at last with them whose lives had been so wrought into his own.

That day came. At last the engineer stepped from a train onto the station platform of the town where these two women lived. His years upon the rail had ended. He was a pensioned servant of his company, with no more work to do. The engineer walked slowly through the station and out into the streets of the town. Everything was as strange to him as if he had never seen this town before. As he walked on, his sense of bewilderment and confusion grew. Could this be the town he had passed ten thousand times? Were these the same houses he had seen so often from the high windows of his cab? It was all as unfamiliar, as disquieting, as a city in a dream, and the perplexity of his spirit increased as he went on.

Presently the houses thinned into the straggling outposts of the town, and the street faded into a country road—the one on which the women lived. And the man plodded on slowly in the heat and dust. At length he stood before the house he sought. He knew at once that he had found the proper place. He saw the lordly oaks before the house, the flower beds, the garden and the arbor, and farther off, the glint of rails.

Yes, this was the house he sought, the place he had passed so many times, the destination he had longed for with such happiness. But now that he had found it, now that he was here, why did his hand falter on the gate; why had the town, the road, the earth, the very entrance to this place he loved, turned unfamiliar as the landscape of some ugly dream? Why did he now feel this sense of confusion, doubt, and hopelessness?

At length he entered by the gate, walked slowly up the path, and in a moment more had mounted three short steps that led up to the porch and was knocking at the door. Presently he heard steps in the hall, the door was opened, and a woman stood facing him.

And instantly, with a sense of bitter loss and grief, he was sorry he had come. He knew at once that the woman who stood there looking at him with a mistrustful eye was the same woman who had waved to him so many thousand times. But her face was harsh and pinched and meager; the flesh sagged wearily in sallow folds, and the small eyes peered at him with timid suspicion and uneasy doubt. All the brave freedom, the warmth and the affection that he had read into her gesture, vanished in the moment that he saw her and heard her unfriendly tongue.

And now his own voice sounded unreal and ghastly to him as he tried to explain his presence, to tell her who he was and the reason he had come. But he faltered on, fighting stubbornly against the horror of regret, confusion, disbelief, that surged up in his spirit, drowning all his former joy and making his act of hope and tenderness seem shameful to him.

At length the woman invited him almost unwillingly into the house, and called her daughter in a harsh shrill voice. Then, for a brief agony of time, the man sat in an ugly little parlor, and he tried to talk while the two women stared at him with a dull, bewildered hostility, a sullen, timorous restraint.

And finally, stammering a crude farewell, he departed. He walked away down the path and then along the road toward town, and suddenly he knew that he was an old man. His heart, which had been brave and confident when it looked along the familiar vista of the rails, was now sick with doubt and horror as it saw the strange and unsuspected visage of an earth which had always been within a stone's throw of him, and which he had never seen or known. And he knew that all the magic of that bright lost way, the vista of that shining line, the imagined corner of that small good universe of hope's desire, was gone forever, could never be got back again.

—1935

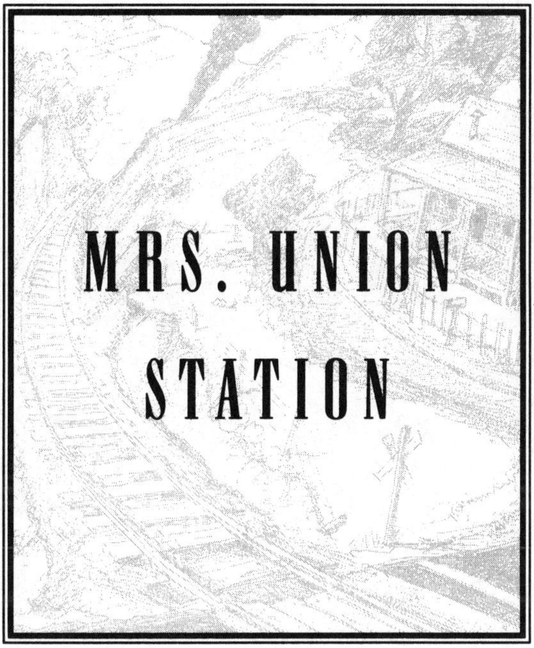

MRS. UNION STATION

DOUGLASS WELCH

WITH HIS WATCH in hand, and with an expression of vast displeasure on his usually placid face, John H. Alston, superintendent of the Lonely Valley Division of the Chicago, Omaha, Salt Lake & Pacific Railway, watched the locomotive and ten sleek cars of Number Six eastbound, otherwise known as the Hurricane, slowly thread their way into the Grand River station.

"Twenty-seven and a half minutes late," he informed Conductor A. L. Benson and the world in general. "What the hell do you think you're running? A streetcar?"

"We had trouble up the line," said Conductor Benson softly, with the prim satisfaction of a man who has a perfectly valid excuse.

"What kind of trouble?"

"A woman passenger pulled the air on us."

"I don't believe it," said Superintendent Alston flatly. "I don't believe there is a woman anywhere in the world who knows how to pull the air on a train."

"That's what I thought," said Conductor Benson. "But I found out."

"If she was here," said Superintendent Alston, brightening at the thought, "I would punch her right square in the nose."

"Oh, no, you wouldn't," said Conductor Benson dreamily. "Not this little pretty, you wouldn't!"

"Here we spend a million bucks to cut the running time over our division by twenty-one minutes," said Superintendent Alston, "and then some Jane with a two-dollar ticket pulls the air on us because she forgot to turn off the gas heater or leave a note for the milkman, I suppose."

"It's a very sad story," said Conductor Benson, "and it will take me some time to tell it."

"Well, we missed our connections here with the Dixie Mail," said Superintendent Alston, "so you can just come into my office and dictate your story to my stenographer, and I will let you do the explaining to the general manager's office instead of me."

A YOUNG WOMAN passenger [dictated Conductor Benson] pulled the air on us at Junction at 12:19 P.M. today, and pretty near stood the train on end. She got on at Salsburg only about nine minutes before. We have a slow order over the P. B. & T. crossover at Junction, and we were approaching this crossover at greatly reduced speed—I would say not faster than eight miles an hour—when this young pretty makes an emergency application from the rear parlor car. We stop with a hard jolt, but we don't pull any draw-bars and we don't slide the wheels much. Engineer John Hadley claims he finds a flat on one of his drivers as big as a dot, and he comes back and says he is going to spank this passenger personally, right now. He even starts toward one of the Pullmans to borrow a hairbrush, but the passenger begins to cry, so he doesn't. I wouldn't have let him, anyway, on account of our slogan, The Passenger Is Always Right, Except When He Doesn't Have His Fare. We are delayed twenty-four minutes at Junction while we look the train over. A couple of passengers took headers in the aisle, but nobody was really hurt.

The young pretty who makes this emergency application is a Mrs. Steven Applebee, of 4531 Wandon Drive, Salsburg, and although she wants to get off the train at Junction, I make her stay aboard until we reach Central City. We don't usually make Central City on this run, but after I hear the little lady's story, I figure it will be all right with the company if we let her off, so she can grab Number Eleven back to Salsburg. She is a very fetching little package, this

Mrs. Applebee, and she is practically up to her ears in trouble if she don't catch Number Eleven.

I ask this pretty how she knows where the emergency air valve is located on the parlor car, and she says her husband is a model-railway fan, and she knows where everything is, including the patch on the fireman's jumper.

"But, madam," I say, "don't you know that when you make an emergency application from the back of a train, you are liable to break that train right in half, and also maybe flatten every wheel?"

"Certainly I know it," she replies, "but I wanted to get off."

There is a fellow in the car who tries to break in to the conversation a couple of times, and she says to him: "Go away. I don't ever want to see you again. You are hateful."

"But, Helene," he protests, "what have I done?"

"You are a wolf in sheep's clothing."

This surprises me greatly, because he is only wearing a double-breasted blue serge suit. Well, the passenger begins to cry again, so I take her into an unoccupied compartment in the Chicago sleeper, and she tells me the whole story. This is a very sad story, and I practically have my handkerchief out a couple of times, and I will not omit any of the details, because I think it will help explain the frame of mind of a pretty who makes an emergency application on a fine train like Number Six.

"HAVE I MENTIONED that she is a very classy looking little doll?" asked Conductor Benson.

"You haven't been talking about anything else," said Superintendent Alston. "Go on!"

WELL, THIS MRS. APPLEBEE [continued Conductor Benson] is not what you call the thinking type, but she is certainly a choice piece of scenery, equal to anything we have got on the Mountain or Coast Divisions. She is a cuddly little pretty with great big eyes, and she is very innocent and trusting.

"I am going to tell you everything," she says, "because you have a kind face. And if you don't let me off this train pretty soon, the line will be responsible for breaking up a family, and I know it doesn't want to be pointed out as a home wrecker."

"I should say not," I reply, "because we always advertise as 'The Family Line.' "

Well, it seems like this Mrs. Applebee has been married about a year, and her husband is a salesman. He is also a model-railway fan, but she never suspected it until after they were engaged. She says love must have made her blind. She says being married to a model-railway fan is a very terrible thing, and there isn't anything you can do for it except take an occasional headache tablet.

It seems like before they are married, her husband—his name is Steve—drives her every evening to a spot on Ransom Hill where there is a first-rate view of the Salsburg depot and the lower yards, and also the city dump. At first she thinks he only goes there because it is a quiet place to park. But it seems like very often, right in the middle of a pretty speech, he pulls out his watch and says: "It's just about time for the 7:23." And even while he is holding her hand he counts the cars on the 7:23, and if there is an extra diner or a private car, he can't talk about anything else the rest of the night.

She says he also takes her to all the moving pictures which have trains in them. And after the show, maybe she says: "I don't think that girl is much of an actress." But he says: "Yes, but did you see that big articulated 2884 Northern Pacific freight locomotive?" And once, she has to sit through a double bill twice, so he can get a second look at the inside of a Wabash signal tower.

Well, before the wedding he spends two solid weeks reading timetables. They are going to New York City on their honeymoon. And on the afternoon of the wedding, the best man says to him: "Now, there isn't anything to be nervous about." And Steve says: "I'm worried about those connections in Chicago. Maybe I ought to have taken the Baltimore and Ohio."

Well, the ceremony is over, and they get aboard our train, and they are pulling out of Salsburg. Mrs. Applebee reaches over and pats his hand. "And now I belong to you, Steve, dear," she says. "I am your own little Helene and I don't belong to anybody else."

But he is looking out the window at a switch engine, and he says: "I can tell one of those a mile away."

"One of what, dear?"

"That goat," he says. "That yard hog. It's a rebuilt job. Used to be a road engine once. You can tell by the big boiler and the firebox. They've put small drivers under her, but she still has a road engine's lines."

"Well, that's very nice, dear, I am sure," she says.

"HE MUST HAVE seen old 768," commented Superintendent Alston. "She's a fine old engine. Yes sir, a fine engine."

"Yes," said Conductor Benson, "but listen."

IT TAKES THEM about four days to get to New York City [said Conductor Benson] because they don't stay on one road more than a couple of hours or so. I can hardly believe it, but Mrs. Applebee tells me they use our line to Chicago, and then go to New York by way of the New York Central, the Pennsylvania, the Nickel Plate, and the Lackawanna. She thinks they are also in the Erie, too, but it is late at night. Anyway, they get on and off trains so many times that she begins to feel like they are being followed by someone.

"Are you sure, Steve dear," she asks, "that we aren't running away from something?"

"No, lovey-dovey," he says; "as long as I am in this part of the country, I want to see as much as possible of the railroads and their equipment."

And another day, when they have two hours to wait for a connection, she suggests they take a bus.

"Good heavens," he says. "Do you think I want it to get back to the Salsburg Model-Railway Club that I rode on a bus!"

When they finally get to New York, the very first night he takes her down to the Grand Central Terminal to listen to the train-announcing. And the next morning while he is shaving in their hotel room, which overlooks the Pennsylvania Station, he calls out all the stations between New York and Boston on the New York, New Haven & Hartford's shore line, and all the stations between New York and Washington, D.C., on the Pennsylvania.

By this time, of course, any other woman would either call in the house physician or a lawyer, but, like I said before, this Mrs. Applebee is a sweet little thing just trying to get along, and she doesn't realize that coming events cast their shadows before. She tries to get into the spirit of things. She shrieks with girlish glee, she tells me, when Steve takes her up into New England and upper New York State to ride on the Central Vermont and the Rutland. He likes the Central Vermont all right, but he is somewhat disappointed in the Rutland because the brakeman wants to talk baseball instead of block signals.

In New York City, of course, they ride all the subways. Sometimes they wait a half hour at Times Square until a train comes along which has a front window and a vacant seat. Steve sits in this seat and peers into the tunnel ahead, and he don't say much except, "We are coming up on that red block pretty fast," or "It doesn't seem to me they allow enough headway between trains." He tries to involve a motorman at the Coney Island station in an argument as to which is best, straight air or automatic air. But the motorman doesn't seem to care whether he has to stop his train with straight air or automatic air, or by dragging his feet.

"That bum ought to be driving a milk wagon," Steve says. "I bet he don't know a brake shoe from a pair of kid's rubbers."

Mrs. Applebee makes a big hit with her husband one morning by imitating a news butcher.

"Cigars, cigarettes, tobacco, candy, fresh fruit, and souvenir postcards," she says.

"Honey," he tells her, "you're wonderful."

"It sounds like a great honeymoon," commented Superintendent Alston.

"Wait until you hear what happened when they got home," said Conductor Benson. "This is where it really gets sad."

WELL, THEY NO sooner arrive in Salsburg [continued Conductor Benson] and settle down in their new house than he invites her to a meeting of the model-railway club. Of course, he has talked almost constantly about the club ever since he met her, but she hasn't any clear idea of it. She thinks maybe they all get down on their hands and knees and pull choo-choos around. To tell the truth, whenever he starts talking about locomotives and draw-bars and valve gears and three-percent grades, she just sits and looks at him with awe, and thinks how handsome he is, and how nice and kind his eyes are, and what a lucky, lucky girl she is to be married to such a splendid creature.

"I have asked some of the other fellows to invite their wives, too," he says. "I don't see why we can't all work and enjoy the system together. I think you girls will get as much fun out of it as we do. Of course, you won't be able to run trains right away. You will have to start by operating some of our manual switches and crossing gates, but after a while you can work your way up into an occasional local freight."

From what Mrs. Applebee tells me, the club has an O-gauge system in the basement of the Johnson home. You know, Johnson, the Salsburg banker. Each man has contributed something like a locomotive or a string of boxcars or maybe a couple of Pullmans. The track and the equipment—even the stations, crossing gates, bridges, and signal towers—are built strictly according to scale, about a fourth of an inch to a foot in real life. They call this railroad the Chicago, Alton & West Coast, and it has about five hundred feet of track arranged in loops. One of these loops runs out of the basement and circles through the Johnson rock garden.

Mrs. Applebee says the club meets three times a week. One man sits at a table and acts as dispatcher, writing up train orders. Another makes up passenger and freight trains in the Chicago yards, and each of the others has a division, and is responsible for the trains that run over it.

The locomotives are powered with electric motors and they pick up their juice from a third rail. The idea is never to touch a train with your hands if you can help it.

Well, the Applebees hurry through dinner this night because it is a terrible thing to be late and delay the trains. In fact, Mrs. Applebee says the only reason her friends, the Browns, are hardly speaking to one another is because Mrs. Brown had to go and have her baby on the very night that Mr. Brown was supposed to sit in as relief dispatcher.

When the Applebees arrive at the Johnson home, she finds the crowd down in the basement, the ladies gathered politely off in one corner, pretty breathless about the whole business. Mrs. Applebee says her first reaction to what she sees is that Mrs. Johnson must be a very patient woman to let her husband and his friends muss her basement up that way. Mrs. Applebee says Mrs. Johnson's laundress is probably a contortionist. There are tracks at various levels all around the walls, across the floor, and even suspended from the ceiling. It doesn't make much sense to Mrs. Applebee.

Steve walks over to this banker, who is sitting at the table, and he says: "Let's have the order for Number Seventeen."

"Number Seventeen," says the banker, "meets Number Sixteen at Alton and Number Four-oh-two at East Kansas City. You've also got a slow order over two sections east of Alton on account of track repairs."

Well, Steve walks over to the Chicago depot and yards, which is on top of the Johnson workbench, and he stands beside a locomotive and seven Pullmans.

"Train Number Seventeen!" he calls out. "The Continental Limited! Now leaving on Track Four for Pontiac, Atlanta, Springfield, Alton, Kansas City, Denver, Salt Lake City, San Francisco, and all points west! All a-b-o-a-r-d!"

"I THINK YOU'RE making some of this up," protested Superintendent Alston.

"No, I'm not," replied Conductor Benson. "I'm telling it just like she did, only I'm not so bitter about it."

STEVE THROWS A switch [continued Conductor Benson] and the train starts moving. Mrs. Applebee notices that all the men have their watches out. It seems like the running time is figured in seconds, and any member who turns a train over to another division late has to have a pretty good reason. Like, for instance, the night the Johnson Airedale tried to take a bite out of the observation-lounge car of Number Fifteen, the Kansas City Flyer, when it was swinging around his kennel at a good seventy-mile clip. They keep the Airedale chained up during the club meetings now.

The Continental Limited races around the wall behind the furnace, speeds toward the washtubs, and disappears into a tunnel in the wall of the fruit closet. It comes out again at a higher level and stops at a small, lighted station.

"Number Seventeen arriving at Alton on time!" says Steve. And, according to Mrs. Applebee, his face is glowing like the night he proposed.

The ladies follow this train over the other divisions all the way to San Francisco, which is at the foot of the garden, and they utter glad little cries over the locomotive's headlight and the way the light shines out of the car windows. And pretty soon some of the ladies are assigned to various duties. Mrs. Applebee gets a manual switch in the Chicago yards.

She doesn't understand the operation of this switch very well, and she gives it a yank while a freight train is passing through. It seems like seven cars are derailed.

"For goodness' sakes," she laughs. "I guess I am not much of a switchman, am I?"

And she picks up one of the cars and starts to put it back on the track.

"Don't touch those cars!" her husband shouts.

She says her husband is acting like he just caught her making eyes at the iceman. His tone is quite sharp.

"The only way we can get those reefers back on the rails," he says, "is with the wrecker."

Well, they bring the wrecking train down from Alton, and the other men gather around, shaking their heads and saying, "Tch, tch, tch!" It appears that what Mrs. Applebee has done is a very terrible thing indeed. It is the first derailment on the Chicago, Alton & West Coast Railway in three weeks, they tell her. They spend a solid hour getting those cars back on the track without using their hands.

"Oh, let's have something to drink," one of the ladies suggests.

"I should say not," says Johnson. "Didn't you ever hear of Rule G?"

"Why no," says the lady.

"Well, Rule G is the no-drinking rule on every railway in the country," says the banker, "and we don't drink while we are on duty. Not on the C. A. and W. C., we don't!"

"No," explains the banker's wife, "not since old Judge Semple got liquored up one night and staged a head-on collision in Tunnel Five. He was expelled!"

When the Applebees are leaving that night, it is this same Mrs. Johnson who gives Mrs. Applebee a warm, sympathetic little squeeze of the hand.

"Poor dear," she whispers. "You'll learn to be a railroad man's wife one of these days, but the period of learning is terrible. When I was getting accustomed to it, I used to have hideous dreams. I was always being chased by a timetable. And don't think that I don't have to be constantly on guard, even now. For three years I have been fighting to keep Mr. Johnson from building a trestle right across the goldfish pond. The goldfish pond is Great Salt Lake."

"Of course, I don't blame you, dear," says Steve, on the way home, "but did you ever see anyone turn a switch on a regular railroad while a train was passing over it?"

"I guess not," she says.

"All right, then," he says. "Why did you do it?"

"I don't know, Steve," she replies, "and let's not discuss the matter anymore."

The next time the club meets she pleads a headache, and she is not surprised when Steve later reports that all the other wives seem to have headaches, too.

It isn't long after this that the club decides to change over from a third-rail to a two-rail system, which involves a good deal of rewiring and some track re-laying. Steve is busy at the Johnsons' every weekday night, and all day Sunday he spends his time at his own kitchen table, putting together a New York Central Hudson–type locomotive. The parts for this cost him fifty-eight dollars, and it means that Mrs. Applebee has to struggle along another month without drapes for the living room.

Mrs. Applebee says she sometimes wishes Steve would be attracted to another woman, because she would know what to do about that. She would get herself some snappy new clothes and try doing her hair differently. But she says there is nothing a woman can do whose husband is suddenly that way about a New York Central Hudson–type locomotive with a feed-water heater, a Baker valve gear, alligator crossheads, and a booster on the trailer truck.

"YES," COMMENTED Superintendent Alston, profoundly stirred, "you take these Hudson-type engines—they're pretty, all right, but one of our 5200 Mallets can outpull two of them."

"Yes," agreed Conductor Benson, "but I never yet heard of anyone going nuts over a Mallet."

WELL, ANYWAY [said Conductor Benson], Mrs. Applebee wants to go upstate to attend the university homecoming, but Steve is just putting the paint job on his new engine, and he can't possibly leave it. So Mrs. Applebee drives up with a girlfriend. And it is there she meets this Tommy Germaine. From what I gather, this Tommy Germaine is Mrs. Applebee's sugar-pie when she is in college. He spots her at the alumni dance the night before the big game, and he prances right over.

"Well, if it isn't the lovely lady again," he says. "I swear, you grow more beautiful every day!"

"Oh, Tommy!" she says. "The same old Tommy! Even the same old line."

"You're married!" he pouts. "I read about it in the papers. I sulked for weeks. Wouldn't eat anything but a little barley broth. People tell me I almost faded away."

"Oh, Tommy," she laughs. He sweeps her out on the dance floor.

"By the way," he says, "what does your lord and master do, besides hurry home every night to his sweet little wife?"

"He's assistant to the vice president of the Chicago, Alton and West Coast Railway," she says.

"I never heard of it," he says.

"It's a model railway," she explains. "He's really district sales manager for International Small Appliances Company, but the model railway is his life's work."

"I should think," says this Tommy Germaine, "that you would be his life's work."

"Oh, hush up," she giggles.

Well, he takes her to the game next day, and that evening they go with two other couples to a little roadhouse to dance. Mrs. Applebee says that it's just like a month at the beach. She feels young and attractive and appreciated again.

"I'm going to see more of you, I hope," this Tommy says. "My company has assigned me to the Salsburg office, and I move next week. I'd like to meet your husband."

"You'll love Steve," she tells him. "And if you want to make a real hit with him, bring along a couple of timetables or the picture of a caboose."

She has such a good time at the homecoming that she feels almost guilty when she returns home. She tells Steve everything.

He listens to her kind of impatiently and says: "Well, that's fine. I wish I could have gone up there myself. Do you know what Johnson said about my engine?"

"No," she says. "What?"

"He claims the paint is too black. He says it ought to be more of a gunmetal shade. What do you think?"

"The first coat looked perfectly all right to me," she assures him.

"I'm glad you say that," Steve says, very pleased.

This Tommy Germaine doesn't lose any time. He isn't in Salsburg two days before he telephones.

"It's me," he says. "And hungering for a real old-fashioned home-cooked meal, if I may be so suggestive."

"You may be, Tommy," she says, "and you may come right out tonight, if you don't mind corned beef and cabbage."

Steve and this Tommy hit it off from the start.

"I hear you're interested in railroads," says Tommy. "An uncle of mine works in the passenger department of the Sante Fe."

"Is that so?" comments Steve with great interest. "That's a mighty good road, the Sante Fe. They put out a very readable timetable."

Steve has Tommy out to the model-railway club as his guest a couple of times, and gets him admitted to the Forward Salsburg and Wide Awake Luncheon clubs. It is not long before this Tommy is practically a member of the family, and he thinks nothing of dropping in unannounced. Mrs. Applebee also sees a good deal of this Tommy at country-club dances and on the golf course. From what I gather, Steve is not only busy with the model-railway gang but his company has also extended his sales territory and he has to spend considerable time away from home. So he begins to rely more and more on this Tommy to keep his social end up.

No matter what the neighbors and the old boys and girls on the clubhouse porch say, however, Mrs. Applebee is not too pleased with the arrangement. She doesn't mind Steve's trips out of town, but she is certainly reaching what she calls "the saturation point" concerning locomotives and railroad trains. The big blow-off comes the night of the country-club formal.

Mrs. Applebee goes to some trouble and expense to get her hair done differently, but all Steve says is: "What's the matter? You look kind of funny tonight." He dances with her a couple of times, then turns her over to this Tommy. Steve ducks away to the bar, where the model-railway club is having a special meeting. It seems like one of the boys wants to introduce a streamlined engine into the system, like the Milwaukee uses on the Hiawatha on the Twin City run out of Chicago. The rest of the boys are thumbs-down. What is the sense, they are asking, of building a beautiful model engine, then covering it with a piece of painted tin which hides all the working parts?

"I don't know," says Steve, stepping into the argument. "If all the other lines are going into streamlining, I don't think the Chicago, Alton and West Coast can afford to hold off. Don't forget we are running through highly competitive territory. I think it will be all right to have one streamline job, and maybe call it the Albatross."

"Who ever heard," one of the boys says, "of naming a train after a bird?"

"All right, smart guy," says Steve. "Didn't you ever hear of the famous Flying Crow on the Kansas City Southern? Or the Gull on the Boston and Maine?"

"You've got me there," the guy admits.

"WHILE HE WAS listing trains which are named after birds," said Superintendent Alston, "why didn't he mention the Flamingo on the Louisville and Nashville, and the Southern Pacific's Lark, and the New Haven's Owl?"

"I guess he didn't think about them," apologized Conductor Benson.

WHILE STEVE IS all wrapped up in this discussion [continued Conductor Benson], Mrs. Applebee is dancing with Tommy and getting madder every minute. Finally she sends Tommy to get Steve.

"Steve," she says sharply, "I want to go home!"

"What's the matter?" he asks.

"Never mind," she says. "I want to go home."

In the automobile he details all this streamlining argument, but she makes no comment. When he puts the car away and comes into the house, he finds her standing in the middle of the living-room floor, looking pretty grim.

"Steve," she says, "sit down!"

"Why, what's the matter honey?" he asks.

"Steve," she says, "you and I are going to have a talk."

"Have I done something?" he asks, getting alarmed.

"Steve," she says, "we have been married eleven months. Am I still as pretty as you used to say I was?"

"Why, of course, honey," he replies, puzzled.

"And I keep a nice, clean, comfortable house for you, too, don't I?"

"Why, sure," he replies. "Look, if I've done something that—"

"And I'm economical and helpful and sympathetic and encouraging, am I not, Steve?"

"Sure you are, honey," he says. "I don't understand—"

"All right," she says. "Then why don't you pay more attention to me? Don't you love me anymore?"

"Oh, I see what you mean," he says. "I guess you're sore about tonight. I did disappear for quite a long time. We got to talking about that new train, whether we ought to have a beavertail-end or a conventional open-end observation car."

"It isn't just tonight, Steve," she says. "It's every day and every night."

"Why, gosh, Helene," he says. "I had no idea that—"

"That's all you talk about from breakfast until bedtime. I sometimes feel as if I were married to a union station."

"But, Helene," he says. "I had no idea—"

"And I try to be patient and understanding," she says, "but now I have reached the point where I will throw my things into a suitcase and walk right out of this house if I ever hear you speak of a locomotive and coal car again."

"Not a coal car, Helene," he says gently. "Call it a tender. Coal cars are called hoppers and have nothing to do with a locomotive."

"You see?" she says, and she bursts into tears.

Well, he puts his arm around her, and he says: "Gosh, Helene, I never realized. I won't ever look at another train again. I will even turn my head when we drive by the depot."

"No, I don't want that," she says. "I just want you to love me a little more."

So for a couple of weeks they have a regular love nest. Of course, every so often he will speak of something crude like a seventy-ton Lehigh Valley hopper or a New York, Ontario & Western caboose, but she realizes this is purely force of habit. She isn't too severe with him. As long as he is in a flowers-and-candy mood ninety percent of the time, she is not going to begrudge him the other ten percent. She knows that some men are solitary drinkers, she says, and that some men chase after other women, and that some men spill cigar ashes down the front of their vests, and that there are no absolutely perfect husbands on the market.

In fact, Steve is so nice to her that she feels maybe she has been almost cruel; she catches him one night, sitting on a soapbox in the garage, reading a new issue of the Missouri Pacific timetable. He folds it up quick with a guilty expression, like she had caught him smoking corn silk.

"I was just wondering what time the Scenic Limited runs out of St. Louis," he says.

"You poor, dear, and abused man," she says. "I didn't mean that you couldn't read timetables in the house if you want to. And, as a matter of fact, I see no reason why you shouldn't attend the regular meetings of the club."

She is feeling, she tells me, perhaps too generous at the moment, because you can't taper off a model-railway fan like you can a drug addict. Show him an eccentric rod and he's off again. You've got to keep him away from machinery and the sound of locomotive whistles, and put him on a soft diet.

Well, they coast along happily until today, which is their wedding anniversary. Mrs. Applebee says they are figuring on driving up to Reflection Lake for the day. It's about a hundred miles, and they plan to start at nine o'clock this morning. Well, they are just locking up the house when the phone rings. He answers it.

"Helene," he shouts. "Barkerville is in town!"

"Who is Barkerville?" she asks, with a sinking feeling.

"He's the owner of the famous Sunrise Valley Model Railway in California," Steve says, "and that's the line that the movies use for all their trick shots of railway wrecks. He's at the Johnsons', looking our system over, and the boys want me to come over."

"Oh, Steve," she says, very sadly.

"I'll just be a minute," he promises. "I only want to shake hands with him."

"Steve," she says, "today is our wedding anniversary."

"Don't you worry, honey," he says. "I'll be back in no time. You wait in the house until I honk the horn."

Well, this is nine o'clock. At ten o'clock she telephones the Johnson house and Mrs. Johnson says the whole crowd has gone down to the Talbot home to look at a tin-plater Talbot is converting into a scale job. She calls the Talbot home, and Mrs. Talbot says yes, they were there, but they have gone somewhere else, and she doesn't care where they have gone, and she doesn't care if they never come back, because Barkerville woke up the baby by imitating the way the Western Pacific sounds in the Feather River Canyon.

At eleven o'clock Mrs. Applebee is fighting mad. And then the doorbell rings. It isn't Steve. It's this Tommy Germaine.

"Oh, Tommy," she sobs. Well, she tells him the whole story, and he sits there looking like he has just found out that Steve spends his evenings going around peeping into windows.

"This is no way to treat a sensitive, pretty, and high-spirited woman like yourself," Tommy Germaine says. "This is ghastly."

"I am going away," she says, "to teach him a lesson. He can't do this to me."

"I think you are right," says this Tommy.

She writes Steve a note and props it up on the living-room table.

"Where are you going?" Tommy asks her while she is packing a few clothes.

"I'm going to Grand River, to Mother," she says.

"It's not far," Tommy says. "I will accompany you a little way. You need a friend along at a time like this."

"Good old Tommy," she says. "You are a real friend, aren't you?"

When he is getting their tickets at the depot, he says: "I hate trains. Stuffy old cars and green plush seats. Smoke and cinders and jolting and bumping."

"It's not quite so bad as that," she assures him. "In fact, this is a new train we're going on. Aluminum alloy and air-conditioned."

And when we get under way, she looks out the window and spots this same yard hog.

"It used to be a road engine," she says idly. "You can tell by the firebox and the big boiler."

"Helene," he says, not hearing her, "there is something I want to tell you. I couldn't have told you before. Perhaps I ought not to tell you now. But I've always had a certain feeling about you, and that feeling lately has grown into something pretty important."

"Please, Tommy," she says.

"Helene," he says, "for the past few weeks I haven't been able to think of anything else but how nice it would be to settle down in the country, in a sweet little house—"

"Tommy," she says, "you mustn't say such things. Not now, anyway. Later perhaps. You are very sweet, Tommy, and I like you very much."

"—and just settle down," he continued dreamily, "with a sweet wife and my workbench, and—"

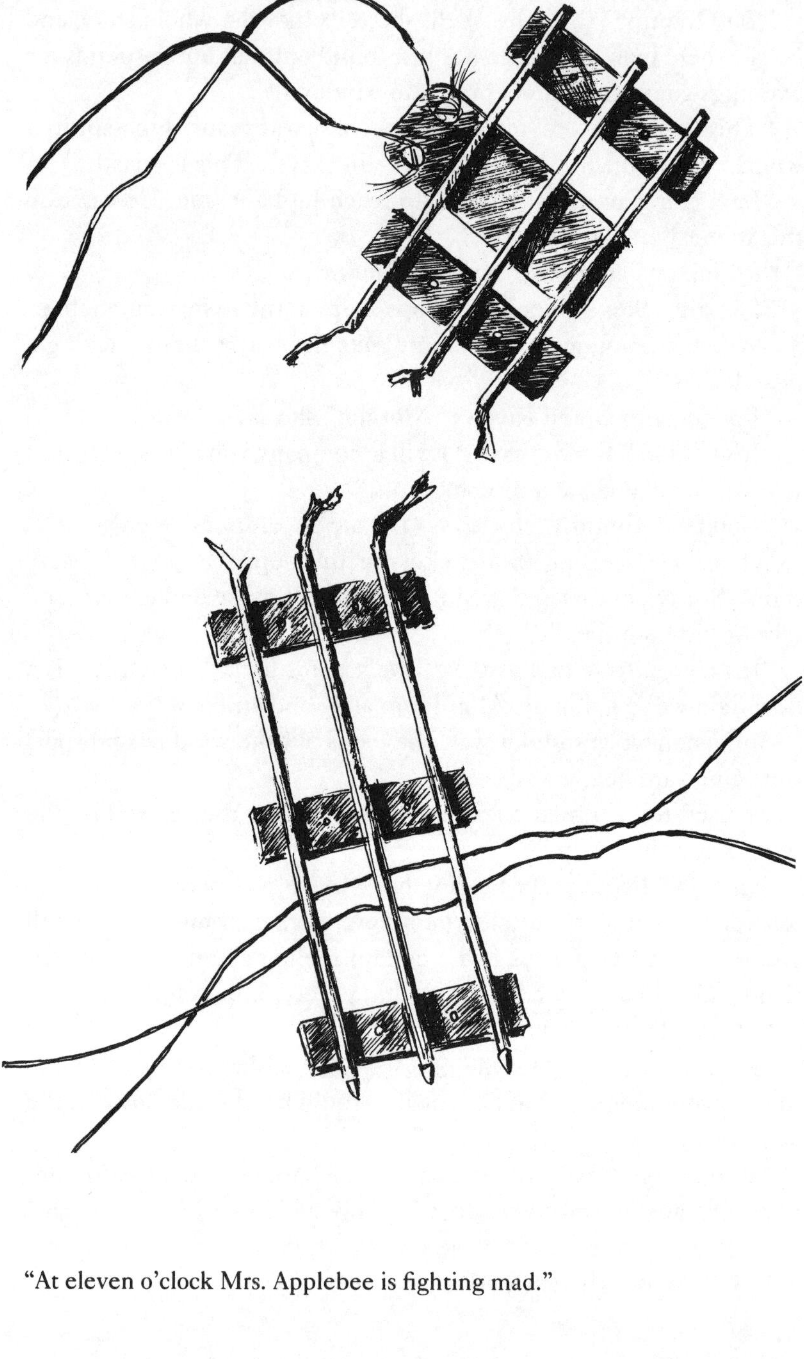

“At eleven o’clock Mrs. Applebee is fighting mad.”

"Your workbench?" she echoes. "What do you do with a workbench?"

"I make model ships," he says.

"You make what?" she demands, half rising in her seat.

"Model ships," he replies. "I've got over fifty already. Some of them have been exhibited in the greatest—"

"Why, you heel!" she storms. "You insufferable heel!"

And she runs back in the car and pulls the air on us. She says she realizes then that all men are nuts in one way or another, and Steve is no worse than average.

"WHY, YOU fathead!" roared Superintendent Alston. "Why didn't you let her off at Junction? You left her in a pretty mess. Her husband probably got that note she left!"

"Don't get so hot!" shouted Conductor Benson. "That's why I stopped at Central City. She went into the station to telephone a neighbor to get the key under the back-door mat and take the letter off the living-room table."

"Did the neighbor get it?" demanded Superintendent Alston.

"Certainly," said Conductor Benson. "I held the train until she came out of the station to tell me. And I told the agent to flag down Number Eleven and put her on board. She was home again in only an hour."

"Well, that's better," said Superintendent Alston. "We railroad men have got to stick together."

"But the funny thing to me," said Conductor Benson, "is the idea of all these grown men playing with model trains. It amused me so much that the next time I am in Salsburg, I'm going to run over to the Johnson house to see what they've got."

"You and me both," said Superintendent Alston. "We may be able to give them some pointers."

—1901

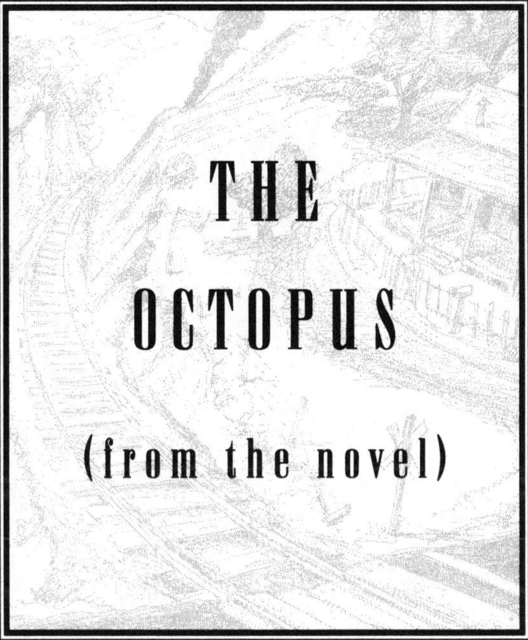

THE OCTOPUS

(from the novel)

FRANK NORRIS

EDITOR'S NOTE: *Norris's novel* The Octopus *concerns the battle between wheat farmers and a railroad magnate in California's Central Valley. Preceding this excerpt, Dyke has been fired as an engineer, but, ever optimistic, the German immigrant goes on to make a success of himself by experimenting with growing hops. In this excerpt, buoyed by his bumper crop, he goes to the railroad office to confirm the price of shipping the hops.*

THAT MORNING Dyke's mother had awakened him according to his instructions at daybreak. A consignment of his hop poles from the north had arrived at the freight office of the P. & S. W. in Bonneville, and he was to drive in on his farm wagon and bring them out. He would have a busy day.

"Hello, hello," he said, as his mother pulled his ear to arouse him; " 'morning, Mama."

"It's time," she said; "after five already. Your breakfast is on the stove."

He took her hand and kissed it with great affection. He loved his mother devotedly, quite as much as he did the little tad. In their little cottage, in the forest of green hops that surrounded them on every hand, the three led a joyous and secluded life, contented, industrious, happy, asking nothing better. Dyke, himself, was a big-hearted, jovial man who spread an atmosphere of good humor wherever he went. In the evenings he played with Sidney like a big boy, an older brother, lying on the bed or the sofa, taking her in his arms. Between them they had invented a great game. The ex-engineer, his boots removed, his huge legs in the air, hoisted the little tad on the soles of his stockinged feet like a circus acrobat, dandling her there, pretending he was about to let her fall. Sidney, choking with delight, held on nervously, with little screams and chirps of excitement, while he shifted her gingerly from one foot to another, and thence, the final act, the great gallery play, to the palm of one great hand. At this point, Mrs. Dyke was called in, father and daughter, children both, crying out that she was to come in and look, look. She arrived out of breath from the kitchen, the potato masher in her hand.

"Such children," she murmured, shaking her head at them, amused for all that, tucking the potato masher under her arm and clapping her hands.

In the end, it was part of the game that Sidney should tumble down upon Dyke, whereat he invariably vented a great bellow as if in pain, declaring that his ribs were broken. Gasping, his eyes shut, he pretended to be in the extreme of dissolution—perhaps he was dying. Sidney, always a little uncertain, amused but distressed, shook him nervously, tugging at his beard, pushing open his eyelid with one finger, imploring him not to frighten her, to wake up and be good.

On this occasion, while yet he was half dressed, Dyke tiptoed into his mother's room to look at Sidney fast asleep in her little iron cot, her arm under her head, her lips parted. With infinite precaution he kissed her twice and then, finding one little stocking hung with its mate very neatly over the back of a chair, dropped into it a dime, rolled up in a wad of paper. He winked all to himself and went out again, closing the door with exaggerated carefulness.

He breakfasted alone, Mrs. Dyke pouring his coffee and handing him his plate of ham and eggs, and half an hour later took himself off in his springless skeleton wagon, humming a tune behind his beard and cracking the whip over the backs of his staid and stolid farm horses.

The morning was fine, the sun just coming up. He left Guadalajara, sleeping and lifeless, on his left and, going across lots, over an angle of Quien Sabe, came out upon the Upper Road, a mile below the Long Trestle. He was in great spirits, looking about him over the brown fields, ruddy with the dawn. Almost directly in front of him, but far off, the gilded dome of the courthouse at Bonneville was glinting radiant in the first rays of the sun, while a few miles distant, toward the north, the venerable campanile of the Mission San Juan stood silhouetted in purplish black against the flaming east. As he proceeded, the great farm horses jogging forward, placid, deliberate, the countryside waked to another day. Crossing the irrigating ditch farther on, he met a gang of Portuguese, with picks and shovels over their shoulders, just going to work.

The ex-engineer reached the post office in Bonneville toward eleven o'clock; but he did not at once present his notice of the arrival of his consignment at Ruggles's office. It entertained him to indulge in an hour's lounging about the streets. It was seldom he got into town, and when he did, he permitted himself the luxury of enjoying his evident popularity. He met friends everywhere, in the post office, in the drugstore, in the barbershop, and around the courthouse. With each one he held a moment's conversation; almost invariably this ended in the same way:

"Come on 'n have a drink."

"Well, I don't care if I do."

And the friends proceeded to the Yosemite Bar, pledging each other with punctilious ceremony. Dyke, however, was a strictly temperate man. His life on the engine had trained him well. Alcohol he never touched, drinking instead ginger ale, sarsaparilla-and-iron—soft drinks.

At the drugstore, which also kept a stock of miscellaneous stationery, his eye was caught by a "transparent slate," a child's toy, where, upon a little pane of frosted glass, one could trace with considerable elaboration outline-figures of cows, plows, bunches of fruit, and even rural watermills that were printed on slips of paper underneath.

"Now, there's an idea, Jim," he observed to the boy behind the soda-water fountain; "I know a little tad that would just about jump out of her skin for that. Think I'll have to take it with me."

"How's Sidney getting along?" the other asked while wrapping up the package.

Dyke's enthusiasm had made of his little girl a celebrity throughout Bonneville.

The ex-engineer promptly became voluble, assertive, doggedly emphatic.

"Smartest little tad in all Tulare County, and more fun! A regular whole show in herself."

"And the hops?" inquired the other.

"Bully," declared Dyke, with a good-natured man's readiness to talk of his private affairs to anyone who would listen. "Bully. I'm dead sure of a bonanza crop by now. The rain came *just* right. I actually don't know as I can store the crop in those barns I built, it's going to be so big. That foreman of mine was a daisy. Jim, I'm going to make money in that deal. After I've paid off the mortgage—you know I had to mortgage; yes, crop and homestead both, but I can pay it off and all the interest to boot, lovely—well, and as I was saying, after all expenses are paid off I'll clear big money, m'son. Yes sir. I *knew* there was a boodle in hops. You know the crop is contracted for already. Sure, the foreman managed that. He's a daisy. Chap in San Francisco will take it all and at the advanced price. I wanted to hang on, to see if it wouldn't go to six cents, but the foreman said, 'No, that's good enough.' So I signed. Ain't it bully, hey?"

"Then what'll you do?"

"Well, I don't know. I'll have a layoff for a month or so and take the little tad and Mother up and show 'em the city—Frisco—until it's time for the schools to open, and then we'll put Sid in the seminary at Marysville. Catch on?"

"I suppose you'll stay right by hops now?"

"Right you are, m'son. I know a good thing when I see it. There's plenty others going into hops next season. I set 'em the example. Wouldn't be surprised if it came to be a regular industry hereabouts. I'm planning ahead for next year already. I can let the foreman go, now that I've learned the game myself, and I think I'll buy a piece of land off Quien Sabe and get a bigger crop, and build a couple more barns, and, by George, in about five years' time I'll have things humming. I'm going to make *money*, Jim."

He emerged once more into the street and went up the block leisurely, planting his feet squarely. He fancied that he could feel he was considered of more importance nowadays. He was no longer a subordinate, an employee. He was his own man, a proprietor, an owner of land, furthering a successful enterprise. No one had helped him; he had followed no one's lead. He had struck out unaided for himself, and his success was due solely to his own intelligence, industry, and foresight. He squared his great shoulders till the blue gingham of his jumper all but cracked. Of late, his great blond beard had grown and the work in the sun had made his face very red. Under the visor of his cap—relic of his engineering days—his blue eyes twinkled with vast good nature. He felt that he made a fine figure as he went by a group of young girls in lawns and muslins and garden hats on their way to the post office. He wondered if they looked after him, wondered if they had heard that he was in a fair way to become a rich man.

But the chronometer in the window of the jewelry store warned him that time was passing. He turned about and, crossing the street, took his way to Ruggles's office, which was the freight as well as the land office of the P. & S. W. Railroad.

As he stood for a moment at the counter in front of the wire partition, waiting for the clerk to make out the order for the freight agent at the depot, Dyke was surprised to see a familiar figure in conference with Ruggles himself, by a desk inside the railing.

The figure was that of a middle-aged man, fat, with a great stomach, which he stroked from time to time. As he turned about, addressing a remark to the clerk, Dyke recognized S. Behrman. The banker, railroad agent, and political manipulator seemed to the ex-engineer's eyes to be more gross than ever. His smooth-shaven jowl stood out big and tremulous on either side of his face; the roll of fat on the nape of his neck, sprinkled with sparse, stiff hairs, bulged out with great prominence. His great stomach, covered with a light brown linen vest stamped with innumerable interlocked horseshoes, protruded far in advance, enormous, aggressive. He wore his inevitable round-topped hat of stiff brown straw, varnished so bright that it reflected the light of the office windows like a helmet, and even from where he stood, Dyke could hear his loud breathing and the clink of the hollow links of his watch chain upon the vest buttons of imitation pearl, as his stomach rose and fell.

Dyke looked at him with attention. There was the enemy, the representative of the Trust with which Derrick's League was locking horns. The great struggle had begun to invest the combatants with interest. Daily, almost hourly, Dyke was in touch with the ranchers, the wheat growers. He heard their denunciations, their growls of exasperation and defiance. Here was the other side—this placid fat man, with a stiff straw hat and linen vest, who never lost his temper, who smiled affably upon his enemies, giving them good advice, commiserating with them in one defeat after another, never ruffled, never excited, sure of his power, conscious that in back of him was the Machine, the colossal force, the inexhaustible coffers of a mighty organization, vomiting millions to the League's thousands. The League was clamorous, ubiquitous, its objects known to every urchin on the streets; but the Trust was silent, its ways inscrutable—the public saw only results. It worked on in the dark—calm, disciplined, irresistible. Abruptly Dyke received the impression of the multitudinous ramifications of the colossus. Under his feet the ground seemed mined; down there below him in the dark, the huge tentacles went silently twisting and advancing, spreading out in every direction, sapping the strength of all opposition, quiet, gradual, biding the time to reach up and out and grip with a sudden unleashing of gigantic strength.

"I'll be wanting some cars of you people before the summer is out," observed Dyke to the clerk as he folded up and put away the order that the other had handed him. He remembered perfectly well that he had arranged the matter of transporting his crop some months before, but his role of proprietor amused him and he liked to busy himself again and again with the details of his undertaking.

"I suppose," he added, "you'll be able to give 'em to me. There'll be a big wheat crop to move this year and I don't want to be caught in any car famine."

"Oh, you'll get your cars," murmured the other.

"I'll be the means of bringing business your way," Dyke went on; "I've done so well with my hops that there are a lot of others going into the business next season. Suppose," he continued, struck with an idea, "suppose we went into some sort of pool, a sort of shippers' organization; could you give us special rates, cheaper rates—say, a cent and a half?"

The other looked up.

"A cent and a half! Say *four* cents and a half and maybe I'll talk business with you."

"Four cents and a half," returned Dyke, "I don't see it. Why, the regular rate is only two cents."

"No, it isn't," answered the clerk, looking him gravely in the eye, "it's five cents."

"Well, there's where you are wrong, m'son," Dyke retorted genially. "You look it up. You'll find the freight on hops from Bonneville to Frisco is two cents a pound for carload lots. You told me that yourself last fall."

"That was last fall," observed the clerk. There was a silence. Dyke shot a glance of suspicion at the other. Then, reassured, he remarked: "You look it up. You'll see I'm right."

S. Behrman came forward and shook hands politely with the ex-engineer. "Anything I can do for you, Mr. Dyke?"

Dyke explained. When he had done speaking, the clerk turned to S. Behrman and observed respectfully: "Our regular rate on hops is five cents."

"Yes," answered S. Behrman, pausing to reflect; "yes, Mr. Dyke, that's right—five cents."

The clerk brought forward a folder of yellow paper and handed it to Dyke. It was inscribed at the top *Tariff Schedule No. 8,* and underneath these words, in brackets, was a smaller inscription: *Supersedes No. 7 of Aug. 1.*

"See for yourself," said S. Behrman. He indicated an item under the head of *Miscellany.*

" 'The following rates for carriage of hops in carload lots,' " read Dyke, " 'take effect June 1, and will remain in force until superseded by a later tariff. Those quoted beyond Stockton are subject to changes in traffic arrangements with carriers by water from that point.' "

In the list that was printed below, Dyke saw that the rate for hops between Bonneville or Guadalajara and San Francisco was five cents.

For a moment Dyke was confused. Then swiftly the matter became clear in his mind. The Railroad had raised the freight on hops from two cents to five.

All his calculations as to a profit on his little investment he had based on a freight rate of two cents a pound. He was under contract to deliver his crop. He could not draw back. The new rate ate up every cent of his gains. He stood there ruined.

"Why, what do you mean?" he burst out. "You promised me a rate of two cents and I went ahead with my business with that understanding. What do you mean?"

S. Behrman and the clerk watched him from the other side of the counter.

"The rate is five cents," declared the clerk doggedly.

"Well, that ruins me," shouted Dyke. "Do you understand? I

won't make fifty cents. *Make!* Why, I will *owe*—I'll be— That ruins me, do you understand?"

The other raised a shoulder. "We don't force you to ship. You can do as you like. The rate is five cents."

"Well—but— Damn you, I'm under contract to deliver. What am I going to do? Why, you told me—you promised me a two-cent rate."

"I don't remember it," said the clerk. "I don't know anything about that. But I know this: I know that hops have gone up. I know the German crop was a failure and that the crop in New York wasn't worth the hauling. Hops have gone up to nearly a dollar. You don't suppose we don't know that, do you, Mr. Dyke?"

"What's the price of hops got to do with you?"

"It's got *this* to do with us," returned the other with a sudden aggressiveness, "that the freight rate has gone up to meet the price. We're not doing business for our health. My orders are to raise your rate to five cents, and I think you are getting off easy."

Dyke stared back in blank astonishment. For the moment, the audacity of the affair was what most appealed to him. He forgot its personal application.

"Good Lord," he murmured, "good Lord! What will you people do next? Look here. What's your basis of applying freight rates, anyhow?" he suddenly vociferated with furious sarcasm. "What's your rule? What are you guided by?"

But at the words, S. Behrman, who had kept silent during the heat of the discussion, leaned abruptly forward. For the only time in his knowledge, Dyke saw his face inflamed with anger and with the enmity and contempt of all this farming element with whom he was contending.

"Yes, what's your rule? What's your basis?" demanded Dyke, turning swiftly to him.

S. Behrman emphasized each word of his reply with a tap of one forefinger on the counter before him: "All—the—traffic—will—bear."

The ex-engineer stepped back a pace, his fingers on the ledge of the counter, to steady himself. He felt himself grow pale, his heart become a mere leaden weight in his chest, inert, refusing to beat.

In a second the whole affair, in all its bearings, went speeding before the eye of his imagination like the rapid unrolling of a panorama. Every cent of his earnings was sunk in this hop business of his. More than that, he had borrowed money to carry it on, certain of success—borrowed of S. Behrman, offering his crop and his little home as security. Once he failed to meet his obligations, S. Behrman would foreclose. Not only would the Railroad devour every morsel of his profits, but also it would take from him his home; at a blow he would be left penniless and without a home. What would then become of his mother—and what would become of the little tad? She, whom he had been planning to educate like a veritable lady. For all that year he had talked of his ambition for his little daughter to everyone he met. All Bonneville knew of it. What a mark for gibes he had made of himself. The workingman turned farmer! What a target for jeers—he who had fancied he could elude the Railroad! He remembered he had once said the great Trust had overlooked his little enterprise, disdaining to plunder such small fry. He should have known better than that. How had he ever imagined the Road would permit him to make any money?

Anger was not in him yet; no rousing of the blind, white-hot wrath that leaps to the attack with prehensile fingers moved him. The blow merely crushed, staggered, confused.

He stepped aside to give place to a coatless man in a pink shirt who entered, carrying in his hands an automatic door-closing apparatus.

"Where does this go?" inquired the man.

Dyke sat down for a moment on a seat that had been removed from a worn-out railway car to do duty in Ruggles's office. On the back of a yellow envelope he made some vague figures with a stump of blue pencil, multiplying, subtracting, perplexing himself with many errors.

S. Behrman, the clerk, and the man with the door-closing apparatus involved themselves in a long argument, gazing intently at the top panel of the door. The man who had come to fix the apparatus was unwilling to guarantee it, unless a sign was put on the outside of the door, warning incomers that the door was self-closing. This sign would cost fifteen cents extra.

"But you didn't say anything about this when the thing was ordered," declared S. Behrman. "No, I won't pay it, my friend. It's an overcharge."

"You needn't think," observed the clerk, "that just because you are dealing with the Railroad you are going to work us."

Dyke, studying the figures on the back of the envelope, came forward again. "Say," he hazarded, "how about this? I make out—"

"We've told you what our rates are, Mr. Dyke," exclaimed the clerk angrily. "That's all the arrangement we will make. Take it or leave it."

Dyke moved away and stood for a moment in the center of the room, staring at the figures on the envelope.

"I don't see," he muttered, "just what I'm going to do. No, I don't see what I'm going to do at all."

Dyke went down the stairs to the street and proceeded onward aimlessly in the direction of the Yosemite House, fingering the yellow envelope and looking vacantly at the sidewalk.

There was a stoop to his massive shoulders. His great arms dangled loosely at his sides, the palms of his hands open.

As he went along, a certain feeling of shame touched him. Surely his predicament must be apparent to every passerby. No doubt everyone recognized the unsuccessful man in the very way he slouched along. The young girls in lawns, muslins, and garden hats, returning from the post office, their hands full of letters, must surely see in him the type of the failure, the bankrupt.

Then brusquely his tardy rage flamed up. By God, *no,* it was not his fault; he had made no mistake. His energy, industry, and foresight had been sound. He had been merely the object of a colossal trick, a sordid injustice, a victim of the insatiate greed of the monster, caught and choked by one of those millions of tentacles suddenly reaching up from below, from out of the dark beneath his feet, coiling around his throat, throttling him, strangling him, sucking his blood. For a moment he thought of the courts, but instantly laughed at the idea. What court was immune from the power of the monster? Ah, the rage of helplessness, the fury of impotence! No help, no hope—ruined in a brief instant—he a veritable giant, built of great sinews, powerful, in the full tide of his manhood, having all his health, all his wits. How could he now face his home? How could he tell his mother of this catastrophe? And Sidney—the little tad; how could he explain to her this wretchedness—how soften her disappointment? How keep the tears from out her eyes—how keep alive her confidence in him—her faith in his resources?

"What a target for jeers—he who had fancied he could elude the Railroad!"

Bitter, fierce, ominous, his wrath loomed up in his heart. His fists gripped tight together, his teeth clenched. Oh, for a moment to have his hand upon the throat of S. Behrman, wringing the breath from him, wrenching out the red life of him—staining the street with the blood sucked from the veins of the People!

To the first friend that he met, Dyke told the tale of the tragedy, and to the next, and to the next. The affair went from mouth to mouth, spreading with electrical swiftness, overpassing and running ahead of Dyke himself, so that by the time he reached the lobby of the Yosemite House, he found his story awaiting him. A group formed about him. In his immediate vicinity business for the instant was suspended. The group swelled. One after another of his friends added themselves to it. Again and again, Dyke recounted the matter, beginning with the time when he was discharged from the same corporation's service for refusing to accept an unfair wage. His voice quivered with exasperation; his heavy frame shook with rage; his eyes were injected, bloodshot, his face flamed vermilion; while his deep bass rumbled throughout the running comments of his auditors like the thunderous reverberation of diapason.

From all points of view, the story was discussed by those who listened to him, now in the heat of excitement, now calmly, judicially. One verdict, however, prevailed:

"You're stuck. You can roar till you're black in the face, but you can't buck against the Railroad. There's nothing to be done."

"You can shoot the ruffian, you can shoot S. Behrman," clamored one of the group. "Yes sir; by the Lord, you can shoot him."

Nothing to be done. No, there was nothing to be done—not one thing. Dyke, at last alone and driving his team out of the town, turned the business confusedly over in his mind from end to end. Advice, suggestion, even offers of financial aid had been showered upon him from all directions. Friends were not wanting who heatedly presented to his consideration all manner of ingenious plans, wonderful devices. They were worthless. The tentacle held fast. He was stuck.

—1901

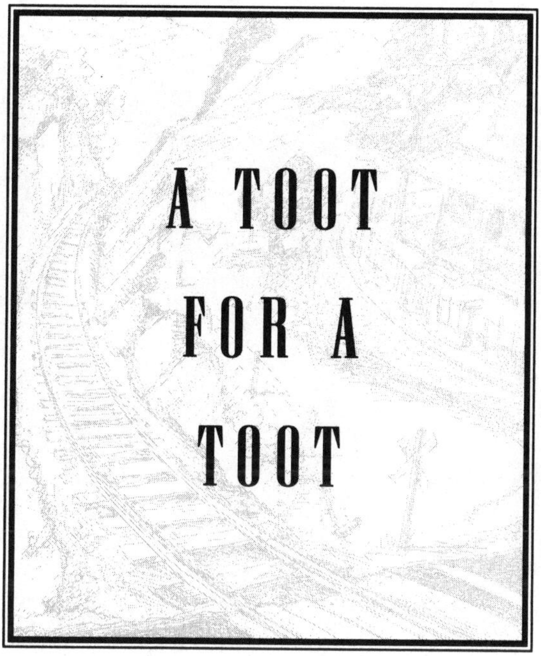

A TOOT FOR A TOOT

OCTAVUS ROY COHEN

EPIC PETERS'S INSTINCT was at work. "I got a hunch," he murmured apprehensively, "that this ain't gwine be the swellest run I ever took." Two factors contributed to the hunch of the elongated Pullman porter. For one thing, there had been a ghastly dearth of tips from passengers boarding the midnight train at Birmingham. For another, the buzzer of his call board had been sounding incessantly since the "All aboard."

Somewhat peeved with the world in general, and his job in particular, Mr. Peters took his own sweet time about closing his vestibule as the Limited nosed out into the chilly, murky night. He poked unenthusiastically at an occasional bit of dust, arranged his car step meticulously in the vestibule corner and then lurched unhappily into the car.

Just as he suspected, the board indicated that Lower Six required service. The training of many years came to the assistance of Epic Peters. As a sterling porter who was popular with Pullman and railroad conductors and whose name appeared frequently on the honor roll, Epic had learned to gauge the quality of those who traveled with him between the Alabama metropolis and New York.

"An' that feller in Lower Six," reflected Mr. Peters, "is the mos' kind I detest."

The person in question had waddled down the platform a half hour since, in the wake of a redcap who was loaded down with many heavy bags. He was a large man with a florid complexion and an officious manner. His voice was shrill and penetrating. He wore a blue suit, gaily cut, and it was quite evident that he fancied himself considerable of a sheik.

The trousers were full, the socks fancy, the shoes of two-tone leather. His vest was piped with white braid and he sported a scarlet necktie in which reposed a huge pearl. He carried a silver-headed cane, a gaudy topcoat, and wore a gray felt hat at a rakish angle. And Epic Peters saw him tip the staggering redcap a nickel.

Mr. Peters groaned.

"Tips nickels!" he grated. "I bet if he buys a ice-cream soda he wants a rebate when he returns the glass an' spoon."

The newcomer talked loudly and frequently as Epic escorted him to his berth and sought to satisfy the gentleman in the arrangement of his bags. Once, Epic dared designate the sign hanging at the end of the aisle: QUIET. The traveler glared at Mr. Peters and announced that he was paying full fare and reckoned he'd talk if he wanted to—besides, the service was rotten.

Now, as Mr. Peters reluctantly answered the summons from the fat gentleman's berth, it was to find the big head poked out between the curtains. The passenger glared at Epic and anathematized the service. It seemed that some cinders were creeping in through the screen, that there was a wrinkle in the sheet, and that his spare blanket was not properly folded.

Epic bore up under the tirade with the dignity becoming a colored gentleman and philosopher. He did not even deign to inform the man that he was the best berthmaker on the Birmingham station and known throughout the Southeast as one of the finest colored men ever to receive a monthly wage from the Pullman Company. With vast and disdainful patience he performed the tasks required by the exacting traveler, and heard that gentleman say peevishly:

"Well, I hope to goodness I can get some sleep."

As Epic moved away he endorsed the wish: "Lawsy knows, I hope so, too. Dawg-gone that feller. He buys one ticket an' thinks he's Mistuh Pullman Illinois hisse'f."

As Epic moved down the aisle he was conscious of certain movements in Section Eight. He turned quickly—just in time to see a ratlike face and a pair of beady eyes withdrawn quickly. "That feller in Lower Eight," Epic told himself, "also ain't the craziest sort I is about."

As a matter of fact, the gentleman in Lower Eight would have rasped Epic's nerves intensely had not the fat person in Lower Six been so obtrusively obnoxious. And, had Epic known it, his instinctive antipathy for the ratlike little man in Eight was not unfounded.

The person in Lower Eight was about five feet four inches in height. He had a slender, wiry figure on which cheap clothes fitted uncertainly. His eyes were beady and he had a disturbing habit of talking out of the side of his mouth. His hands were amazing, however; strong and long-fingered and amazingly deft.

At birth the little man had been christened Aloysius Bryan by a doting and unsuspecting mother. Since that time he had, in the pursuit of his chosen profession, used other names as convenience suggested. The police of various cities knew him as Danny the Dip, Dan Bryan, the Runt, and Dippy Dan. The name Aloysius had departed with his last short trousers.

To give Aloysius full credit, it must be admitted that he was an expert pickpocket. He operated alone—and frequently. He had few friends and no confidants, and only a too-great fondness for large diamonds steered him into trouble with the police. He could scissor or reef a victim with the best of them, leaving the unwitting contributor ignorant of financial loss until a considerable time after.

Birmingham had offered an excellent field for Aloysius. Pickings had been reasonably easy. But that very day a certain embarrassing situation had arisen on the First National Bank corner—something which informed Danny the Dip that he'd be wise to seek other fields for his nefarious activities. So this night found him on the Limited with a New York ticket in his pocket and a profound hope that no plainclothes bull would impede his departure from the South.

Epic's trained eye had warned him against Aloysius when that furtive gentleman sidled onto the train and slipped into his berth. Mr. Peters was not unfamiliar with gentlemen who make a living by nimble wits, fingers, and conscience. Mr. Peters boasted that he could spot a train hustler as far as he could see one, and something told him from the first that this ratlike gentleman was worth observing.

Yet, as the train roared through the chilly night and sleep refused to come to Epic, that person sat in the smoking room, and reflected that of the two gentlemen—the one in Lower Six and the one in Lower Eight—he'd prefer a half dozen of Aloysius to one of the former. After all, Epic was not personally concerned with undersized persons who looked and acted like crooks, but the blatant officious type brought him agony of soul and misery of spirit.

Quite early in the morning the train rolled under the shed of the Atlanta station. The Atlanta Pullman was cut out and the train made up anew for the run to New York. There Captain Sandifer, the grizzled and veteran Pullman conductor of whom Epic was extremely fond, took over the diagrams and chatted briefly with his favorite porter.

"Things going all right, Epic?"

"Not so many, Cap'n. I got on my car one of them white folks that thinks he boughten the comp'ny when he paid his money fo' a ticket."

"Been riding you, eh?"

"Nos-suh, not me, he ain't. But he sho ain't the fondest kind of passenger I is of."

"I don't blame you, Epic. But, cheer up! The run won't last forever."

"Nos-suh, maybe not. But it seems mos' that long."

By the time the train pulled out of Atlanta half the passengers had risen and wandered into the diner—among them the stout gentleman and Aloysius. When they returned their sections were already arranged for the day and Epic was busy elsewhere in the car.

The stout person summoned Epic. "Porter," he snapped, "what do you mean by putting my small bag under the seat?"

"I don't mean nothin', white folks. Always puts the bags under the seats."

"Hmph! Get it out immediately."

"Yas-suh, cap'n."

Epic bent over and wrestled with the bag. He rose and bowed.

"That all, mistuh?"

"No, it isn't. I want two pillows and a hat bag."

"Y-y-yas-suh, boss; right away. I aims to give service, which is how come they to call me Hop Sure."

"I'm not interested in your nicknames. What I want is the pillows."

Epic was shuddering with futile rage as he went on the errand. And while he was extracting pillowcases from the linen cabinet at the end of the aisle, he saw Captain Sandifer come through the car and answer the summons of the obtrusive stout person. Epic listened in.

"Impertinent porter you have on this car," rasped the person with the white piping on his vest.

Sandifer frowned. "Epic Peters?"

"I don't know his name or anything about him. I know he is inefficient and impertinent."

The eyes of the Pullman conductor narrowed. He knew the type of man he was conversing with, and one of the great regrets in his life was that duty prohibited him from exterminating such insects.

"Epic is never impertinent," he defended frigidly.

"He was impertinent to me."

"How?"

"Do I have to give details? Isn't my word sufficient?"

Sandifer's face was dead white with anger. The man was simply insufferable.

"Perhaps," said the conductor coldly.

"I'll file a report of this with the Pullman Company," raged the person in Section Six. "It is outrageous."

"Sorry," said Sandifer as he moved away.

It was with difficulty that Epic concealed his elation as he climbed to the upper berth in search of two pillows. Bless Cap'n Sandifer's heart! There was sho'nuff quality white folks. Reckon he knowed when a feller was pertinent or not. Wou'n't let no trash like this pouter pigeon put nothin' over on him! Not Cap'n Sandifer, nos-suh!

The florid person seemed to enjoy his futile anger. He snatched the pillows from Epic's hand and tried to stare frostily, but Mr. Peters's genial countenance was wreathed in a smile of sheer good humor. It seemed that nothing could ruffle his calm—a fact that served to annoy the man in Lower Six more than ever.

Humming gaily, Epic gave his attention to Section Seven. The lady who had occupied the lower had left the train at a little station beyond Atlanta. The upper berth of that section had not been occupied. Mr. Peters worked swiftly and well, rather happily conscious that two pairs of eyes were focused upon him. One pair of eyes belonged to the fat person. The other was the property of Danny the Dip, né Aloysius.

Mr. Peters bent joyfully to his task. He adjusted the two mattresses in the upper berth, discarded used linen, neatly folded baskets, and arranged pillows. Then he snapped the upper berth shut and commenced arranging the cushions of the lower.

He snapped the backrests into place and shoved one of the seat cushions back, and as he did so a glitter caught his eye. From the green-carpeted floor something twinkled up at him. A frown creased his mahogany forehead as he bent to pick it up.

When he straightened he was possessed of a queer excitement. He was holding in his hand a platinum ring which was set with a single gorgeous diamond.

Hop Sure's heart missed a beat. He knew that he cradled a young fortune in his palm, and his thoughts flashed ahead to the possibility of a sizable reward. It never occurred to him to do anything save report the matter to Captain Sandifer and turn in the ring to the Pullman office. Epic's honesty was unswerving. But he would have been less than human had he failed to speculate upon the value of his finding and the reward which a grateful and generous owner might bestow. His tremendous hand closed over the ring and he dropped it into the pocket of his coat. Then he turned quickly.

The stout man in Section Six was staring straight at him. Unquestionably that gentleman had witnessed the discovery of the ring, and Epic experienced a sense of annoyance. He glanced elsewhere about the car, curious to know whether anyone else had observed the finding of the ring. No one seemed interested. Even Aloysius, alias Danny the Dip, was staring out of the window, apparently absorbed in the speeding landscape.

Epic swung back to his work. His heart sang within him, for it seemed that his early hunch that this was to be an unpleasant and unprofitable trip was only half right. Unpleasant, yes, but unprofitable—

"Hot ziggity dam!" exclaimed Mr. Peters. "Di'monds is the most thing I love to find."

Some passengers had been late in rising. Two or three had eaten breakfast in their berths and were only now showing signs of stepping into their clothes. Consequently the labor of straightening the car had dragged interminably.

When Captain Sandifer next passed through the car Epic didn't even see him. He was perched on the arm of a lower, arranging mattresses in an upper. But the fat man in Section Six noticed that Epic did not report the finding of the diamond to the Pullman conductor, and the fact took on a sinister significance to the officious traveler.

With an armful of used linen Hop Sure made his way to the end of the car. And there, standing in the aisle, someone pressed sharply against him. He raised his head, to stare into the beady eyes of Danny the Dip.

Aloysius was trying to be affable. He spoke out of the corner of his mouth:

"Are we on time, porter?"

"Yas-suh, right on the minute."

"Yeah? Nice day, ain't it?"

"Pretty nice, boss man."

Aloysius looked around. "Where's the drinking water?"

Epic designated the cooler and hastened to secure for his undersized passenger a paper drinking cup. "There you is, cap'n."

Danny the Dip thanked Hop Sure and inhaled a cupful of ice water. Then he returned to his place in Section Eight while Epic engrossed himself once more in the task of fixing his car.

Eventually the job was completed and Epic sank into an unused section for a well-earned rest. He tried to make himself comfortable, but in spite of his best efforts he fidgeted with the consciousness that the eyes of the fat man were focused upon him.

Captain Sandifer came through the car. Epic determined to turn the diamond ring over to him then and there. But before he could speak to the Pullman conductor, that individual was stopped by the rasping voice of the fat person in Section Six:

"Conductor!"

Sandifer stopped in the aisle. It was obvious that the passenger was not overly popular with him.

"Well?" he asked bleakly.

"I consider it my duty to report something to you."

"What?"

"I very much question the honesty of your porter."

"Well," snapped Sandifer, "I don't!"

"You wouldn't, of course." The pursy lips of the traveler creased into a sneer. "Has he turned over to you anything which he found in the car this morning?"

Sandifer shook his head. "No. But if he found anything of value he will."

"Evidently your confidence is very great—much greater than mine. I shall write a report of this to the Pullman Company and—"

The conductor was furious. "Now, listen here!" he said curtly. "You've done a lot of insinuating and haven't backed it up with a fact. If you've got any accusations to make, make 'em. But I'm not going to be bothered with your infernal hot air any longer."

"Oh, is that so! For all I know, you're in cahoots—"

"Mister," warned Sandifer sweetly, "I value my job very highly, but not so highly that it would be safe for you to finish that sentence."

Epic wriggled with glee. That was the way to talk to uppity folks. Trust Cap'n Sandifer for that.

"Just the same," said the fat person, "when your porter made up Section Seven he found something which seemed to me to be a valuable diamond ring."

"He did, eh?"

"He certainly did."

"Was it your ring?"

"No-o-o."

"Belong to any friend of yours?"

"No, but—"

"Then it's none of your business."

Sandifer turned on his heel and strode from the car, white-faced with anger. He refused to give the fat man the satisfaction of accepting from Hop Sure at that time the ring which had been found.

Having known Epic for years, there was no question in the mind of the conductor that Mr. Peters possessed an ineluctable honesty. And he took a keen satisfaction in the look of thwarted anger which had come into the fishlike eyes of the man in Section Six.

Epic himself was very happy. Cap'n Sandifer was his friend—always had been and always would be. He knew the captain for a rigid taskmaster, but one who appreciated efficient and honest effort.

The train was approaching Charlotte, and Epic noticed a bit of activity in Section Eight. Aloysius was strapping his suitcase very carefully. It was evident that he was making preparations to leave the train. This occasioned mild surprise in the breast of Mr. Peters, for he happened to know that the ratlike person held a ticket for New York.

But the destination of Danny the Dip did not interest Mr. Peters for very long. He lounged in his seat and turned his thoughts into pleasant channels which had to do with the discomfiture of the fat man. Epic understood and appreciated the delicacy of feeling which had prompted the conductor to say nothing about the ring in the presence of the protuberant gentleman in Section Six.

Plenty of time to return the diamond ring. Smiling broadly, Epic dropped his hand into his pocket to assure himself that everything was all right.

Quite suddenly, and with comprehensive completeness, the smile vanished from Epic's countenance and in its stead there came an expression of abysmal consternation. His fingers fumbled frantically and he was stricken by a chill.

"Oh, whoa is me!" he mourned as the potentialities of the situation were thrust upon him. "That ring has went!"

Gone—vanished—completely and absolutely departed somewhere else!

It required less than a split second for Epic Peters to realize that he was in a horrid dilemma. His distaste for the fat man in Section Six now flamed to a violent and aggressive hatred.

He had found the ring, and the fat man had seen him find it. Bulwarked behind the knowledge of his own honesty, he had taken his own time about reporting the discovery to Cap'n Sandifer, and the fat man had made a bad matter worse by suggesting to the Pullman conductor that Epic intended to steal the ring.

Now the ring was gone, and Cap'n Sandifer knew that he had found it. Sooner or later Sandifer would ask for the ring, and Epic groaned at the prospect of telling him that it had disappeared. Sandifer might believe Epic, but by the same token the conductor would make a report of the whole affair to the company officials. In addition to that, the fat man would also see to it that the matter came to the most unfortunate ears.

There would be an investigation—perhaps a trial. Epic knew that he would be dismissed from the service—kicked out of the profession to which he had devoted his life. The very least that could be proved against him was gross carelessness, and there was grave danger that he might be convicted of dishonesty.

The spirit of Mr. Epic Peters groveled. He hit bottom and continued going down. "Oh gosh," he moaned, "Ol' Man Disaster has sho slapped me right in the face!"

At first Epic was unable to do anything but reflect upon the ghastly situation. Then he commenced to hunt. He hunted violently for that ring, searching every nook and cranny of the car. The fat man was regarding him sneeringly. And the beady eyes of Danny the Dip never left the wriggling figure of the distraught porter.

The ring was nowhere to be found. Epic now was in terror lest Cap'n Sandifer choose this inopportune time to demand it. To avoid such a catastrophe, Hop Sure retired to the unoccupied drawing room. He desired solitude and lots of it. He left the door open, but managed to keep out of sight.

He commenced thinking. Never in all his eventful career had the brain of Mr. Peters functioned with such amazing speed. Logic hammered insistently. The ring was lost. It hadn't jumped out of the window, it wasn't on the floor of the car, nor was it concealed in the upholstery. Unquestionably, however, it was still in the car.

Epic's thoughts flashed to the fat man, but he immediately discarded the thought that that person had anything to do with it. Then he remembered the ratlike individual in Section Eight.

From the very first moment that he set eyes on Aloysius, Epic had felt an antipathy to that gentleman. He knew there was something wrong about Danny the Dip—something fearfully and radically wrong.

He cocked his head on one side so as to command a view of the car. Danny the Dip was undoubtedly planning to get off at Charlotte. The significance of this impressed Hop Sure.

The man had a ticket to New York. Why, then, should he suddenly alter his plans and leave the train in North Carolina? Something queer—dawg-goned queer, too. Instinct informed Epic that Danny the Dip was in some manner connected with that ring. He thought Danny had witnessed the finding. He wasn't sure, but he thought so. Apparently Danny had been looking out of the window at the time, but Epic had a hunch that those beady eyes hadn't missed much.

Epic remembered something else. He recalled the queer actions of Aloysius near the water cooler. Danny the Dip had accosted him and engaged him in conversation about matters of no importance whatever. During that conversation the Dip had stood very, very close to Epic—so close, reflected the porter, that he could very easily have slipped nimble fingers into the capacious pocket of Epic's coat and extracted therefrom the diamond ring.

Epic set his feet squarely on the floor. He felt certain that he had hit upon the correct solution; facts dovetailed perfectly.

Mr. Peters was desperate. He knew that he had only a few minutes of grace. Very shortly the train would be in Charlotte and Aloysius would leave. Once away, Epic knew he'd never again set eyes on the man or the ring.

Mr. Peters was spurred to drastic action. He summoned a genial, disarming smile and plastered it on his face. Then he approached Danny the Dip.

"Gittin' off at Charlotte, boss man?"

The ratlike eyes darted to Epic's countenance.

"Yes."

"Lemme brush you off, suh."

Epic held a whisk broom insinuatingly before the eyes of Aloysius. The wiry little man hesitated, then rose. Immediately Epic stepped toward the end of the car.

"Right this way, cap'n, so's the dust won't bother nobody."

Aloysius frowned, but followed. To have reseated himself might have attracted attention.

Epic stopped at the door of the drawing room and motioned Aloysius to enter. The professional pickpocket hesitated briefly, then stepped inside. Immediately Epic extracted a cloth from his pants pocket and knelt on the floor before the little man. He polished his shoes assiduously.

The heart of Mr. Peters was pounding. Ordinarily none-too-well-supplied with physical courage, he was now daring everything to avert personal disaster. He rose, pocketed the dust cloth and turned.

His slim, angular body functioned smoothly. One skinny arm

reached out and slammed the drawing-room door. Well-trained fingers snapped the lock. Then Hop Sure turned upon the astounded Danny an expression which had lost all of its mild good nature.

Danny the Dip stepped back defensively. His eyes narrowed to pinpoints and the color drained from his cheeks.

"What the—"

"Just a minute, white folks!" Epic's words came like drops from an icicle. "You got somethin' I want."

"Why, you—"

"No need swearin' at me, neither. I never aim to be nothin' but respectful, an' my rule ain't gwine he broke, but you got somethin' that I'se gwine have, no matter how you forces me to git it."

Danny was thinking swiftly. The lengthy porter showed no hint of weakness or lack of courage.

Epic spoke again. Words seemed to restore his fast-ebbing bravery.

"Gimme that di'mond ring!" he commanded harshly, extending his hand.

"Wh-what diamond ring?"

"Don't try no fumadiddles with me, white folks. You know good an' well what di'mond ring you has got. An' I crave to have it."

"You're talking crazy."

"H'm, I reckon not. Mistuh, I ain't no fool—honest I ain't. Somethin' seemed wrong with you right fum the first, an' it don't look reasonable to me that no man would buy a ticket to New Yawk an' git off at Charlotte less'n he had a good reason. So if you just gimme the ring—"

"I won't give you anything."

Epic shrugged.

"A'right, mistuh. If you won't, you won't, an' I ain't gwine argufy."

Danny the Dip stepped forward. "Let me out of here."

"Not so's you could observe it, mistuh. Heah you stays until you gimme that ring, or else until the police gits you."

"Police?"

"You di'n't misunderstan' me none. I said police, an' b'lieve me, mistuh, I meant police."

"But—but, porter—"

"I don't aim to git butted, neither. If you gimme that ring I promise to let you leave the train at Charlotte an' not say nothin' to nobody. If you refuse, I han's you over to the police right at the station. An' don't think I won't tell 'em why."

"Now, listen." The voice of Aloysius had taken on a whiny, wheedling note. "A little cash—"

"Cash don't mean nothin' to me, or even less than that. It's di'mond ring fo' Hop Sure or jail fo' you. Now, which?"

Danny's lip curled. "If I had a gun—"

"Man, tha's the mos' thing I was scared of when I brung you in heah. You ain't never gwine know how frightened I was of that. I sho despises to git kilt."

Aloysius glanced out of the window. The train was slowing down. Already they were within the corporate limits of Charlotte.

Epic interpreted the thoughts of the man and grinned cheerfully. "Take all the time you want," he invited. "But the minute us stops at that station with you still havin' that ring, I yells fo' the police."

Aloysius knew when he was beaten. Threats, cajolery, and bribery had failed.

"You promise you won't even hint to anybody?"

"Gosh—yes, I promise. All I crave is that jool."

Danny the Dip probed into his watch pocket and extracted therefrom a gleaming diamond ring. He placed it resentfully in Epic's palm.

"There!" he rasped. "And if you break your promise I'll get you if it's the last thing I do."

"Don't you worry, mistuh. I wou'n't break that promise if I wanted to."

Intoxicated with happiness, Epic sped to the platform, where he busied himself arranging suitcases for the departing passengers. He felt the need of company and lots of it. Aloysius would never dare start anything while others were watching.

The train stopped at the station in Charlotte. A half dozen passengers alighted, and foremost among them was Danny the Dip.

Epic was on the platform, and it was he who handed Danny's suitcase to that slender gentleman. The pickpocket grabbed it from the porter and strode swiftly away. Epic gazed ruefully after him.

"Well, I'll be dawg-bit! He didn't even gimme a tip."

The train pulled out. As Epic reentered his car he was conscious of the fishy, suspicious glance of the fat man in Section Six.

But that glance failed to annoy Mr. Peters now. He felt an enormous disdain for the fat person. Interfere in his affairs, eh? Reckon he'd show him something!

Epic settled into the seat recently vacated by Danny the Dip. And suddenly he felt the ghastly effects of what medical men technically term a nervous reaction.

Mr. Peters was cold and limp all over. He had battled bravely through a crisis and achieved victory, but the strain exacted its toll now, and Epic could actually feel the strength flow out of his finger ends.

His mind dwelt on terrible things. Suppose Aloysius had drawn a gun. Suppose Aloysius had attacked him. Suppose—oh, most horrid of thoughts!—suppose he had been wrong and Aloysius had not possessed the ring.

But it was all over now. The sun was shining and the little birdies were warbling their gayest tunes. Mr. Peters planned every little detail of the triumphal moment when—before the suspicious eyes of the fat man in Section Six—he would present to Captain Sandifer the gorgeous diamond ring which had caused him such agony.

He had it again, safe and sound. Brain had triumphed over dishonest cunning. Epic permitted himself to smile as he slipped his right hand into his pocket and felt for the diamond.

He blinked—he blinked again. He sat up straight in his seat, conscious of a terrible sinking sensation at the pit of his tummy.

"Great wigglin' tripe," he gasped, "that ring has gone again!"

And now Mr. Epic Peters knew that all the suffering which he had already experienced was mere rehearsal. For every ounce of misery which had been his before reaching Charlotte, there was now a ton to rack and torture him. He thought of the nimble-fingered Aloysius—gone out of his life forever—and of the diamond ring for which he had blithely risked total extermination.

Epic uncoiled himself and searched the section in which he sat. Then he crawled the length of the car on hands and knees. A sweet-faced old lady questioned him.

"What's the matter, porter?"

Epic raised a haggard face.

"Ev'ything, ma'am."

"Lost something?"

"Lady, I sho has. Seems like I has los' my lease on life."

The ring did not appear. More and more certainly the conviction grew upon Epic that Aloysius had double-crossed him. He returned to the vacant section and flung himself down on the seat. Forlornly he plunged his hand into the pocket of his coat.

The index finger touched something. A hole!

Instantly an expression of eager hope crossed the troubled brow of Mr. Peters. With decisive strength he ripped the hole to several times its size. He dropped his entire hand into the cavity which existed between coat and lining.

And then something startling happened to his countenance. His jaw sagged, his eyes popped, a cold perspiration stood out on his brow.

He withdrew from his pocket a hand which trembled with an excess of excitement. Slowly he opened his fist. Sunlight, streaming in through the window, was reflected dazzlingly into the eyes of the lengthy Pullman porter.

Gleaming gloriously in his hand there lay not one diamond ring but two. Two rings! Two diamonds! Two platinum settings!

"Great sufferin' stew-meat," gasped Epic, "the ring has done twinned!"

Captain Sandifer appeared. Epic did not hesitate. He slipped one of the rings into his trousers pocket as he rose to full length.

He accosted the conductor, and before the disappointed eyes of the fat person in Section Six, Mr. Peters extended to his superior the identical diamond ring which had been discovered early that morning in Lower Seven.

"Cap'n Sandifer," he announced in a bored tone, "heah's a li'l trifle I found this mawnin' while I was performin' my chores."

Sandifer accepted the ring and thanked Epic. Then he flashed a gleeful glance at the thoroughly cowed fat gentleman in Section Six. Words seemed unnecessary. But Epic Peters insisted on speaking:

"Cap'n Sandifer?"

"What is it, Hop Sure?"

"Is you willin' to do me a favor?"

"Certainly."

"Some folks is always th'owin' away aspersions. Would you mind walkin' th'oo the train an' askin' ev'ybody if they has lost a di'mond ring?"

"But I'm sure this was lost by the lady in Lower Seven."

"Yas-suh, boss, so'm I. But I want to feel sure there ain't nobody else in the train lost no other di'mond."

More to discomfort the man in Lower Six than to please Epic, Captain Sandifer agreed. He canvassed the train and was back in ten minutes.

"All clear, Epic," he announced. "Nobody else on the train has lost anything."

"You got that positively, Cap'n?"

"Absolutely."

Epic trailed the Pullman conductor the length of the car. They stood together on the vestibule platform.

"Cap'n Sandifer," said Epic, "I craves to ask you a question."

"All right, Hop Sure. What is it?"

"It's just this, Cap'n. Suppose while I was porterin', a passenger on my car happened to give me—of his own free will an' discord—a swell di'mond ring—just give it to me! Would that ring belong to me, or should I turn it in to the company?"

The conductor grinned.

"If he gave it to you, Epic, it would be yours."

Mr. Peters nodded beatifically.

"Thanks, Cap'n. Tha's all I yearned to know."

The Pullman conductor passed on. Epic stood motionless, busy with his thoughts. He understood everything now. He even understood why Danny the Dip had left the train at Charlotte. Danny had seen trouble brewing, and, being a professional crook, was not desirous of being discovered among the passengers should police be called upon to investigate.

Mr. Peters gazed at the gorgeous stone which glittered up at him. Then his lips twisted into a smile.

"All I got to do now," he reflected happily, "is find a gal to fit this."

—1928

THE NERVE OF FOLEY

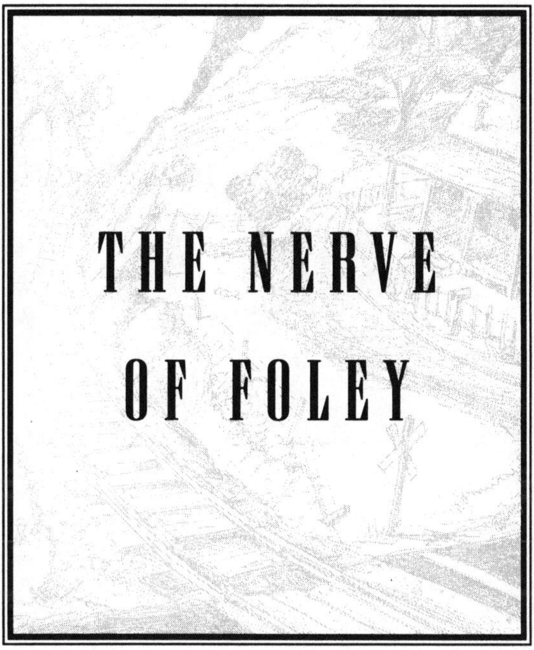

FRANK H. SPEARMAN

THERE HAD BEEN rumors all winter that the engineers were going to strike. Certainly we of the operating department had warning enough. Yet, in the railroad life there is always friction in some quarter; the railroad man sleeps like the soldier, with an ear alert—but just the same he sleeps, for with waking comes duty.

Our engineers were good fellows. If they had faults, they were American faults—rashness, a liberality bordering on extravagance, and a headstrong, violent way of reaching conclusions—traits born of ability and self-confidence and developed by prosperity.

One of the best men we had on a locomotive was Andrew Cameron; at the same time he was one of the hardest to manage, because he was young and headstrong. Andy, a big, powerful fellow, ran opposite Felix Kennedy on the Flyer. The fast runs require young men. If you will notice, you will rarely see an old engineer on a fast passenger run; even a young man can stand only a few years of that kind of work. High speed on a locomotive is a question of nerve and endurance—to put it bluntly, a question of flesh and blood.

"You don't think much of this strike, do you, Mr. Reed?" said Andy to me one night.

"Don't think there's going to be any, Andy."

He laughed knowingly.

"What actual grievance have the boys?" I asked.

"The trouble's on the east end," he replied evasively.

"Is that any reason for calling a thousand men out on this end?"

"If one goes out, they all go."

"Would you go out?"

"Would I? You bet!"

"A man with a home and a wife and a baby boy like yours ought to have more sense."

Getting up to leave, he laughed again, confidently. "That's all right. We'll bring you fellows to terms."

"Maybe," I retorted as he closed the door. But I hadn't the slightest idea they would begin the attempt that night. I was at home and sound asleep when the caller tapped on my window. I threw up the sash; it was pouring rain and dark as a pocket.

"What is it, Barney? A wreck?" I exclaimed.

"Worse than that. Everything's tied up."

"What do you mean?"

"The engineers have struck."

"Struck? What time is it?"

"Half past three. They went out at three o'clock."

Throwing on my clothes, I floundered behind Barney's lantern to the depot. The superintendent was already in his office talking to the master mechanic.

Bulletins came in every few minutes from various points announcing trains tied up. Before long we began to hear from the east end. Chicago reported all engineers out; Omaha wired, no trains moving. When the sun rose that morning our entire system, extending through seven states and territories, was absolutely paralyzed.

It was an astounding situation, but one that must be met. It meant either an ignominious surrender to the engineers or a fight to the death. For our part, we had only to wait for orders. It was just six o'clock when the chief train-dispatcher who was tapping at a key, said: "Here's something from headquarters."

We crowded close around him. His pen flew across the clip; the message was addressed to all division superintendents. It was short; but at the end of it he wrote a name we rarely saw in our office. It was that of the railroad magnate we knew as "the Old Man," the president of the system, and his words were few: "Move the trains."

"Move the trains!" repeated the superintendent. "Yes; but trains can't be moved by pinch-bars nor by main force."

We spent the day arguing with the strikers. They were friendly, but firm. Persuasion, entreaties, threats, we exhausted; and ended just where we began, except that we had lost our tempers. The sun set without the turn of a wheel. The victory of the first day was certainly with the strikers.

Next day it looked pretty blue around the depot. Not a car was moved; the engineers and firemen were a unit. But the wires sung hard all that day and all that night. Just before midnight Chicago wired that Number One—our big passenger train, the Denver Flyer—had started out on time, with the superintendent of motive power as engineer, and a wiper for fireman. The message came from the second vice president. He promised to deliver the train to our division on time the next evening, and he asked, "Can you get it through to Denver?"

We looked at each other. At last all eyes gravitated toward Neighbor, our master mechanic.

The train dispatcher was waiting. "What shall I say?" he asked.

The division chief of the motive power was a tremendously big Irishman, with a voice like a foghorn. Without an instant's hesitation the answer came clear:

"Say yes!"

Every one of us started. It was throwing the gage of battle. Our word had gone out; the division was pledged; the fight was on.

Next evening the strikers, through some mysterious channel, got word that the Flyer was expected. About nine o'clock a crowd of them began to gather round the depot.

It was after one o'clock when Number One pulled in and the foreman of the Omaha roundhouse swung down from the locomotive cab. The strikers clustered around the engine like a swarm of angry bees; but that night, though there was plenty of jeering, there was no actual violence. When they saw Neighbor climb into the cab to take the run west, there was a sullen silence.

Next day a committee of strikers, with Andy Cameron, very cavalier, at their head, called on me.

"Mr. Reed," said he officiously, "we've come to notify you not to run any more trains through here till this strike's settled. The boys won't stand it; that's all." With that he turned on his heel to leave with his following.

"Hold on, Cameron," I replied, raising my hand as I spoke; "that's not quite all. I suppose you men represent your grievance committee?"

"Yes sir."

"I happen to represent, in the superintendent's absence, the management of this road. I simply want to say to you, and to your committee, that I take my orders from the president and the general manager—not from you nor anybody you represent. That's all."

Every hour the bitterness increased. We got a few trains through, but we were terribly crippled. As for freight, we made no pretense of moving it. Trainloads of fruit and meat rotted in the yards. The strikers grew more turbulent daily. They beat our new men and crippled our locomotives. Then, our troubles with the new men were almost as bad. They burned out our crown sheets; they got mixed up on orders all the time. They ran into open switches and into each other continually, and had us very nearly crazy.

I kept tabs on one of the new engineers for a week. He began by backing into a diner so hard that he smashed every dish in the car, and ended by running into a siding a few days later and setting two tanks of oil on fire, which burned up a freight depot. I figured he cost us forty thousand dollars the week he ran. Then he went back to selling windmills.

After this experience I was sitting in my office one evening, when a youngish fellow in a slouch hat opened the door and stuck his head in.

"What do you want?" I growled.

"Are you Mr. Reed?"

"What do you want?"

"I want to speak to Mr. Reed."

"Well, what is it?"

"Are you Mr. Reed?"

"Confound you, yes! What do you want?"

"Me? I don't want anything. I'm just asking, that's all."

His impudence staggered me so that I took my feet off the desk.

"Heard you were looking for men," he added.

"No," I snapped. "I don't want any men."

"Wouldn't be any show to get on an engine, would there?"

A week earlier I would have risen and fallen on his neck. But there had been others.

"There's a show to get your head broke," I suggested.

"I don't mind that, if I get my time."

"What do you know about running an engine?"

"Run one three years."

"On a threshing machine?"

"On the Philadelphia and Reading."

"Who sent you in here?"

"Just dropped in."

"Sit down."

I eyed him sharply as he dropped into a chair.

"When did you quit the Philadelphia and Reading?"

"About six months ago."

"Fired?"

"Strike."

I began to get interested. After a few more questions I took him into the superintendent's office. But at the door I thought it well to drop a hint.

"Look here, my friend, if you're a spy you'd better keep out of this. This man would wring your neck as quick as he'd suck an orange. See?"

"Let's tackle him anyhow," replied the fellow, eyeing me coolly.

I introduced him to Mr. Lancaster, and left them together. Pretty soon the superintendent came into my office.

"What do you make of him, Reed?" said he.

"What do you make of him?"

Lancaster studied a minute.

"Take him over to the roundhouse and see what he knows."

I walked over with the new find, chatting warily. When we reached a live engine I told him to look it over. He threw off his coat, picked up a piece of waste, and swung into the cab.

"Run her out to the switch," said I, stepping up myself.

He pinched the throttle, and we steamed slowly out of the house. A minute showed he was at home on an engine.

"Can you handle it?" I asked as he shut off after backing down to the roundhouse.

"You use soft coal," he replied, trying the injector. "I'm used to hard. This injector is new to me. Guess I can work it, though."

"What did you say your name was?"

"I didn't say."

"What is it?" I asked curtly.

"Foley."

"Well, Foley, if you have as much sense as you have gall, you ought to get along. If you act straight, you'll never want a job again as long as you live. If you don't, you won't want to live very long."

"Got any tobacco?"

"Here, Baxter," said I, turning to the roundhouse foreman, "this is Foley. Give him a chew, and mark him up to go out on Seventy-seven tonight. If he monkeys with anything around the house, kill him."

Baxter looked at Foley, and Foley looked at Baxter; and, Baxter not getting the tobacco out quick enough, Foley reminded him he was waiting.

We didn't pretend to run freights, but I concluded to try the fellow on one, feeling sure that if he was crooked he would ditch it and skip.

So Foley ran a long string of empties and a car or two of rotten oranges down to Harvard Junction that night, with one of the dispatchers for pilot. Under my orders they had a train made-up at the junction for him to bring back to McCloud. They had picked up all the strays in the yards, including half a dozen cars of meat that the local board of health had condemned after it had lain out in the sun for two weeks, and a car of butter we had been shifting around ever since the beginning of the strike.

When the strikers saw the stuff coming in next morning behind Foley they concluded I had gone crazy.

"What do you think of the track, Foley?" said I.

"Fair," he replied, sitting down on my desk. "Stiff hill down there by Zanesville."

"Any trouble to climb it?" I asked, for I had purposely given him a heavy train.

"Not with that car of butter. If you hold that butter another week it will climb a hill without any engine."

"Can you handle a passenger train?"

"I guess so."

"I'm going to send you west on Number One tonight."

"Then you'll have to give me a fireman. That guy you sent out last night is a lightning-rod peddler. The dispatcher threw most of the coal."

"I'll go with you myself, Foley. I can give you steam. Can you stand it to double-back tonight?"

"I can stand it if you can."

When I walked into the roundhouse in the evening, with a pair of overalls on, Foley was in the cab getting ready for the run.

Neighbor brought the Flyer in from the east. As soon as he had uncoupled and got out of the way, we backed down with the 448. It was the best engine we had left, and, luckily for my back, an easy steamer. Just as we coupled to the mailcar, a crowd of strikers swarmed out of the dusk. They were in an ugly mood, and when Andy Cameron and Bat Nicholson sprang up into the cab, I saw we were in for trouble.

"Look here, partner," exclaimed Cameron, laying a heavy hand on Foley's shoulder; "you don't want to take this train out, do you? You wouldn't beat honest workingmen out of a job."

"I'm not beating anybody out of a job. If you want to take out this train, take it out. If you don't, get out of this cab."

Cameron was nonplussed. Nicholson, a surly brute, raised his fist menacingly.

"See here, boss," he growled, "we won't stand no scabs on this line."

"Get out of this cab."

"I'll promise you you'll never get out of it alive, my buck, if you ever get into it again," cried Cameron, swinging down. Nicholson followed, muttering angrily. I hoped we were out of the scrape, but to my consternation Foley, picking up his oil can, got right down behind them, and began filling his cups without the least attention to anybody.

Nicholson sprang on him like a tiger. The onslaught was so sudden that they had him under their feet in a minute. I jumped down, and Ben Buckley, the conductor, came running up. Between us we gave the little fellow a life. He squirmed out like a cat and instantly backed up against the tender.

"One at a time, and come on," he cried hotly. "If it's ten to one, and on a man's back at that, we'll do it different." With a quick, peculiar movement of his arm he drew a pistol and, pointing it squarely at Cameron, cried, "Get back!"

I caught a flash of his eye through the blood that streamed down his face. I wouldn't have given a switch-key for the life of the man who crowded him at that minute. But just then Lancaster came up, and before the crowd realized it we had Foley, protesting angrily, back in the cab again.

"For heaven's sake, pull out of this before there's bloodshed, Foley," I cried; and, nodding to Buckley, Foley opened the choker.

It was a night run and a new track to him. I tried to fire and pilot both, but after Foley suggested once or twice that if I would tend to the coal he would tend to the curves, I let him find them—and he found them all, I thought, before we got to Athens. He took big chances in his running, but there was a superb confidence in his bursts of speed, which marked the fast runner and the experienced one.

At Athens we had barely two hours to rest before doubling back. I was never tired in my life till I struck the pillow that night, but before I got it warm the caller routed me out again. The eastbound Flyer was on time, or nearly so, and when I got into the cab for the run back, Foley was just coupling on.

"Did you get a nap?" I asked as we pulled out.

"No; we slipped an eccentric coming up, and I've been under the engine ever since. Say, she's a bird, isn't she? She's all right. I couldn't run her coming up; but I've touched up her valve motion a bit, and I'll get action on her as soon as it's daylight."

"Don't mind getting action on my account, Foley; I'm shy on life insurance."

He laughed.

"You're safe with me. I never killed man, woman, or child in my life. When I do, I quit the cab. Give her plenty of diamonds, if you please," he added, letting her out full.

He gave me the ride of my life; but I hated to show scare, he was so coolly audacious himself. We had but one stop—for water—and after that, all down grade. We bowled along as easy as ninepins, but the pace was a hair-raiser. After we passed Arickaree we never touched a thing but the high joints. The long, heavy train behind us flew round the bluffs once in a while like the tail of a very capricious kite; yet somehow—and that's an engineer's magic—she always lit on the steel.

Day broke ahead, and between breaths I caught the glory of a sunrise on the plains from a locomotive-cab window. When the smoke of the McCloud shops stained the horizon, remembering the ugly threats of the strikers, I left my seat to speak to Foley.

"I think you'd better swing off when you slow up for the yards, and cut across to the roundhouse," I cried, getting close to his ear, for we were on terrific speed. He looked at me inquiringly. "In that way you won't run into Cameron and his crowd at the depot," I added. "I can stop her all right."

He didn't take his eyes off the track. "I'll take the train to the platform," said he. "Isn't that a crossing-cut ahead?" he added suddenly as we swung round a fill west of town.

"Yes; and a bad one."

He reached for the whistle and gave the long, warning screams. I set the bell ringer and stooped to open the furnace door to cool the fire, when—*chug!*

I flew up against the water gauges like a coupling-pin. The monster engine reared right up on her head. Scrambling to my feet, I saw the new man clutching the air lever with both hands, and every wheel on the train was screeching. I jumped to his side and looked over his shoulder. On the crossing just ahead, a big white horse, dragging a buggy, plunged and reared frantically. Standing on the buggy seat, a baby boy clung bewildered to the lazyback; not another soul in sight. All at once the horse swerved sharply back; the buggy lurched half over; the lines seemed to be caught around one wheel. The little fellow clung on; but the crazy horse, instead of running, began a hornpipe right between the deadly rails.

I looked at Foley in despair. From the monstrous quivering leaps of the great engine I knew the drivers were in the clutch of the mighty air-brake; but the resistless momentum of the train was nonetheless sweeping us down at deadly speed on the baby. Between the two tremendous forces the locomotive shivered like a gigantic beast. I shrank back in horror; but the little man at the throttle, throwing the last ounce of air on the burning wheels, leaped from his box with a face transfigured.

"Take her!" he cried, and, never shifting his eyes from the cut, he shot through his open window and darted like a cat along the running board to the front.

Not a hundred feet separated us from the crossing. I could see the baby's curls blowing in the wind. The horse suddenly leaped from across the track to the side of it; that left the buggy quartering with the rails, but not twelve inches clear. The way the wheels were cramped, a single step ahead would throw the hind wheels into the train; a step backward would shove the front wheels into it. It was appalling.

Foley, clinging with one hand to a headlight bracket, dropped down on the steam chest and swung far out. As the cowcatcher shot past, Foley's long arm dipped into the buggy like the sweep of a connecting-rod, and caught the boy by the breeches. The impetus of our speed threw the child high in the air, but Foley's grip was on the little overalls, and as the youngster bounded back he caught it close. I saw the horse give a leap. It sent the hind wheels into the corner of the baggage car. There was a crash like the report of a hundred rifles, and the buggy flew in the air. The big horse was thrown fifty feet; but Foley, with a great light in his eyes and the baby boy in his arm, crawled laughing into the cab.

Thinking he would take the engine again, I tried to take the baby. Take it? Well, I think not!

"Hi there, buster!" shouted the little engineer wildly; "that's a corking pair of breeches on you, son. I caught the kid right by the seat of the pants," he called over to me, laughing hysterically. "Heavens, little man! I wouldn't've struck you for all the gold in Alaska. I've got a chunk of a boy in Reading as much like him as a twin brother. What were you doing all alone in that buggy? Whose kid do you suppose it is? What's your name, son?"

At his question I looked at the child again—and I started. I had certainly seen him before; and had I not, his father's features were too well stamped on the childish face for me to be mistaken.

"Foley," I cried, all amazed, "that's Cameron's boy—little Andy!"

He tossed the baby the higher; he looked the happier; he shouted the louder.

"The deuce it is! Well, son, I'm mighty glad of it." And I certainly was glad.

In fact, mighty glad, as Foley expressed it, when we pulled up at the depot, and I saw Andy Cameron with a wicked look pushing to the front through the threatening crowd. With an ugly growl he made for Foley.

"I've got business with you—you—"

"I've got a little with you, son," retorted Foley, stepping leisurely down from the cab. "I struck a buggy back here at the first cut, and

I hear it was yours." Cameron's eyes began to bulge. "I guess the outfit's damaged some—all but the boy. Here, kid," he added, turning for me to hand him the child, "here's your dad."

The instant the youngster caught sight of his parent he set up a yell. Foley, laughing, passed him into his astonished father's arms before the latter could say a word. Just then, a boy running and squeezing through the crowd cried to Cameron that his horse had run away from the house with the baby in the buggy, and that Mrs. Cameron was having a fit.

Cameron stood like one gone daft—and the boy, catching sight of the baby that instant, panted and stared in an idiotic state.

"Andy," said I, getting down and laying a hand on his shoulder, "if these fellows want to kill this man, let them do it alone—you'd better keep out. Only this minute he has saved your boy's life."

The sweat stood out on the big engineer's forehead like dew. I told the story. Cameron tried to speak; but he tried again and again before he could find his voice.

"Mate," he stammered, "you've been through a strike yourself—you know what it means, don't you? But if you've got a baby—" He gripped the boy tighter to his shoulder.

"I have, partner; three of 'em."

"Then you know what this means," said Andy huskily, putting out his hand to Foley. He gripped the little man's fist hard, and turning, walked away through the crowd.

Somehow it put a damper on the boys. Bat Nicholson was about the only man left who looked as if he wanted to eat somebody; and Foley, slinging his blouse over his shoulder, walked up to Bat and tapped him on the shoulder.

"Stranger," said he gently, "could you oblige me with a chew of tobacco?"

Bat glared at him an instant; but Foley's nerve won.

Flushing a bit, Bat stuck his hand into his pocket; took it out; felt hurriedly in the other pocket; and, with some confusion, acknowledged he was short. Felix Kennedy intervened with a slab, and the three men fell at once to talking about the accident.

A long time afterward some of the striking engineers were taken back, but none of those who had been guilty of actual violence. This barred Andy Cameron, who, though not worse than many others, had been less prudent; and while we all felt sorry for him after the other boys had gone to work, Lancaster repeatedly and positively refused to reinstate him.

Several times, though, I saw Foley and Cameron in confab; and one day up came Foley to the superintendent's office, leading little Andy, in his overalls, by the hand. They went into Lancaster's office together, and the door was shut a long time.

When they came out, little Andy had a piece of paper in his hand.

"Hang on to it, son," cautioned Foley; "but you can show it to Mr. Reed if you want to."

The youngster handed me the paper. It was an order directing Andrew Cameron to report to the master mechanic for service in the morning.

I HAPPENED OVER at the roundhouse one day nearly a year later, when Foley was showing Cameron a new engine just in from the east. The two men were become great cronies; that day they fell to talking over the strike.

"There was never but one thing I really laid up against this man," said Cameron to me.

"What's that?" asked Foley.

"Why, the way you shoved that pistol into my face the first night you took out Number One."

"I never shoved any pistol into your face." So saying, he stuck his hand into his pocket with the identical motion he used that night of the strike, and leveled at Andy—just as he had done then—a plug of tobacco. "That's all I ever pulled on you, son; I never carried a pistol in my life."

Cameron looked at him, then he turned to me with a tired expression:

"I've seen a good many men, with a good many kinds of nerve, but I'll be splintered if I ever saw any one man with all kinds of nerve till I struck Foley."

—1901

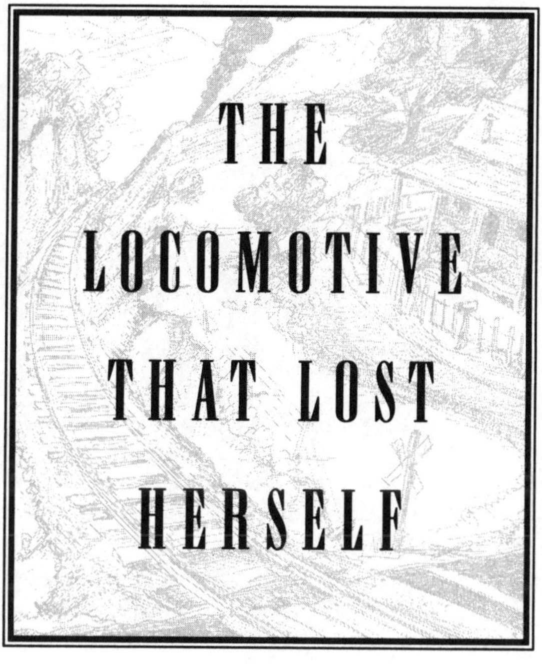

THE LOCOMOTIVE THAT LOST HERSELF

CY WARMAN

ENGINE 13 had been designed by a genius who was called a crank. He was the inventor of some of the most useful tools and appliances in use in the shops. He was an enthusiast. If he had not been, his design would never have been accepted by the superintendent of motive power and machinery. He claimed that his new locomotive would steam better, pull harder, and run faster than any engine on the K.P. She was so constructed that she could run farther on a tank of water, the enthusiast said, than an ordinary locomotive would run on two; and that was good, for water was scarce on the plains. She had patent lubricators and balanced valves—new inventions at that time—and being fresh-painted and handsome, she was regarded as a good "catch" by the engineers of the Smoky Hill Division. The genius who designed her had been sent out East to the locomotive works, to superintend her construction; and long before the engine was completed, the mechanics employed upon her had arrived at the conclusion that the Western engineer was as crazy as a jacksnipe.

As the locomotive neared completion the enthusiasm of her designer increased. A quiet, undemonstrative enthusiasm it was, that seemed to possess the soul of the inventor and to fill his life with all that he needed. Upon her growing skeleton he worked himself weary, and then rested himself in quiet contemplation of his ideal engine; and finally, when the wheels were placed beneath her frame, he began to see her as she should appear when completed. One morning when the workmen came, they found Hansen's bed in the engine tank. From that day forward he worked about her by day, and slept, if he slept at all, upon her at night.

Oscar Hansen, a Dane, had yellow hair and a very poor stand of clay-colored whiskers. Like writing and painting geniuses, he allowed his hair and beard to grow and blow as they would, and the result was that he was about as unhandsome a man as one would meet in a lifetime. All this was nothing to Hansen. He lived in his work, and believed that in time he would run away from Stephenson, Franklin, and all the rest.

When the 13 arrived at Kansas City, Hansen was with her, and he remained with her day and night until she was taken out to be limbered up for her trial trip. He insisted upon handling her himself, and would not allow the locomotive engineer to touch the throttle until the master mechanic came to him personally and remonstrated. It was evident from the very first that the engine was not right, and the engineer told Hansen so at the close of the first day with her. Hansen became so angry that he threatened to kill the engineer if he ever dared to repeat what he had said. Every day for nearly a week the new engine was raced around the yards, and never for a moment did Hansen leave her. His wild hair became wilder, his deep eyes sank deeper into his head, and his thin white face became almost horrible to see. At the end of a week it was decided to put the 13 on the Denver Express for her trial trip, and Hansen surprised the master mechanic by asking to be allowed to run her.

"But you are not a locomotive engineer," urged the official, "and I couldn't think of allowing you to handle the engine. You may go with her, if you wish; but the engineer must have full control of the locomotive."

Hansen went sullenly out, and climbed up into the cab.

When the conductor came with the orders, he glanced up, and asked: "Who's His Whiskers?"

"That fellow with the tired look and troubled tresses," answered the engineer, "is the idiot who designed this machine."

Hansen had, by insisting upon running the new locomotive himself, incurred the displeasure of every engineer on the road, and as this remark was meant for him to hear, he heard it. When the conductor left the engine, Hansen crossed over to the driver's side and said: "If you don't make time today, I'll run her myself, and I'll send you where you won't want a fireman."

The driver only laughed, for the sanity of the inventor had been a debatable question ever since his return with the new engine.

The train to which the 13 was coupled was a heavy one, for Colorado was at that time just beginning to "boom." In the first run, of seven miles, they lost five minutes, but Hansen was too much taken up with watching his machine to take note of the time. Her boiler was foaming, as new boilers usually do; her main pins were hot, and so was her engineer. The first stop was at a small town, and when the conductor gave the signal to go, the engineer was still on the ground pouring tallow on the pins. Hansen became frantic at what, to him, seemed unnecessary delay and, springing to the driver's side, he pulled the throttle wide open without releasing the air-brakes. The engine lurched forward, and when the slack was gone, her wheels began to revolve at a frightful rate. The engineer sprang into the cab and found Hansen working frantically in a vain effort to shut off steam, and concluded at a glance that the throttle had been left partly open, and that the high pressure of steam had forced it out.

Now, when the engineer, fireman, and Hansen all seized the lever to force the throttle in, they sprang the stem, and the thing could not be closed. The engineer released the air with the hope that the train might be started, and in that way the engine could be cooled down without doing any great damage. But the wheels were now revolving at such a rate that the engine had no adhesive power, and the train stood still. Five, ten, fifteen seconds went by, and still the three men worked, each in another's way, trying to shut off steam. A solid stream of fire was rolling out of the stack, and such sprays of sparks came from the drivers that they looked like living flames.

Pushing Hansen and the fireman out of his way, the engineer opened both injectors; what with the cold water going in and the fire going out, the mad machine cooled rapidly, and in a few moments, ground harshly and came to a stop. It was found, upon examination, that the drivers had dug great holes in the steel rails, and that the tires on the back pair of driving-wheels, already well heated by the furnace, had loosened by expansion and slipped nearly off the wheels. In a little while the throttle was cooled and closed, and a fresh fire was made; but when they gave the engine steam, she refused to move. She was uncoupled, and still refused to go; and then they saw that her tires had cooled and clasped the firebox, and the firebox, expanding, held them there and locked the wheels.

When they had put out her fire, the wheels let loose, so that a yard engine could drag her back to the roundhouse. All the way her scarred wheels ground and ground against her frame, while Hansen sat in the tank with his thin yellow whiskers full of coal dust, and nobody but he knew that he had opened the throttle.

During the weeks that followed, while the 13 was being repaired, having her tires turned down to remove the slivers of steel, and getting reset and repainted, Hansen never left her for a single hour. His condition became so pitiable that the engineers, who had at first looked upon him with contempt, now spoke kindly to him or gave him no attention at all. He rarely washed now; his yellow beard was dark with coal dust, and his death-hued face was splotched with soot and black oil. By the time the 13 was ready for the road, Hansen was almost ready for an undertaker; and when the master mechanic saw him, he gave orders that the inventor must not be allowed to go out on the engine, which was to take out the fast freight, a night run of some importance.

Hansen had hoped, even boasted, that the 13 should never be coupled into anything plainer than a mail car, and now when he learned that she was going out on a freight run he was frantic. Formerly he had insisted upon running the engine only; now he wanted to run the road. When the foreman told him, as kindly as he could, that no one would be allowed in the cab of the 13 except the engineer and the fireman, the inventor glared fiercely for a moment, then turned and entered the office of the master mechanic. He did not wait to be ushered in, but strode to the chief's desk, and informed the head of the motive power department that Engine 13 would not go out on freight; that when she did go out, she would pull a passenger train, and that he, Hansen, would be the engineer.

The master mechanic was forced to be firm with the man whom, up to now, he had avoided or humored; and he told him plainly that the orders given concerning the new engine would certainly be carried out, and that if he became too troublesome he would be locked up. Hansen raved like a madman, and all the clerks in the office were unable to seize and hold him. "She is my life!" he shrieked. "I have put my soul into her, and I will never allow her to go out of my sight—you will be guilty of murder if you separate us."

As the mad inventor fought, he frothed at the mouth, and the perspiration that almost streamed from his forehead washed white furrows down his face. It was not until the special officer came with handcuffs that Hansen could be controlled; and as the 13 rolled slowly across the turntable he was led away to the lockup. He became perfectly quiet now, and when they reached "the Cooler," as it was called, the officer removed the handcuffs and turned to unlock the door. Hansen, taking advantage of this opportunity, turned quickly and bolted, and was many yards away before the officer, rattling away at the padlock, knew that his prisoner had escaped.

The officer very naturally supposed that Hansen would return to the shops, but he did not. He made straight for the freight yards, where the 13 stood steaming, all coupled up and ready to pull out on her night run over the plains. The engineer had finished oiling, and had gone into the little telegraph office where the conductor was getting orders. The fireman, who was in the cab looking after the engine, saw Hansen come leaping over the strings of flat and coal cars, with his beard sweeping round his neck and his yellow hair blown back from his bare head. As the inventor sprang upon the engine the fireman seized him, only to be hurled out over the coal tank by the desperate Dane.

Having freed himself from the fireman, Hansen gave two sharp blasts— "Off brakes"—and opened the throttle. The sudden jerk broke the train in two, four cars from the engine; and before the astonished engineer could reach the head end, the engine was in motion. The mad driver knew enough to open the sand lever, and with a few exhausts the short train was moving so fast that the trainmen were unable to reach it. Out over the switches, already set for the fast freight, and down the main line dashed the wild driver, while a flood of fire came from the stack and rained upon the roofs of cars and switch shanties along the line. Flagmen, coming out at crossings to cheer the fast freight with a white signal of "All right," saw the grim face of Hansen leaning from the cab; saw his white teeth shining, and his yellow hair streaming back over his shoulders, as the engine dashed by. Farmers along the line saw a great shower of sparks falling in their fields, and in her wake the wild engine left a sea of burning stubble where red flames leaped from shock to rick.

When the fireman, dazed and stunned, had been picked up and revived, he told them what had happened, and a dispatch was sent to the first station out to "ditch" the 13, which had broken loose from her train and was running wild. This station was the meeting point for the fast freight and the incoming express, and if the wild engine was allowed to pass, she must surely collide with the passenger train. The operator, who was on duty looking out for these two important trains, realized the situation at a glance, and opened the switch at the farther end of the siding to allow the 13 to go into the ditch beyond the depot.

Because it was a junction point, the station was located at the foot of a long slope, down which Hansen drove at a frightful rate. Whatever speed he had lost by losing fire and wasting steam, he now regained on the downward grade. So great was the speed of the train that when the engine struck the first switch she left the track and plunged into the depot, carrying the four loaded cars with her. The fourth car contained giant powder for the miners in the mountains, and this now exploded with terrific force. The agent and his assistant had stationed themselves near the other switch to witness the performance of the wild engine when she should leave the rail, and so escaped death. Hansen's escape was almost miraculous. The engine, in turning over, threw him upon the roof of the low station, the roof was blown away by the explosion, and Hansen was carried out into the prairie. The special engine and crew that followed upon her blazing trail found the 13 buried in the burning station, and Hansen lying unconscious upon the starlit plain.

THE BLACKENED FIELDS had been plowed and prepared for another crop, the station was being rebuilt, and the company's claim agent was busy settling with the farmers along the line, before Hansen was able to walk out in the garden in back of the company's hospital. It seemed to him, he said, that he had been ill all his life, and that all he knew was the short life he had lived in the hospital. Back of that, all was a blank, save that he had a faint notion that he had lived before, and that the world out of which he had come was made up of one great sorrow from which he had narrowly escaped.

"Is that my name?" he asked of the attendant one day when his reason had returned.

"Sure," said the nurse; "your name was Oscar—don't you know your own name?"

"Oh yes!" said the patient wearily. "I had forgotten. What's my other name, Oscar what?"

The attendant was about to reply when the surgeon, entering, gave sign for the man to be quiet. "Restless," said the doctor, taking the patient's hand; and the sick man caught at the word, the meaning of which his wreck of a mind scarcely comprehended, and repeated: "Reslis—Oscar Reslis—that's a nice-sounding name."

"Yes," said the surgeon, deciding to let it go at that; "Oscar Reslis is a very pretty name."

The physical condition of the patient improved rapidly enough now, but his mental condition continued to puzzle the chief surgeon and his staff. He was quiet enough, and seemed anxious to be alone—away from the other patients and the attendants. He would sit for hours thinking, thinking, hard and long, upon the great problem of Life, and trying to make out how he came to be. The attendants had been instructed to keep a close watch upon the sick man, and this, as his reasoning powers returned, Hansen detected. "Why do you follow me all the while?" he asked of his German keeper one day, when the latter had trailed him down in the garden.

"To see so dot you don' skedattle—flew der coop—see? Dat vos it."

"Tell me, Fritz," Hansen pleaded, "where did I live before I came here?"

"Oh ho!" exclaimed the German. "You dink I vos one fool? Der doc tell me I shall not speak mit you about your past life. He say I must-use say, nix, une blay as I don't listen, see?"

"Then tell me why they brought me here."

"Oh! I mus'nit, I mus'nit speak mit you about your sickness, der doc says; because, he say, it will make you nut fly off. You see it is nit goot for you to know so much, because you been kronk in der cope—see? Dot vos it. Doc says you must not told a man vat is crazy dot he been crazy, for dot makes him sometimes still more crazy yet again already. Dot is it. So I vill not say anodder vord from you."

Oscar thought a great deal over his conversation with Fritz, and as the days went by he began to realize that he was a prisoner; that he had been a prisoner once before, either in this world or the other; that he had escaped, and he must escape again. All his time was now occupied in forming plans by which he might free himself from his captors, who had no right, according to his way of reasoning, to hold him.

One night when Fritz was asleep, Oscar dressed himself, slid down the rainspout, and reached the garden. By the help of some grapevines that grew there, he was able to scale the wall; and, once free, he ran away with all his might, not caring where his legs carried him so long as they bore him away from his prison. It happened that, as he reached the yard, a freight train was pulling out, and seeing that it was leaving the town, he boarded it and rode away. Upon some flat cars in this train there were a number of narrow-gauge locomotives going out to a mountain road then being built in the new West, and in the firebox of one of these engines Hansen hid. The train had been out three days, and was almost in sight of the Rocky Mountains, when Hansen was forced by hunger from his hiding place.

He was put off at an eating station, and the boarding boss took care of him. He said his name was Oscar Reslis; and when he was strong enough to work he was put into the kitchen as dishwasher. But being sober and industrious, he was soon promoted to be second cook. At the end of the year, when the cook got drunk and lost his place, Oscar was made chief cook at one of the best-known eating houses on the K.P. He was a little queer in his actions, but they all attributed his eccentricities to his long fast in the firebox of the dead engine, and treated him with greater consideration than he would otherwise have received.

WHEN THEY HAD hammered the kinks out of her warped and twisted frame, and smoothed the dents out of her boiler, the luckless locomotive was rebuilt, painted, and rolled out over the turntable with the same unlucky number on her headlight. Nobody wanted her now. New and beautiful as she was, not an engineer asked to be allowed to run her. After she had been broken in again, and the traveling engineer had passed on her fitness for the road, she was ordered out on local freight.

She had no serious trouble for some months, but any number of minor accidents were charged up to her in the conductor's delay reports, and the workbook in the roundhouse was written full of her troubles. At the end of the year it was found that she had burned more coal, used more oil, had more repairs, cost more money, made less mileage, and injured more people, than any engine on the Smoky Hill Division. She was placed in the hands of one of the most experienced engineers, but she made the same bad record, if not a worse one; and neither engineer nor master mechanic was able to put a hand upon her and say: "Here she is wrong." Her trouble could not be located, and most of the men gave it up, declaring that Hansen had "hoodooed" her. One day her throttle flew open and stuck as it had upon her first trip, causing her to run away, kill her engineer, and injure a number of trainmen. After that she was put on a construction train, and made to drag outfit cars from station to station along the line. But even here she had to be followed up by a machine shop to keep her on her wheels.

In time she came to be the talk of the whole system. If a man had a special or a fast freight behind him, he would invariably ask the dispatcher where the 13 was, and he looked for her at every curve until he had found and passed her. She was always "due" to jump the track or lie down between stations in the face of the fast express. She became so notoriously unlucky that men were hardly held responsible for her capers. Wrecks that would have cost the driver of another engine ten days were not reported; and even serious accidents her engineer was not called upon to explain. So long as she remained at the other end of the line, the master mechanic was satisfied. She was a "hoodoo."

MEANWHILE OSCAR RESLIS had become an expert cook, and had many friends at the little Western town that had been a flag

"The train had been out three days, and was almost in sight of the Rocky Mountains, when Hansen was forced by hunger from his hiding place."

station when he stopped there to break his long fast. His mind seemed clearer, but he was less cheerful. A settled melancholy seemed fixed upon him, which none of his associates was able to understand. He believed in the transmigration of souls. Where he had lived, he said, he had been deeply wronged and persecuted. He had passed through a great sorrow, and to his acquaintances it seemed that he had been purified by pain.

He lived such a simple, sinless life that those about him believed in him and in the faith he held, and in time he had a number of converts to what they called "the Reslis religion." He was constantly preaching. "Strive hard, strive hard," he would say to those about him. "Remember that all the good you do in this life will count for you in the life to come. The more you suffer here the more you will enjoy there—be patient."

One sultry summer day, when all the help were complaining of the heat in the kitchen, the patient cook surprised them by beginning to sing as he went about his work, a thing he had never done before.

"I think I shall go away soon," he said, when the second cook asked the cause of his apparent happiness.

"Where? Oh! That I do not know; but to a better place than this, I hope. Not that this is a bad world; but we must advance—go on and up, up and on, until we reach the perfect life."

Suddenly there came through the open windows two shrill blasts of a locomotive whistle, and instantly Hansen's face grew joyously bright.

"There she is! There she is!" he cried, bounding out of the kitchen, and clearing the back fence at a single leap. And now he beheld the old 13 just pulling out with three or four outfit cars and an old, rickety caboose behind her. She was so covered with alkali, dust, and grease, that her number could not be seen; but he had heard her voice and knew her.

The fireman was busy at the furnace, the engineer was looking back to see that the yardmen closed the switch behind him; and so the cook climbed into the cab unobserved. When the fireman came out of the coal tank and found the man there, he concluded that the engineer had given him permission to ride; and when the engineer looked over and saw the fireman fixing a seat for the "deadhead," he thought the two men must be friends and, as few people ever came into the cab, he was rather pleased to find a man reckless enough to ride the 13.

The Dane's face told plainly how glad he was to find the lost idol of his heart. Dirty, disgraced—almost despised—drudging along in front of her wretched train of rickety, dust-covered cars, she was still beautiful to him.

The engineer was doing the best he could with the old scrap-heap, for there was a passenger train coming from the west, and the first siding was nearly ten miles away. It had been raining down the line the night before, and the parched plain was fresh and cool. Both the engineer and the fireman were much interested in the bare-headed passenger, who seemed about as happy as a man can get and live. He took note of every move made by the engineer, smiling when the engine blew off steam, and frowning when the driver handled the throttle or lever in a rough or careless manner.

"Guess this is your first ride on a locomotive, eh?" asked the driver.

"My first ride?" cried Hansen. "Don't you know me? I made this engine, and they took her from me, and locked me up in a prison; but I shall never leave her again. I shall scour her jacket, polish her bell, repaint her, and she shall pull the Denver Express."

"If I don't b'lieve, it's the crazy Dane," said the engineer. "Where'd you git 'im?"

"I didn't git 'im at all," said the fireman. "Where'd you git 'im?"

"Is that what they call me over there—back there where we used to live?" asked Hansen, almost pathetically.

The engineer made no reply; the fireman shook the grates and looked out over the plain, where the scant grass, taking courage from the recent rain, made a feeble effort to look green and cheerful.

"Open her up," shouted Hansen. "Don't be afraid of her. We shall push right on to the end of the run—until we find a roundhouse, and some tools—and then we will rebuild her. How handsome she will look when she comes out. We will paint her black this time—all black—all but her bell; and that shall shine like burnished gold. Black will become us now, for we have passed through great trials since our separation. How they have abused you, my noble steed," continued the man, glancing along the boiler and up at the stack.

The engine began to roll and plunge fearfully now, and the driver, looking out, saw that the rain had been very heavy, and that the track was almost unsafe. But he dared not slow down, because of his close meeting-point with the eastbound express. Instead of being frightened at the capers of the rolling, plunging engine, the Dane seemed delighted, and leaned far out on the fireman's side, and shouted and laughed as the world went by. Although the track was clear and straight, the driver kept a constant lookout, for he had no air, and the way the train was rolling, it would be difficult for the trainmen to get to the brakes, and when they did get to them they were apt to be out of repair.

Occasionally they crossed deep, narrow gullies on wooden bridges that shook as the engine struck them. These waterless streams in the West are treacherous. It is not enough to say that they are dry one hour and bank-full the next; for they will often fill to overflowing in a single minute. The water at times will roll down in a solid wall ten or twelve feet high. There had been a cloudburst here, and suddenly the driver saw the sagging rails hanging over a deep ravine. The bridge was gone, and there was no possible show for them. "Jump!" he shouted, and the fireman leaped out into the prairie, and the engine plunged headfirst into the stream, now almost dry. The three or four outfit cars piled in on top of the engine and filled up the gap, while the caboose, breaking her coupling, leaped over the wreck and was thrown out on the plain beyond the washout.

When the fireman had pulled himself together, and the conductor and brakemen had crawled from the wrecked caboose, bruised and bleeding, they went in search of the engineer and the crazy Dane. What they found, and failed to find, is well known to thousands of railroad men. It has become a part of the history of the road and of the West.

There in the bed of the narrow stream, they found the outfit cars all in a heap. The stream—only eight or ten inches of clear water—was rippling through and around the wreck; but the locomotive was gone, and so was her driver, and so was the Dane. The men stared at one another, and when the fireman told them that the crazy inventor was on the engine, they were seized with a strange terror, and they all turned and scrambled up the bank. Far down the plain they saw the smoke of a locomotive, and they thought that the crazy Dane must have caused the 13 to leap over the washout. It must be so, for the engine had disappeared, and this discovery served only to increase their bewilderment.

Presently the conductor thought of his running orders and of the eastbound express, which they were running to meet at the siding only a mile beyond the washout; and, securing a soiled flag from the old caboose, he ran with all his might to meet and flag the approaching train. The arrival of the express explained away the smoke they had seen, and made it plain to the crew of the work train that their engine had not escaped, but that she was somewhere in the quicksand of the little stream. It was some time before the crew and the passengers of the express could bring themselves to believe the story told by the bewildered freight crew. They went down into the stream, waded into the water, and found the sand firm enough to hold a man up, and some of the passengers said the men were crazy, and would not believe the tale they told. What wonder, then—if these men, who were there only a few minutes after the wreck, doubted this story—that men laugh today when the enterprising newsboy points out the place where the engine went down and disappeared in the sand.

The railway officials, however, did not doubt the story, and they came and dug and drifted, prospected, and plowed around in the desert sands all night and all the next day. After the bridge had been rebuilt they went at it in earnest. For days and weeks and months they worked away, digging and sounding in the sand, and when thousands of dollars had been expended they gave it up. The lost locomotive has never been found.*

*The following letters, recently received by the author, will be of interest to the reader:

OFFICE OF THE GENERAL SUPERINTENDENT
UNION PACIFIC RAILWAY COMPANY
DENVER, COLORADO

March 1, 1896
Cy Warman, Esq., Washington, D.C.

The lost locomotive of which you inquire went down in Sand Creek, a few hours' run east of Denver; and although thousands of dollars have been expended by the company, the engine has never been found.

Respectfully yours,
W. A. Deuel, General Supt., U. P. Ry.

THE DENVER & RIO GRANDE RAILROAD COMPANY
TREASURY DEPARTMENT
DENVER, COLORADO

March 21, 1896
Mr. Cy Warman, Washington, D.C.

My Dear Cy,

I remember the story of the engine going down in Sand Creek; and, so far as I know, it has never been recovered.

With best wishes, I am, hastily, sincerely yours,
J. W. Gilluly, Treasurer of the D. & R. G. RR.

—1897

HOBOES THAT PASS IN THE NIGHT

JACK LONDON

IN THE COURSE of my tramping I encountered hundreds of hoboes, whom I hailed or who hailed me, and with whom I waited at water-tanks, "boiled up," cooked "mulligans," "battered" the "drag" or "privates," and beat trains, and who passed and were seen never again. On the other hand, there were hoboes who passed and repassed with amazing frequency, and others still, who passed like ghosts, close at hand, unseen, and never seen.

It was one of the latter that I chased clear across Canada over three thousand miles of railroad, and never once did I lay eyes on him. His "monica" was Skysail Jack. I first ran into it at Montreal. Carved with a jackknife was the skysail yard of a ship. It was perfectly executed. Under it was *Skysail Jack.* Above was *B.W. 10–15–94.* This latter conveyed the information that he had passed through Montreal bound west, on October 15, 1894. He had one day the start of me. "Sailor Jack" was my monica at that particular time, and promptly I carved it alongside of his, along with the date and the information that I, too, was bound west.

I had misfortune in getting over the next hundred miles, and eight days later I picked up Skysail Jack's trail three hundred miles west of Ottawa. There it was, carved on a water-tank, and by the date I saw that he likewise had met with delay. He was only two days ahead of me. I was a "comet" and "tramp-royal," so was Skysail Jack; and it was up to my pride and reputation to catch up with him.

I "railroaded" day and night, and I passed him; then in turn he passed me. Sometimes he was a day or so ahead, and sometimes I was. From hoboes, bound east, I got word of him occasionally, when he happened to be ahead; and from them I learned that he had become interested in Sailor Jack and was making inquiries about me.

We'd have made a precious pair, I am sure, if we'd ever got together; but get together we couldn't. I kept ahead of him clear across Manitoba, but he led the way across Alberta, and early one bitter gray morning, at the end of a division just east of Kicking Horse Pass, I learned that he had been seen the night before between Kicking Horse Pass and Rogers' Pass. It was rather curious the way the information came to me. I had been riding all night in a "side-door Pullman" (boxcar), and nearly dead with cold had crawled out at the division to beg for food. A freezing fog was drifting past, and I "hit" some firemen I found in the roundhouse. They fixed me up with the leavings from their lunch pails, and in addition I got out of them nearly a quart of heavenly "java" (coffee). I heated the latter, and, as I sat down to eat, a freight pulled in from the west. I saw a side door open and a road-kid climb out. Through the drifting fog he limped over to me. He was stiff with cold, his lips blue. I shared my java and grub with him, learned about Skysail Jack, and then learned about him. Behold, he was from my own town, Oakland, California, and he was a member of the celebrated Boo Gang—a gang with which I had affiliated at rare intervals. We talked fast and bolted the grub in the half hour that followed. Then my freight pulled out, and I was on it, bound west on the trail of Skysail Jack.

I was delayed between the passes, went two days without food, and walked eleven miles on the third day before I got any, and yet I succeeded in passing Skysail Jack along the Fraser River in British Columbia. I was riding "passengers" then and making time; but he must have been riding passengers, too, and with more luck or skill than I, for he got into Mission ahead of me.

Now Mission was a junction, forty miles east of Vancouver. From the junction one could proceed south through Washington and Oregon over the Northern Pacific. I wondered which way Skysail Jack would go, for I thought I was ahead of him. As for myself, I was still bound west to Vancouver. I proceeded to the water-tank to leave that information, and there, freshly carved, with that day's date upon it, was Skysail Jack's monica. I hurried on into Vancouver. But he was gone. He had taken ship immediately and was still flying west on his world-adventure. Truly, Skysail Jack, you were a tramp-royal, and your mate was the "wind that tramps the world." I take off my hat to you. You were "blowed-in-the-glass," all right. A week later I, too, got my ship, and on board the steamship *Umatilla*, in the forecastle, was working my way down the coast to San Francisco. Skysail Jack and Sailor Jack—gee!—if we'd ever got together . . .

Water-tanks are tramp directories. Not all in idle wantonness do tramps carve their monicas, dates, and courses. Often and often have I met hoboes earnestly inquiring if I had seen anywhere such and such a "stiff" or his monica. And more than once I have been able to give the monica of recent date, the water-tank, and the direction in which he was then bound. And promptly the hobo to whom I gave the information lit out after his pal. I have met hoboes who, in trying to catch a pal, had pursued clear across the continent and back again, and were still going.

"Monicas" are the *nom-de-rails* that hoboes assume or accept when thrust upon them by their fellows. Leary Joe, for instance, was timid, and was so named by his fellows. No self-respecting hobo would select Stew Bum for himself. Very few tramps care to remember their pasts during which they ignobly worked, so monicas based upon trades are very rare, though I remember having met the following: Moulder Blackey, Painter Red, Chi Plumber, Boiler-maker, Sailor Boy, and Printer Bo. "Chi" (pronounced *shy*), by the way, is the argot for "Chicago."

A favorite device of hoboes is to base their monicas on the localities from which they hail, as: New York Tommy, Pacific Slim, Buffalo Smithy, Canton Tim, Pittsburg Jack, Syracuse Shine, Troy Mickey, K. L. Bill, and Connecticut Jimmy. Then there was "Slim Jim from Vinegar Hill, who never worked and never will." A "shine" is always a Negro, so called, possibly, from the highlights on his countenance. Texas Shine or Toledo Shine convey both race and nativity.

Among those that incorporated their race, I recollect the following: Frisco Sheeny, New York Irish, Michigan French, English Jack, Cockney Kid, and Milwaukee Dutch. Others seem to take their

"Water-tanks are tramp directories. Not all in idle wantonness do tramps carve their monicas, dates, and courses."

monicas in part from the color schemes stamped upon them at birth, such as: Chi Whitey, New Jersey Red, Boston Blackey, Seattle Browney, and Yellow Dick and Yellow Belly—the last a Creole from Mississippi, who, I suspect, had his monica thrust upon him.

Texas Royal, Happy Joe, Bust Connors, Burley Bo, Tornado Blackey, and Touch McCall used more imagination in rechristening themselves. Others, with less fancy, carry the names of their physical peculiarities, such as: Vancouver Slim, Detroit Shorty, Ohio Fatty, Long Jack, Big Jim, Little Joe, New York Blink, Chi Nosey, and Broken-backed Ben.

By themselves come the road-kids, sporting an infinite variety of monicas. For example, the following, whom here and there I have encountered: Buck Kid, Blind Kid, Midget Kid, Holy Kid, Bat Kid, Swift Kid, Cookey Kid, Monkey Kid, Iowa Kid, Corduroy Kid, Orator Kid (who could tell how it happened), and Lippy Kid (who was insolent, depend upon it).

On the water-tank at San Marcial, New Mexico, a dozen years ago, was the following hobo bill of fare:

(1) Main-drag fair.
(2) Bulls not hostile.
(3) Roundhouse good for kipping.
(4) Northbound trains no good.
(5) Privates no good.
(6) Restaurants good for cooks only.
(7) Railroad House good for night-work only.

Number one conveys the information that begging for money on the main street is fair; number two, that the police will not bother hoboes; number three, that one can sleep in the roundhouse. Number four, however, is ambiguous. The northbound trains may be no good to beat, and they may be no good to beg. Number five means that the residences are not good to beggars, and number six means that only hoboes that have been cooks can get grub from the restaurants. Number seven bothers me. I cannot make out whether the Railroad House is a good place for any hobo to beg at night, or whether it is good only for hobo-cooks to beg at night, or whether any hobo, cook or non-cook, can lend a hand at night, helping the cooks of the Railroad House with their dirty work and getting something to eat in payment.

But to return to the hoboes that pass in the night. I remember one I met in California. He was a Swede, but he had lived so long in the United States that one couldn't guess his nationality. He had to tell it on himself. In fact, he had come to the United States when no more than a baby. I ran into him first at the mountain town of Truckee. "Which way, Bo?" was our greeting, and "Bound east" was the answer each of us gave. Quite a bunch of "stiffs" tried to ride out the overland that night, and I lost the Swede in the shuffle. Also, I lost the overland.

I arrived in Reno, Nevada, in a boxcar that was promptly sidetracked. It was Sunday morning, and after I threw my feet for breakfast, I wandered over to the Paiute camp to watch the Indians gambling. And there stood the Swede, hugely interested. Of course we got together. He was the only acquaintance I had in that region, and I was his only acquaintance. We rushed together like a couple of dissatisfied hermits, and together we spent the day, threw our feet for dinner, and late in the afternoon tried to "nail" the same freight. But he was ditched, and I rode her out alone, to be ditched myself in the desert twenty miles beyond.

Of all desolate places, the one at which I was ditched was the limit. It was called a flag station, and it consisted of a shanty dumped inconsequentially into the sand and sagebrush. A chill wind was blowing, night was coming on, and the solitary telegraph operator who lived in the shanty was afraid of me. I knew that neither grub nor bed could I get out of him. It was because of his manifest fear of me that I did not believe him when he told me that eastbound trains never stopped there. Besides, hadn't I been thrown off of an eastbound train right at that very spot not five minutes before? He assured me that it had stopped under orders, and that a year might go by before another was stopped under orders. He advised me that it was only a dozen or fifteen miles on to Wadsworth and that I'd better hike.

I elected to wait, however, and I had the pleasure of seeing two westbound freights go by without stopping, and one eastbound freight. I wondered if the Swede was on the latter. It was up to me to hit the ties to Wadsworth, and hit them I did, much to the telegraph operator's relief, for I neglected to burn his shanty and murder him. Telegraph operators have much to be thankful for. At the end of half a dozen miles, I had to get off the ties and let the eastbound overland go by. She was going fast, but I caught sight of a dim form on the first "blind" that looked like the Swede.

That was the last I saw of him for weary days. I hit the high places across those hundreds of miles of Nevada desert, riding the overlands at night, for speed, and in the daytime riding in boxcars and getting my sleep. It was early in the year, and it was cold in those upland pastures. Snow lay here and there on the level, all the mountains were shrouded in white, and at night the most miserable wind imaginable blew off from them. It was not a land in which to linger. And remember, gentle reader, the hobo goes through such a land, without shelter, without money, begging his way and sleeping at night without blankets. This last is something that can be realized only by experience.

In the early evening I came down to the depot at Ogden. The overland of the Union Pacific was pulling east, and I was bent on making connections. Out in the tangle of tracks ahead of the engine I encountered a figure slouching through the gloom. It was the Swede. We shook hands like long-lost brothers, and discovered that our hands were gloved. "Where'd ye glom 'em?" I asked. "Out of an engine cab," he answered; "and where did you?" "They belonged to a fireman," said I; "he was careless."

We caught the blind as the overland pulled out, and mighty cold we found it. The way led up a narrow gorge between snow-covered mountains, and we shivered and shook and exchanged confidences about how we had covered the ground between Reno and Ogden. I had closed my eyes for only an hour or so the previous night, and the blind was not comfortable enough to suit me for a snooze. At a stop, I went forward to the engine. We had on a "doubleheader" (two engines) to take us over the grade.

The pilot of the head engine, because it "punched the wind," I knew would be too cold; so I selected the pilot of the second engine, which was sheltered by the first engine. I stepped on the cowcatcher and found the pilot occupied. In the darkness I felt out the form of a young boy. He was sound asleep. By squeezing, there was room for two on the pilot, and I made the boy hudge over and crawled up beside him. It was a "good" night; the "shacks" (brakemen) didn't bother us, and in no time we were asleep. Once in a while when hot cinders or heavy jolts aroused me, I snuggled closer to the boy and dozed off to the coughing of the engines and the screeching of the wheels.

The overland made Evanston, Wyoming, and went no farther. A wreck ahead blocked the line. The dead engineer had been brought in, and his body attested the peril of the way. A tramp, also, had been killed, but his body had not been brought in. I talked with the boy. He was thirteen years old. He had run away from his folks in someplace in Oregon, and was heading east to his grandmother. He had a tale of cruel treatment in the home he had left that rang true; besides, there was no need for him to lie to me, a nameless hobo on the track.

And that boy was going some, too. He couldn't cover the ground fast enough. When the division superintendents decided to send the overland back over the way it had come, then up on a cross "jerk" to the Oregon Short Line, and back along that road to tap the Union Pacific the other side of the wreck, that boy climbed upon the pilot and said he was going to stay with it. This was too much for the Swede and me. It meant traveling the rest of that frigid night in order to gain no more than a dozen miles or so. We said we'd wait till the wreck was cleared away, and in the meantime get a good sleep.

Now, it is no snap to strike a strange town, broke, at midnight, in cold weather, and find a place to sleep. The Swede hadn't a penny. My total assets consisted of two dimes and a nickel. From some of the town boys we learned that beer was five cents, and that the saloons kept open all night. There was our meat. Two glasses of beer would cost ten cents, there would be a stove and chairs, and we could sleep it out till morning. We headed for the lights of a saloon, walking briskly, the snow crunching under our feet, a chill little wind blowing through us.

Alas, I had misunderstood the town boys. Beer was five cents in one saloon only in the whole burg, and we didn't strike that saloon. But the one we entered was all right. A blessed stove was roaring white-hot; there were cozy, cane-bottomed armchairs, and a none-too-pleasant-looking barkeeper who glared suspiciously at us as we came in. A man cannot spend continuous days and nights in his clothes, beating trains, fighting soot and cinders, and sleeping anywhere, and maintain a good "front." Our fronts were decidedly against us; but what did we care? I had the price in my jeans.

"Two beers," said I nonchalantly to the barkeeper, and while he drew them, the Swede and I leaned against the bar and yearned secretly for the armchairs by the stove.

The barkeeper set the two foaming glasses before us, and with pride I deposited the ten cents. Now I was dead game. As soon as I learned my error in the price I'd have dug up another ten cents. Never mind if it did leave me only a nickel to my name, a stranger in a strange land. I'd have paid it all right. But that barkeeper never gave me a chance. As soon as his eyes spotted the dime I had laid down, he seized the two glasses, one in each hand, and dumped the beer into the sink behind the bar. At the same time, glaring at us malevolently, he said: "You've got scabs on your nose. You've got scabs on your nose. You've got scabs on your nose. See!"

I hadn't, either, and neither had the Swede. Our noses were all right. The direct bearing of his words was beyond our comprehension, but the indirect bearing was clear as print: He didn't like our looks, and beer was evidently ten cents a glass.

I dug down and laid another dime on the bar, remarking carelessly, "Oh, I thought this was a five-cent joint."

"Your money's no good here," he answered, shoving the two dimes across the bar to me.

Sadly I dropped them back into my pocket, sadly we yearned toward the blessed stove and the armchairs, and sadly we went out the door into the frosty night.

But as we went out the door, the barkeeper, still glaring, called after us, "You've got scabs on your nose, see!"

I have seen much of the world since then, journeyed among strange lands and peoples, opened many books, sat in many lecture halls; but to this day, though I have pondered long and deep, I have been unable to divine the meaning in the cryptic utterance of that barkeeper in Evanston, Wyoming. Our noses *were* all right.

We slept that night over the boilers in an electric-lighting plant. How we discovered that "kipping" place I can't remember. We must have just headed for it, instinctively, as horses head for water or carrier pigeons head for the home cote. But it was a night not pleasant to remember. A dozen hoboes were ahead of us on top the boilers, and it was too hot for all of us. To complete our misery, the engineer would not let us stand around down below. He gave us our choice of the boilers or the outside snow.

"You said you wanted to sleep, and so, damn you, sleep," said he to me, when, frantic and beaten out by the heat, I came down into the fire-room.

"Water," I gasped, wiping the sweat from my eyes, "water."

He pointed out-of-doors and assured me that down there somewhere in the blackness I'd find the river. I started for the river, got lost in the dark, fell into two or three drifts, gave it up, and returned half-frozen to the top of the boilers. When I had thawed out, I was thirstier than ever. Around me the hoboes were moaning, groaning, sobbing, sighing, gasping, panting, rolling and tossing and floundering heavily in their torment. We were so many lost souls toasting on a griddle in hell, and the engineer, Satan Incarnate, gave us the sole alternative of freezing in the outer cold. The Swede sat up and anathematized passionately the wanderlust in man that sent him tramping and suffering hardships such as that.

"When I get back to Chicago," he perorated, "I'm going to get a job and stick to it till hell freezes over. Then I'll go tramping again."

And, such is the irony of fate, next day, when the wreck ahead was cleared, the Swede and I pulled out of Evanston in the iceboxes of an "orange special," a fast freight laden with fruit from sunny California. Of course, the iceboxes were empty on account of the cold weather, but that didn't make them any warmer for us. We entered them through hatchways in the top of the car; the boxes were constructed of galvanized iron, and in that biting weather, were not pleasant to the touch. We lay there, shivered and shook, and with chattering teeth held a council wherein we decided that we'd stay by the iceboxes day and night till we got out of the inhospitable plateau region and down into the Mississippi Valley.

But we must eat, and we decided that at the next division we would throw our feet for grub and make a rush back to our iceboxes. We arrived in the town of Green River late in the afternoon, but too early for supper. Before mealtime is the worst time for "battering" back doors; but we put on our nerve, swung off the side ladders as the freight pulled into the yards, and made a run for the houses. We were quickly separated; but we had agreed to meet in the iceboxes. I had bad luck at first; but in the end, with a couple of handouts poked into my shirt, I chased for the train. It was pulling out and going fast. The particular refrigerator car in which we were to meet had already gone by, and half a dozen cars down the train from it, I swung onto the side ladders, went up on top hurriedly, and dropped down into an icebox.

But a shack had seen me from the caboose, and at the next stop a few miles farther on, Rock Springs, the shack stuck his head into my box and said: "Hit the grit, you son of a toad! Hit the grit!" Also he grabbed me by the heels and dragged me out. I hit the grit all right, and the orange special and the Swede rolled on without me.

Snow was beginning to fall. A cold night was coming on. After dark I hunted around in the railroad yards until I found an empty refrigerator car. In I climbed—not into the iceboxes, but into the car itself. I swung the heavy doors shut, and their edges, covered with strips of rubber, sealed the car airtight. The walls were thick. There was no way for the outside cold to get in. But the inside was just as cold as the outside. How to raise the temperature was the problem. But trust a "profesh" for that. Out of my pockets I dug up three or four newspapers. These I burned, one at a time, on the floor of the car. The smoke rose to the top. Not a bit of the heat could escape, and, comfortable and warm, I passed a beautiful night. I didn't wake up once.

In the morning it was still snowing. While throwing my feet for breakfast, I missed an eastbound freight. Later in the day I nailed two other freights and was ditched from both of them. All afternoon no eastbound trains went by. The snow was falling thicker than ever, but at twilight I rode out on the first blind of the overland. As I swung aboard the blind from one side, somebody swung aboard from the other. It was the boy who had run away from Oregon.

Now, the first blind of a fast train in a driving snowstorm is no summer picnic. The wind goes right through one, strikes the front of the car, and comes back again. At the first stop, darkness having come on, I went forward and interviewed the fireman. I offered to "shove" coal to the end of his run, which was Rawlins, and my offer was accepted. My work was out on the tender, in the snow, breaking the lumps of coal with a sledge and shoveling it forward to him in the cab. But as I did not have to work all the time, I could come into the cab and warm up now and again.

"Say," I said to the fireman, at my first breathing spell, "there's a little kid back there on the first blind. He's pretty cold."

The cabs on the Union Pacific engines are quite spacious, and we fitted the kid into a warm nook in front of the high seat of the fireman, where the kid promptly fell asleep. We arrived at Rawlins at midnight. The snow was thicker than ever. Here the engine was to go into the roundhouse, being replaced by a fresh engine. As the train came to a stop, I dropped off the engine steps plumb into the arms of a large man in a large overcoat. He began asking me questions, and I promptly demanded who he was. Just as promptly he informed me that he was the sheriff. I drew in my horns and listened and answered.

He began describing the kid who was still asleep in the cab. I did some quick thinking. Evidently the family was on the trail of the kid, and the sheriff had received telegraphed instructions from Oregon. Yes, I had seen the kid. I had met him first in Ogden. The date tallied with the sheriff's information. But the kid was still behind somewhere, I explained, for he had been ditched from that very overland that night when it pulled out of Rock Springs. And all the time I was praying that the kid wouldn't wake up, come down out of the cab, and put the "kibosh" on me.

The sheriff left me in order to interview the shacks, but before he left he said: "Bo, this town is no place for you. Understand? You ride this train out, and make no mistake about it. If I catch you after it's gone . . ."

I assured him that it was not through desire that I was in his town; that the only reason I was there was that the train had stopped there; and that he wouldn't see me for smoke the way I'd get out of his darn town.

While he went to interview the shacks, I jumped back into the cab. The kid was awake and rubbing his eyes. I told him the news and advised him to ride the engine into the roundhouse. To cut the story short, the kid made the same overland out, riding the pilot, with instructions to make an appeal to the fireman at the first stop for permission to ride in the engine. As for myself, I got ditched.

The new fireman was young and not yet lax enough to break the rules of the Company against having tramps in the engine; so he turned down my offer to shove coal. I hope the kid succeeded with him, for all night on the pilot in that blizzard would have meant death.

Strange to say, I do not at this late day remember a detail of how I was ditched at Rawlins. I remember watching the train as it was immediately swallowed up in the snowstorm, and of heading for a saloon to warm up. Here was light and warmth. Everything was in full blast and wide open. Faro, roulette, craps, and poker tables were running, and some mad cowpunchers were making the night merry. I had just succeeded in fraternizing with them and was downing my first drink at their expense, when a heavy hand descended on my shoulder. I looked around and sighed. It was the sheriff.

Without a word he led me out into the snow.

"There's an orange special down there in the yards," said he.

"It's a damn cold night," said I.

"It pulls out in ten minutes," said he.

That was all. There was no discussion. And when that orange special pulled out, I was in the iceboxes. I thought my feet would freeze before morning, and the last twenty miles into Laramie I stood upright in the hatchway and danced up and down. The snow was too thick for the shacks to see me, and I didn't care if they did.

My quarter of a dollar bought me a hot breakfast at Laramie, and immediately afterward I was on board the blind baggage of an overland that was climbing to the pass through the backbone of the Rockies. One does not ride blind baggages in the daytime; but in this blizzard at the top of the Rocky Mountains I doubted if the shacks would have the heart to put me off. And they didn't. They made a practice of coming forward at every stop to see if I was frozen yet.

At Ames' Monument, at the summit of the Rockies—I forget the altitude—the shack came forward for the last time.

"Say, Bo," he said, "you see that freight sidetracked over there to let us go by?"

I saw. It was on the next track, six feet away. A few feet more in that storm and I could not have seen it.

"Well, the 'after-push' of Kelly's Army is in one of them cars.

They've got two feet of straw under them, and there's so many of them that they keep the car warm."

His advice was good, and I followed it, prepared, however, if it was a con game the shack had given me, to take the blind as the overland pulled out. But it was straight goods. I found the car—a big refrigerator car with the leeward door wide open for ventilation. Up I climbed, and in. I stepped on a man's leg, next on some other man's arm. The light was dim, and all I could make out was arms and legs and bodies inextricably confused. Never was there such a tangle of humanity. They were all lying in the straw, and over, and under, and around one another. Eighty-four husky hoboes take up a lot of room when they are stretched out. The men I stepped on were resentful. Their bodies heaved under me like the waves of the sea, and imparted an involuntary forward movement to me. I could not find any straw to step upon, so I stepped upon more men. The resentment increased, so did my forward movement. I lost my footing and sat down with sharp abruptness. Unfortunately, it was on a man's head. The next moment he had risen on his hands and knees in wrath, and I was flying through the air. What goes up must come down, and I came down on another man's head.

What happened after that is very vague in my memory. It was like going through a threshing machine. I was bandied about from one end of the car to the other. Those eighty-four hoboes winnowed me out till what little was left of me, by some miracle, found a bit of straw to rest upon. I was initiated, and into a jolly crowd. All the rest of that day we rode through the blizzard, and to while the time away it was decided that each man was to tell a story. It was stipulated that each story must be a good one, and, furthermore, that it must be a story no one had ever heard before. The penalty for failure was the threshing machine. Nobody failed. And I want to say right here that never in my life have I sat at so marvelous a storytelling debauch. Here were eighty-four men from all the world—I made eighty-five; and each man told a masterpiece. It had to be, for it was either masterpiece or threshing machine.

Late in the afternoon we arrived in Cheyenne. The blizzard was at its height, and though the last meal of all of us had been breakfast, no man cared to throw his feet for supper. All night we rolled on through the storm, and next day found us down on the sweet plains of Nebraska and still rolling. We were out of the storm and the mountains. The blessed sun was shining over a smiling land, and we had eaten nothing for twenty-four hours. We found out that the freight would arrive about noon at a town, if I remember right, that was called Grand Island.

We took up a collection and sent a telegram to the authorities of that town. The text of the message was that eighty-five healthy, hungry hoboes would arrive about noon and that it would be a good idea to have dinner ready for them. The authorities of Grand Island had two courses open to them. They could feed us, or they could throw us in jail. In the latter event they'd have to feed us anyway, and they decided wisely that one meal would be the cheaper way.

When the freight rolled into Grand Island at noon, we were sitting on the tops of the cars and dangling our legs in the sunshine. All the police in the burg were on the reception committee. They marched us in squads to the various hotels and restaurants, where dinners were spread for us. We had been thirty-six hours without food, and we didn't have to be taught what to do. After that we were marched back to the railroad station. The police had thoughtfully compelled the freight to wait for us. She pulled out slowly, and the eighty-five of us, strung out along the track, swarmed up the side ladders. We "captured" the train.

We had no supper that evening—at least the "push" didn't, but I did. Just at suppertime, as the freight was pulling out of a small town, a man climbed into the car where I was playing pedro with three other stiffs. The man's shirt was bulging suspiciously. In his hand he carried a battered quart-measure from which arose steam. I smelled java. I turned my cards over to one of the stiffs who was looking on, and excused myself. Then, in the other end of the car, pursued by envious glances, I sat down with the man who had climbed aboard and shared his java and the handouts that had bulged his shirt. It was the Swede.

At about ten o'clock in the evening, we arrived at Omaha.

"Let's shake the push," said the Swede to me.

"Sure," said I.

As the freight pulled into Omaha, we made ready to do so. But the people of Omaha were also ready. The Swede and I hung upon the side ladders, ready to drop off. But the freight did not stop. Furthermore, long rows of policemen, their brass buttons and stars glittering in the electric lights, were lined up on each side of the track. The Swede and I knew what would happen to us if we ever dropped off into their arms. We stuck by the side ladders, and the train rolled on across the Missouri River to Council Bluffs.

"General" Kelly, with an army of two thousand hoboes, lay in camp at Chautauqua Park, several miles away. The after-push we were with was General Kelly's rearguard, and, detraining at Council Bluffs, it started to march to camp. The night had turned cold, and heavy wind squalls, accompanied by rain, were chilling and wetting us. Many police were guarding us and herding us to the camp. The Swede and I watched our chance and made a successful getaway.

The rain began coming down in torrents, and in the darkness, unable to see our hands in front of our faces, like a pair of blind men we fumbled about for shelter. Our instinct served us, for in no time we stumbled upon a saloon—not a saloon that was open and doing business, not merely a saloon that was closed for the night, and not even a saloon with a permanent address, but a saloon propped up on big timbers, with rollers underneath, that was being moved from somewhere to somewhere. The doors were locked. A squall of wind and rain drove down upon us. We did not hesitate. Smash went the door, and in we went.

I have made some tough camps in my time, "carried the banner" in infernal metropolises, bedded in pools of water, slept in the snow under two blankets when the spirit thermometer registered seventy-four degrees below zero (which is a mere trifle of one hundred and six degrees of frost); but I want to say right here that never did I make a tougher camp, pass a more miserable night, than that night I passed with the Swede in the itinerant saloon at Council Bluffs. In the first place, the building, perched up as it was in the air, had exposed a multitude of openings in the floor through which the wind whistled. In the second place, the bar was empty; there was no bottled firewater with which we could warm ourselves and forget our misery. We had no blankets, and in our wet clothes, wet to the skin, we tried to sleep. I rolled under the bar, and the Swede rolled under the table. The holes and crevices in the floor made it impossible, and at the end of half an hour I crawled up on top the bar. A little later the Swede crawled up on top his table.

And there we shivered and prayed for daylight. I know, for one, that I shivered until I could shiver no more, till the shivering muscles exhausted themselves and merely ached horribly. The Swede moaned and groaned, and every little while, through chattering teeth, he muttered, "Never again; never again." He muttered this phrase repeatedly, ceaselessly, a thousand times; and when he dozed, he went on muttering it in his sleep.

At the first gray of dawn we left our house of pain, and outside, found ourselves in a mist, dense and chill. We stumbled on till we came to the railroad track. I was going back to Omaha to throw my feet for breakfast; my companion was going on to Chicago. The moment for parting had come. Our palsied hands went out to each other. We were both shivering. When we tried to speak, our teeth chattered us back into silence. We stood alone, shut off from the world; all that we could see was a short length of railroad track, both ends of which were lost in the driving mist. We stared dumbly at each other, our clasped hands shaking sympathetically. The Swede's face was blue with the cold, and I know mine must have been.

"Never again what?" I managed to articulate.

Speech strove for utterance in the Swede's throat; then, faint and distant, in a thin whisper from the very bottom of his frozen soul, came the words:

"Never again a hobo."

He paused, and, as he went on again, his voice gathered strength and huskiness as it affirmed his will.

"Never again a hobo. I'm going to get a job. You'd better do the same. Nights like this make rheumatism."

He wrung my hand.

"Good-bye, Bo," said he.

"Good-bye, Bo," said I.

The next moment we were swallowed up from each other by the mist. It was our final passing. But here's to you, Mr. Swede, wherever you are. I hope you got that job.

—1907

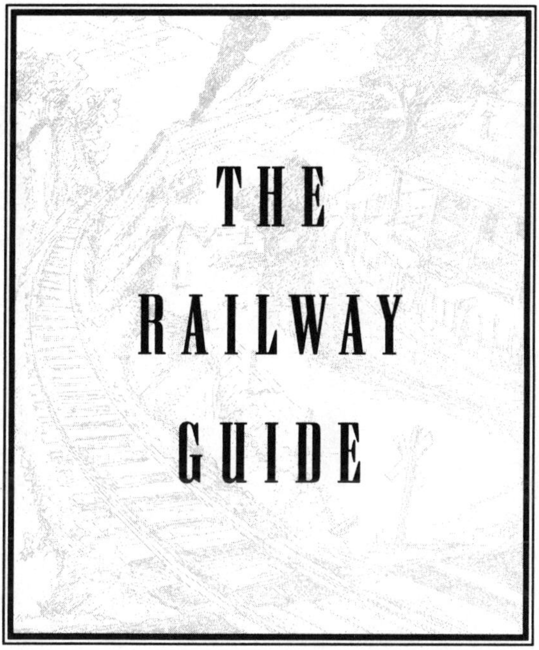

THE RAILWAY GUIDE

CHRISTOPHER MORLEY

NOTE: *Christopher Morley's* Human Being *(1934), from which "The Railway Guide" is excerpted, is the purported biography of a small-time manufacturer named Richard Roe, written by a fictional biographer named Hubbard. In this excerpt, Roe is working as a salesman for a book publisher whose secretary, Miss Mac, infects Roe with a fascination for travel. The passage recalls Owen Wister's opinion that the* Railway Guide *was "the most interesting book in America."*

ANOTHER BOOK WHICH he used to see lying in the office also caught Richard's fancy. It was a thick-bound volume always carefully consulted by the sales boys before going off on their travels. Richard found it more to his taste than most fiction. It was called *The Official Guide of the Railways and Steam Navigation Lines of the United States, Canada, Mexico and Cuba.* It was filled with timetables and the rather violently simplified maps of railroad companies, in which the route of the company under consideration is shown as strong and direct as possible while all the others are very spiderweb. In odd moments Richard would pore over this massive concordance and gathered much miscellaneous information. The names of the famous limited trains sounded to him like bugle calls in the distance.

What a fascinating book it is. The old copy that first enthralled Roe is long since vanished, but Hubbard stopped in at Brentano's to buy a new one—over 1,600 pages of strong American romance for $2.00. His patriotism was a little startled to find advertisements of English railways in the forefront of the work, calmly announcing themselves as "The Fastest Train Service in the World."

It was the smaller railroads of the Middle West or South that seemed like fairy tales to Richard. The Detroit, Toledo & Ironton: You lcavc Dctroit at 8:15 A.M. and arrivc in Ironton 7:05 P.M. (just in time for dinner, he reflected)—no passenger trains on Sundays. Or the Green Bay & Western: You would rise very early, in that bright Wisconsin air, and have coffee and fried ham. The train leaves at 6:50: How clear the birch trees would stand round Lake Winnebago. And after passing through Scandinavia, Plover, Independence, Arcadia, you would be in Winona (213.9 miles) at 2:50 P.M. or maybe take the branch line up to Sturgeon Bay; even more thrilling, see the dotted line across Lake Michigan, the "car ferry" (magic sound) to Ludington. That would lead on toward White Cloud, Owosso, Saginaw, Ann Arbor. Names read in newspapers or seen in the office files or overheard in salesmen's talk suddenly became real.

THE RAILWAY GUIDE became Richard's Outline of History, his Story of Philosophy. There was the Toledo, Peoria & Western ("The Peoria Road"), which doesn't seem to go near Toledo at all on its own rails, but begins at Effner, Indiana. He found himself in imagination on a Mixed Train ("passenger service connections uncertain"), passing a long night on the way to Keokuk. Number Three leaves Effner at 8:30 P.M. It arrives Peoria Yard at 5:20 A.M. There must be a chance for coffee and sinkers at Peoria Yard? And he would go out on Number One-oh-three (good old Number One-oh-three!) at 7:45, arrive at Keokuk 2:30 P.M.—"Is there a bookstore in Keokuk?" he asked Miss Mac.

There were greater names too. Denver & Rio Grande; the Monon Route, more formally listed as the Chicago, Indianapolis & Louisville. That would take you through French Lick, on the Tippecanoe or the Hoosier or the Daylight Limited ("observation library car"). The Norfolk & Western offers the Pocahontas and the Cavalier. Pocahontas leaves Norfolk at 1:20 P.M. and gets you to Cincinnati at 7:55 the next morning—and from the window you see Roanoke, Blue Ridge, Lynchburg, Appomattox, Disputanta. Perhaps you're on the Pocahontas, Goodwill & Wenonah branch—if so, "stops to take revenue passengers, and to leave passengers from Hagerstown and Shenandoah Junction." Surely you are a better American for brooding on these names.

The Nickel Plate was a road he often heard Herman Schmaltz mention with casual familiarity. Herman, he figured out, would be leaving Fostoria at 11:35 A.M. (Eastern time) and proceeding via Arcadia (you'd be surprised how many Arcadias there are), Findley, Lima (Central time here), Coldwater, Fort Recovery, Muncie. Probably he would stop over at Muncie, before going on to Montmorenci, Otterbein, Oxford, Boswell, East Lynn, Arrowsmith, Bloomington.

The Père Marquette, another name to start one reading history. Again an early start: Leave Port Huron 6 A.M., and through Teddo, Palms, Harbor Beach, Tyre, Bad Axe, to Pointe aux Barques. Does the name Bad Axe give a vivid picture of some old lumberman's disgust, now memorized forever?

THE SOUTHERN TIMETABLES were rich in suggestion: He saved up many questions to ask George Work when the latter returned from his "territory." Consider the minor twigs of the Chesapeake & Ohio company: the Hawk's Nest branch, Horse Creek branch, Loup Creek and White Oak branch, Piney River and Paint Creek branch. Or, on the luxurious side, here is the Sportsman to Old Point Comfort ("observation lounge, radio-equipped"—that, of course, is of later era) and the F.F.V. to White Sulphur Springs ("imperial salon cars"). The subsidiaries of the Southern Railway: the Asheville & Craggy Mountain, the State University Railroad. The Crescent Limited to New Orleans ("women's lounge, shower bath, maid and manicure service, movable chairs, magazines, writing desk"); the Ponce de Leon to Florida. Names on the map—Manassas, Brandy, Culpepper, Rapidan, Charlottesville, Sweetbriar, Winesap, Alta Vista. The steamers on the Chesapeake—"leave Baltimore on Tuesday, Thursday, and Saturday for York River Landings. The Old Bay Line: "table d'hôte dinner $1.25—dining room in gallery, upper deck forward." The Mobile & Ohio, Seaboard Air Line (the Orange Blossom Special). The little Maryland & Pennsylvania Railroad, loved as "the Ma and Pa," from Baltimore to York, Pennsylvania, 77 miles in 4½ hours. The Aberdeen & Rockfish in North Ca'lina—leave Aberdeen 8:35 A.M., arrive Fayetteville (45 miles) 10:50. The Mauch Chunk Switchback Railway, "Cable and gravity road to Mount Pisgah: distance of circuit 18 miles. The oldest railroad in the U.S." The Cairo, Truman & Southern, "in operation for freight and passenger service from Weona Junction, Arkansas, to Weona, Arkansas (3.83 miles)." This good little outfit was evidently a family affair. President, J. H. Tschudy. First vice president, Jay Tschudy. Second vice president, E. W. Tschudy. Third vice president, Philip Tschudy. Treasurer and general manager, R. H. Tschudy. Secretary and traffic manager, Fred Tschudy.

Bigger game by contrast: the Atlantic Coast Line with its Florida Special, Palmetto Limited, the Tar Heel (New York to Wilmington, North Carolina), the Flamingo, the Dixie Flyer (to Jacksonville). Illinois Central: the Creole and the Chickasaw. The M.K.T., always known as the Katy, proud of the Blue Bonnet, the Texas Special, the Katy Limited. "There is no pleasanter courtesy," said the Katy, "than to be invited into the diner for afternoon tea and to have the steward suggest and provide chess, checkers, or dominoes for games." Richard thought with renewed admiration of these giants of the traveling leagues who had shared such transcontinental amenities.

There is no end to the lure of these names. You see the little flags fluttering, smoke pouring from squat racing funnels, the flicker of roaring wheels, taillights on a midnight curve. The Sooner, the Alamo Special, the Lone Star. St. Louis Southwestern proclaims the Blue Streak "America's fastest freight train." Chicago & Northwestern is perhaps as poetic as any in its christenings: the Corn King Limited (with "solarium sleeping car"), the Mountain Bluebird, the Columbine, the Gold Coast Limited, the Portland Rose, the Nightingale, the Viking, the Badger State Express. From the "solarium sleeping car" greet Pocatello, Minidoka, Boise, Pendleton, Spokane, Tacoma, Seattle. Or the Union Pacific: the Oregon Trail Express, the Yellowstone Express, the Pony Express, the Owl ("sleepers parked in Seattle for occupancy until 8 A.M."). The Southern Pacific and its proud Sunset Limited and Argonaut, on which "charity, D.V.S., employee, live stock contract, banana messenger, and circus scrip tickets will be honored in coaches only." The Sunbeam, the Lark, the Apache. And here he imagined ventures into Mexico. Leave El Paso 11:15 A.M., and by way of Ciudad Juarez, Montezuma, Chihuahua, Jimenez, Torreon, Aguascalientes, Queretaro, reach Mexico City 10 A.M., two days later.

The Santa Fe, with its Fred Harvey Dining Car Service—how Sam Erskine, who used to "make the Coast," spoke of those royal meals. The Chief, the Navajo, the Missionary. "Because of late hour of arrival at the Petrified Forest detour, trains twenty-three and twenty-four temporarily discontinued." "Frequently the Grand Canyon Limiteds are stopped at dining stations for the evening meal, offering patrons choice of dining aboard the train or at one of our artistic station-hotels." "Hollywood Stars and the Stars in every Profession and Business go Santa Fe and ride the Chief."

Alternative temptation, to go Chicago, Milwaukee & St. Paul—"America's longest electrified railroad." The Olympian, "the first transcontinental roller-bearing train." The Pioneer (Chicago to Minneapolis). The Sioux. The Tomahawk. Or the C. B. & Q. The Aristocrat, the American Royal, the Overland Express. The Great Northern: the Empire Builder "saves a business day between Chicago and Puget Sound." The Canadian Pacific: the Dominion, the Kootenay Express, Soo Express, the Red Wing, the Alouette, the Royal York.

WASN'T THERE ONCE something in Homer known as the Catalogue of Ships? Was it any more thrilling than this muster of trains and stations? Sometimes, studying the *Railway Guide*, you find yourself a long way from Fifth Avenue. Perhaps aboard the Alaska Railroad (run by the Department of the Interior), whose little chart marks coal and gold fields and the Big Game District. Or it may be the Norfolk & Mobjack Bay Steamboat Company; or the Pensacola, St. Andrews, and Gulf steamers, where the *Tarpon*, 450 tons, "connects with all steamers on the Choctawhatchee and Blackwater Rivers." Or, if you're shipping freight, what about "the Poker Fleet, steamers *Ace*, *King*, *Queen*, *Jack*, and *Ten*"—freight service between Buffalo, Detroit, and Duluth? There's the Passamaquoddy Ferry & Navigation Company, of Lubec, Maine; and the Grace Line to Valparaiso, Antofagasta, Tocopilla, Iquique, Cerro Azul, Callao, Guayaquil, Esmeraldas, Buenaventura, Balboa. Queer we make so much of the romance of Europe and forget there's plenty in the two Americas. What of the Compañia Ferrocarril Mexicano del Norte, the Ferrocarriles Unidos de Yucatan ("see the ruins at Uxmal"), the Toluca & San Juan Railroad (narrow gauge), the map and timetables of the Ferrocarriles Nacionales de Mexico: standard gauge, 6,860 miles; narrow gauge, 1,512 miles? (Traffic suspended between Cadena and Dinamita, also between Guadalupe and Ojo Caliente. Wish we knew why.)

The *Railway Guide*, perhaps even more than the *Erskine Atlas*, made the curved and steel-netted surface of the earth actual to Richard. When Miss Mac saw him poring over these timetables she knew he was a Born Salesman.

—1932

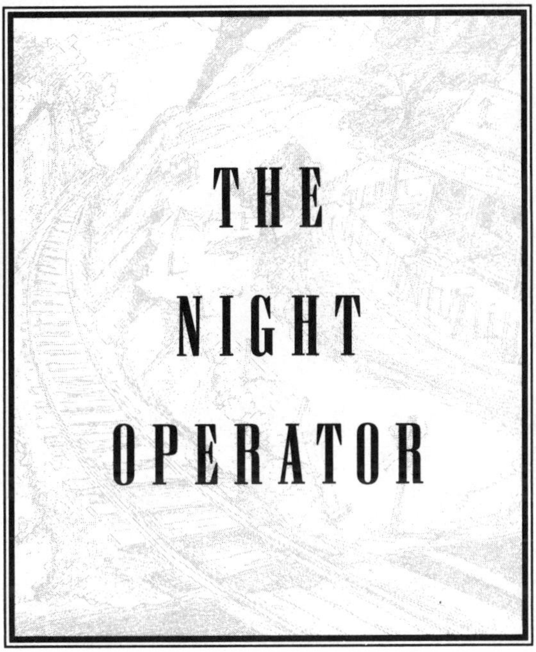

THE NIGHT OPERATOR

FRANK L. PACKARD

TODDLES, IN THE BEGINNING, wasn't exactly a railroadman at all—for several reasons. First, he wasn't a man at all; second, he wasn't, strictly speaking, on the company's payroll; third, which is apparently irrelevant, everybody said he was a bad one; and fourth—because Hawkeye nicknamed him Toddles.

Toddles had another name—Christopher Hyslop Hoogan—but Big Cloud never lay awake at nights losing any sleep over that. On the first run that Christopher Hyslop Hoogan ever made, Hawkeye looked him over for a minute, said, "Toddles," short-like—and, short-like, that settled the matter so far as the Hill Division was concerned. His name was Toddles.

Piecemeal, Toddles wouldn't convey anything to you to speak of. You'd have to see Toddles coming down the aisle of a car to get him at all—and then the chances are you'd turn around after he'd gone by, and stare at him, and it would be even money that you'd call him back and fish for a dime to buy something by way of excuse. Toddles got a good deal of business that way. Toddles had a uniform and a regular run, all right, but he wasn't what he passionately longed to be—a legitimate mate, dyed-in-the-wool railroader. His paycheck, plus commissions, came from the News Company down East which had the railroad concession. Toddles was a newsboy. In his blue uniform and silver buttons, Toddles used to stack up about the height of the back of the car seats as he hawked his wares along the aisles;

and the only thing that was big about him was his head, which looked as though it had got a whopping big lead on his body—and didn't intend to let the body cut the lead down any. This meant a big cap, and, as Toddles used to tilt the visor forward, the tip of his nose, bar his mouth which was generous, was about all one got of his face. Cap, buttons, magazines, and peanuts, that was Toddles—all except his voice. Toddles had a voice that would make you jump if you were nervous the minute he opened the car door, and if you weren't nervous you would be before he had reached the other end of the aisle—it began low down somewhere on high G and went through you shrill as an east wind, and ended like a shriek of a brake shoe with everything the Westinghouse equipment had to offer cutting loose on a quick stop.

Hawkeye? That was what Toddles called his beady-eyed conductor in retaliation. Hawkeye used to nag Toddles every chance he got, and, being Toddles's conductor, Hawkeye got a good many chances. In a word, Hawkeye, carrying the punch on the local passenger, which happened to be the run Toddles was given when the News Company sent him out from the East, used to think he got a good deal of fun out of Toddles—only his idea of fun and Toddles's idea of fun were as divergent as the poles, that was all.

Toddles, however, wasn't anybody's fool, not by several degrees—not even Hawkeye's. Toddles hated Hawkeye like poison; and his hate, apart from daily annoyances, was deep-seated. It was Hawkeye who had dubbed him "Toddles." And Toddles repudiated the name with his heart, his soul—and his fists.

Toddles wasn't anybody's fool, whatever the division thought, and he was right down to the basic root of things from the start. Coupled with the stunted growth that Nature in a miserly mood had doled out to him, none knew better than himself that the name of Toddles, keeping that Nature stuff patently before everybody's eyes, damned him in his aspirations for a bona fide railroad career. Other boys got a job and got their feet on the ladder as call boys, or in the roundhouse; Toddles got . . . a grin. Toddles pestered everybody for a job. He pestered Carleton, the super. He pestered Tommy Regan, the master mechanic. Every time that he saw anybody in authority, Toddles spoke up for a job—he was in deadly earnest—and got a grin. Toddles with a basket of unripe fruit and stale chocolates and his "best-seller" voice was one thing; but Toddles as anything else was just Toddles.

Toddles repudiated the name, and did it forcefully. Not that he couldn't take his share of a bit of guying, but because he felt that he was face-to-face with a vital factor in the career he longed for—so he fought. And if Nature had been niggardly in one respect, she had been generous in others; Toddles, for all his size, possessed the heart of a lion and the strength of a young ox, and he used both, with black and bloody effect, on the eyes and noses of the call boys and younger element who called him Toddles. He fought it all along the line—at the drop of the hat—at a whisper of "Toddles." There wasn't a day went by that Toddles wasn't in a row; and the women, the mothers of the defeated warriors whose eyes were puffed and whose noses trickled crimson, denounced him in virulent language over their washtubs and the back fences of Big Cloud. You see, they didn't understand him, so they called him a "bad one," and, being from the East and not one of themselves, "a New York guttersnipe."

But, for all that, the name stuck. Up and down through the Rockies it was—Toddles. Toddles, with the idea of getting a layover on a siding, even went to the extent of signing himself in full—Christopher Hyslop Hoogan—every time his signature was in order; but the official documents in which he was concerned, being of a private nature between himself and the News Company, did not, in the very nature of things, have much effect on the Hill Division. Certainly the big fellows never knew he had any name but Toddles—and cared less. But they knew him as Toddles, all right! All of them did, every last one of them! Toddles was everlastingly and eternally bothering them for a job. Any kind of a job, no matter what, just so it was real railroading, and so a fellow could line up with everybody else when the paycar came along, and look forward to being something someday.

Toddles, with time, of course, grew older, up to about seventeen or so, but he didn't grow any bigger—not enough to make it noticeable! Even Toddles's voice wouldn't break—it was his young heart that did all the breaking that was done. Not that he ever showed it. No one ever saw a tear in the boy's eyes. It was clenched fists for Toddles, clenched fists and passionate attack. And therein, while Toddles had grasped the basic truth that his nickname militated against his ambitions, he erred in another direction that was equally fundamental, if not more so.

And here, it was Bob Donkin, the night dispatcher, as white a man as his record after years of train-handling was white, a railroad man from the ground up if there ever was one, and one of the best, who set Toddles— But we'll come to that presently. We've got our "clearance" now, and we're off with "rights" through.

Number Eighty-three, Hawkeye's train—and Toddles's—scheduled Big Cloud on the eastbound run at 9:05; and, on the night the story opens, they were about an hour away from the little mountain town that was the divisional point, as Toddles, his basket of edibles in the crook of his arm, halted in the forward end of the second-class smoker to examine again the fistful of change that he dug out of his pants pocket with his free hand.

Toddles was in an unusually bad humor, and he scowled. With exceeding deftness he separated one of the coins from the others, using his fingers like the teeth of a rake, and dropped the rest back jingling into his pocket. The coin that remained he put into his mouth, and bit on it—hard. His scowl deepened. Somebody had presented Toddles with a lead quarter.

It wasn't so much the quarter, though Toddles's salary wasn't so big as some people's who would have felt worse over it, it was his amour propre that was touched—deeply. It wasn't often that anyone could put so bald a thing as lead money across on Toddles. Toddles's mind harked back along the aisles of the cars behind him. He had only made two sales that round, and he had changed a quarter each time—for the pretty girl with the big picture hat, who had giggled at him when she bought a package of chewing gum; and the man with the three-carat diamond tiepin in the parlor car, a little more than on the edge of inebriety, who had got on at the last stop, and who had bought a cigar from him.

Toddles thought it over for a bit; decided he wouldn't have a fuss with a girl anyway, balked at a parlor-car fracas with a drunk, dropped the coin back into his pocket, and went on into the combination baggage and express car. Here, just inside the door, was Toddles's—or rather the News Company's—chest. Toddles lifted the lid; and then his eyes shifted slowly and traveled up the car. Things were certainly going badly with Toddles that night.

There were four men in the car; Bob Donkin, coming back from a holiday trip somewhere up the line; MacNicoll, the baggage master; Nulty, the express messenger—and Hawkeye. Toddles's inventory of the contents of the chest had been hurried—but intimate. A small bunch of six bananas was gone, and Hawkeye was munching them unconcernedly. It wasn't the first time the big, hulking six-foot conductor had pilfered the boy's chest, not by many—and never paid for the pilfering. That was Hawkeye's idea of a joke.

Hawkeye was talking to Nulty, elaborately simulating ignorance of Toddles's presence—and he was talking about Toddles.

"Sure," said Hawkeye, his mouth full of banana, "he'll be a great railroad man someday! He's the stuff they're made of! You can see it sticking out all over him! He's only selling peanuts now till he grows up and—"

Toddles put down his basket and planted himself before the conductor.

"You pay for those bananas," said Toddles in a low voice—which was high.

"When'll he grow up?" continued Hawkeye, peeling more fruit. "I don't know—you've got me. The first time I saw him two years ago, I'm hanged if he wasn't bigger than he is now—guess he grows backwards. Have a banana?" He offered one to Nulty, who refused it.

"You pay for those bananas, you big stiff!" squealed Toddles belligerently.

Hawkeye turned his head slowly and turned his little, beady black eyes on Toddles, then he turned with a wink to the others, and for the first time in two years offered payment. He fished into his pocket and handed Toddles a twenty-dollar bill—there always was a mean streak in Hawkeye, more or less of a bully, none-too-well liked, and whose name on the payroll, by the way, was Reynolds.

"Take fifteen cents out of that," he said, with no idea that the boy could change the bill.

For a moment Toddles glared at the yellow-back, then a thrill of unholy glee came to Toddles. He could just about make it, business all around had been pretty good that day, particularly on the run west in the morning.

Hawkeye went on with the exposition of his idea of humor at Toddles's expense; and Toddles went back to his chest and his reserve funds. Toddles counted out eighteen dollars in bills, made a neat pile of four quarters—the lead one on the bottom—another neat pile of the odd change, and returned to Hawkeye. The lead quarter wouldn't go very far toward liquidating Hawkeye's long-standing indebtedness—but it would help some.

Hawkeye counted the bills carefully, and crammed them into his pocket. Toddles dropped the neat little pile of quarters into Hawkeye's hand—they counted themselves—and Hawkeye put those in his pocket. Toddles counted out the odd change piece by piece, and, as Hawkeye put *that* in his pocket, Toddles put his fingers to his nose.

Queer, isn't it—the way things happen? Think of a man's whole life, aspirations, hopes, ambitions, everything, pivoting on—a lead quarter! But then they say that opportunity knocks once at the door of every man; and, if that be true, let it be remarked in passing that Toddles wasn't deaf!

Hawkeye, making Toddles a target for a parting gibe, took up his lantern and started through the train to pick up the fares from the last stop. In due course he halted before the inebriated one with the glittering tiepin in the smoking compartment of the parlor car.

"Ticket, please," said Hawkeye.

"Too busy to buysh ticket," the man informed him, with heavy confidence. "Wha'sh fare Loon Dam to Big Cloud?"

"One-fifty," said Hawkeye curtly.

The man produced a roll of bills, and from the roll extracted a two-dollar note.

Hawkeye handed him back two quarters, and started to punch a cash-fare slip. He looked up to find the man holding out one of the quarters insistently, if somewhat unsteadily.

"What's the matter?" demanded Hawkeye brusquely.

"Bad," said the man.

A drummer grinned; and an elderly gentleman, from his magazine, looked up inquiringly over his spectacles.

"Bad!" Hawkeye brought his elbow sharply around to focus his lamp on the coin; then he leaned over and rang it on the windowsill—only it wouldn't ring. It was indubitably bad. Hawkeye, however, was dealing with a drunk—and Hawkeye always did have a mean streak in him.

"It's perfectly good," he asserted gruffly.

The man rolled an eye at the conductor that mingled a sudden shrewdness and anger, and appealed to his fellow travelers. The verdict was against Hawkeye, and Hawkeye ungraciously pocketed the lead piece and handed over another quarter.

"Shay," observed the inebriated one insolently, "shay, Conductor, I don't like you. You thought I was—hic!—s'drunk I wouldn't know—eh? Tha'sh where you fooled yerself!"

"What do you mean?" Hawkeye bridled virtuously for the benefit of the drummer and the old gentleman with the spectacles.

And then the other began to laugh immoderately.

"Same ol' quarter," said he. "Same—hic!—ol' quarter back again. Great system—peanut boy—conductor—hic! Pass it off on one—other passes it off on someone else. Just passed it off on—hic!—peanut boy for a joke. Goin' to give him a dollar when he comes back."

"Oh, you did, did you!" snapped Hawkeye ominously. "And you mean to insinuate that I deliberately tried to—"

"Sure!" declared the man heartily.

"You're a liar!" announced Hawkeye, spluttering mad. "And what's more, since it came from you, you'll take it back!" He dug into his pocket for the ubiquitous lead piece.

"Not—hic!—on your life!" said the man earnestly. "You hang on to it, old top. I didn't pass it off on *you*."

"Haw!" exploded the drummer suddenly. "Haw—haw, haw!"

And the elderly gentleman smiled.

Hawkeye's face went red, and then purple.

"Go 'way!" said the man petulantly. "I don't like you. Go 'way! Go an' tell Peanuts I—hic!—got a dollar for him."

And Hawkeye went—but Toddles never got the dollar. Hawkeye went out of the smoking compartment of the parlor car with the lead quarter in his pocket—because he couldn't do anything else—which didn't soothe his feelings any—and he went out mad enough to bite himself. The drummer's guffaw followed him, and he thought he even caught a chuckle from the elderly party with the magazine and spectacles.

Hawkeye was mad; and he was quite well aware, painfully well aware, that he had looked like a fool, which is about one of the meanest feelings there is to feel; and, as he made his way forward through the train, he grew madder still. That change was the change from his twenty-dollar bill. He had not needed to be told that the lead quarter had come from Toddles. The only question at all in doubt was whether or not Toddles had put the counterfeit coin over on him knowingly and with malice aforethought. Hawkeye, however, had an intuition deep down inside of him that there wasn't any doubt even about that, and as he opened the door of the baggage car his intuition was vindicated. There was a grin on the faces of Nulty, MacNicoll, and Bob Donkin that disappeared with suspicious celerity at sight of him as he came through the door.

There was no hesitation then on Hawkeye's part. Toddles, equipped for another excursion through the train with a stack of magazines and books that almost hid him, received a sudden and vicious clout on the side of the ear.

"You'd try your tricks on me, would you?" Hawkeye snarled. "Lead quarters—eh?" Another clout. "I'll teach you, you blasted little runt!"

And with the clouts, the stack of carefully balanced periodicals went flying over the floor; and with the clouts, the nagging, and the hectoring, and the bullying, that had rankled for close on two years in Toddles's turbulent soul, rose in a sudden, all-possessing sweep of fury. Toddles was a fighter—with the heart of a fighter. And Toddles's cause was just. He couldn't reach the conductor's face—so he went for Hawkeye's legs. And the screams of rage from his high-pitched voice, as he shot himself forward, sounded like a cageful of Australian cockatoos on the rampage.

Toddles was small, pitifully small for his age; but he wasn't an infant in arms—not for a minute. And in action Toddles was as near to a wildcat as anything else that comes handy by way of illustration. Two legs and one arm he twined and twisted around Hawkeye's legs; and the other arm, with a hard and knotty fist on the end of it, caught the conductor a wicked jab in the region of the bottom button of the vest. The brass button peeled the skin off Toddles's knuckles, but the jab doubled the conductor forward, and, coincident with Hawkeye's winded grunt, the lantern in his hand sailed ceilingwards, crashed into the center lamps in the roof of the car, and down, in a shower of tinkling glass, dripping oil, and burning wicks, came the wreckage to the floor.

There was a yell from Nulty; but Toddles hung on like grim death. Hawkeye was bawling fluent profanity and seeing red. Toddles heard one and sensed the other—and he clung grimly on. He was all doubled up around Hawkeye's knees, and in that position Hawkeye couldn't get at him very well; and, besides, Toddles had his own plan of battle. He was waiting for an extra heavy lurch of the car.

It came. Toddles's muscles strained legs and arms and back in concert, and for an instant across the car they tottered, Hawkeye staggering in a desperate attempt to maintain his equilibrium—and then down—speaking generally, on a heterogeneous pile of express parcels; concretely, with an eloquent *squnch*, on a crate of eggs, thirty dozen of them, at forty cents a dozen.

Toddles, over his rage, experienced a sickening sense of disaster, but still he clung; he didn't dare let go. Hawkeye's fists, both in an effort to recover himself and in an endeavor to reach Toddles, were going like a windmill; and Hawkeye's threats were something terrifying to listen to. And now they rolled over, and Toddles was underneath; and then they rolled over again; and then a hand locked on Toddles's collar, and he was yanked, terrier-fashion, to his feet.

His face white and determined, his fists doubled, Toddles waited for Hawkeye to get up—the word *run* wasn't in Toddles's vocabulary. He hadn't long to wait.

Hawkeye lunged up, draped in the broken crate—a sight. The road always prided itself on the natty uniforms of its train crews, but Hawkeye wasn't dressed in uniform then—mostly egg yolks. He made a dash for Toddles, but he never reached the boy. Bob Donkin was between them.

"Cut it out!" said Donkin coldly, as he pushed Toddles behind him. "You asked for it, Reynolds, and you got it. Now cut it out!"

And Hawkeye "cut it out." It was pretty generally understood that Bob Donkin never talked much for show, and Bob Donkin was bigger than Toddles, a whole lot bigger—as big as Hawkeye himself. Hawkeye cut it out.

Funny, the egg part of it? Well, perhaps. But the fire wasn't. True, they got it out with the help of the hand extinguishers before it did any serious damage, for Nulty had gone at it on the jump; but while it lasted the burning oil on the car floor looked dangerous. Anyway, it was bad enough so that they couldn't hide it when they got into Big Cloud—and Hawkeye and Toddles went on the carpet for it the next morning in the super's office.

Carleton, "Royal" Carleton, reached for a match, and to keep his lips straight, clamped them firmly on the amber mouthpiece of his brier, and stumpy, big-paunched Tommy Regan, the master mechanic, who was sitting in a chair by the window, reached hurriedly into his back pocket for his chewing and looked out of the window to hide a grin, as the two came in and ranged themselves in front of the super's desk—Hawkeye, six feet and a hundred and ninety pounds, with Toddles trailing him, mostly cap and buttons and no weight at all.

Carleton didn't ask many questions—he'd asked them before—of Bob Donkin—and the dispatcher hadn't gone out of his way to invest the conductor with any glorified halo. Carleton, always a strict disciplinarian, said what he had to say and said it quietly; but he meant to let the conductor have the worst of it, and he did—in a way that was all Carleton's own. Two years' picking on a youngster didn't appeal to Carleton, no matter who the youngster was. Before he was half through he had the big conductor squirming. Hawkeye was looking for something else—besides a galling and matter-of-fact impartiality that accepted himself and Toddles as being on exactly the same plane and level.

"There's a case of eggs," said Carleton at the end. "You can divide up the damage between you. And I'm going to change your runs, unless you've got some good reason to give me why I shouldn't?"

He waited for an answer.

Hawkeye, towering, sullen, his eyes resting bitterly on Regan, having caught the master mechanic's grin, said nothing; Toddles, whose head barely showed over the top of Carleton's desk, and the whole of him sizing up about big enough to go into the conductor's pocket, was equally silent—Toddles was thinking of something else.

"Very good," said Carleton suavely, as he surveyed the ridiculous incongruity before him. "I'll change your runs, then. I can't have you two *men* brawling and prize-fighting every trip."

There was a sudden sound from the window, as though Regan had got some of his blackstrap juice down the wrong way.

Hawkeye's face went black as thunder.

Carleton's face was like a sphinx.

"That'll do, then," he said. "You can go, both of you."

Hawkeye stamped out of the room and down the stairs. But Toddles stayed.

"Please, Mr. Carleton, won't you give me a job on—" Toddles stopped.

So had Regan's chuckle. Toddles, the irrepressible, was at it again—and Toddles after a job, any kind of a job, was something that Regan's experience had taught him to fly from without standing on the order of his flight. Regan hurried from the room.

Toddles watched him go—kind of speculatively, kind of reproachfully. Then he turned to Carleton.

"Please give me a job, Mr. Carleton," he pleaded. "Give me a job, won't you?"

It was only yesterday on the platform that Toddles had waylaid the super with the same demand—and about every day before that as far back as Carleton could remember. It was hopelessly chronic. Anything convincing or appealing about it had gone long ago—Toddles said it parrot-fashion now. Carleton took refuge in severity.

"See here, young man," he said grimly, "you were brought into this office for a reprimand and not to apply for a job! You can thank your stars and Bob Donkin you haven't lost the one you've got. Now, get out!"

"I'd make good if you gave me one," said Toddles earnestly. "Honest, I would, Mr. Carleton."

"Get out!" said the super, not altogether unkindly. "I'm busy."

Toddles swallowed a lump in his throat—but not until after his head was turned and he'd started for the door so the super couldn't see it. Toddles swallowed the lump—and got out. He hadn't expected anything else, of course. The refusals were just as chronic as the demands. But that didn't make each new one any easier for Toddles. It made it worse.

Toddles's heart was heavy as he stepped out into the hall, and the iron was in his soul. He was seventeen now, and it looked as though he never would get a chance—except to be a newsboy all his life.

Toddles swallowed another lump. He loved railroading; it was his one ambition, his one desire. If he could ever get a chance, he'd show them! He'd show them that he wasn't a joke, just because he was small!

Toddles turned at the head of the stairs to go down, when somebody called his name.

"Here—Toddles! Come here!"

Toddles looked over his shoulder, hesitated, then marched in through the open door of the dispatchers' room. Bob Donkin was alone there.

"What's your name—Toddles?" inquired Donkin, as Toddles halted before the dispatcher's table.

Toddles froze instantly—hard. His fists doubled; there was a smile on Donkin's face. Then his fists slowly uncurled; the smile on Donkin's face had broadened, but there wasn't any malice in the smile.

"Christopher Hyslop Hoogan," said Toddles, unbending.

Donkin put his hand quickly to his mouth—and coughed.

"Um-m!" said he pleasantly. "Super hard on you this morning, Hoogan?"

And with the words Toddles's heart went out to the big dispatcher: "Hoogan"—and a man-to-man tone.

"No," said Toddles cordially. "Say, I thought you were on the night trick."

"Double shift—short-handed," replied Donkin. "Come from New York, don't you?"

Yes," said Toddles.

"Mother and father down there still?"

It came quick and unexpected, and Toddles stared for a moment. Then he walked over to the window.

"I haven't got any," he said.

There wasn't any sound for an instant, save the clicking of the instruments; then Donkin spoke again—a little gruffly:

"When are you going to quit making an ass of yourself?"

Toddles swung from the window, hurt. Donkin, after all, was like all the rest of them.

"Well?" prompted the dispatcher.

"You go to blazes!" said Toddles bitterly, and started for the door.

Donkin halted him.

"You're only fooling yourself, Hoogan," he said coolly. "If you wanted what you call a real railroad job as much as you pretend you do, you'd get one."

"Eh?" demanded Toddles defiantly; and went back to the table.

"A fellow," said Donkin, putting a little sting into his words, "never got anywhere by going around with a chip on his shoulder fighting everybody because they called him Toddles, and making a nuisance of himself with the Big Fellows until they got sick of the sight of him."

It was a pretty stiff arraignment. Toddles choked over it, and the angry blood flushed to his cheeks.

"That's all right for you!" he spluttered out hotly. "You don't look too small for the train crews or the roundhouse, and they don't call you Toddles so's nobody'll forget it. What'd *you* do?"

"I'll tell you what I'd do," said Donkin quietly. "I'd make everybody on the division wish their own name was Toddles before I was through with them, and I'd *make* a job for myself."

Toddles blinked helplessly.

"Getting right down to a cash fare," continued Donkin, after a moment, as Toddles did not speak, "they're not so far wrong, either, about you sizing up pretty small for the train crews or the roundhouse, are they?"

"No-o," admitted Toddles reluctantly; "but—"

"Then why not something where there's no handicap hanging over you?" suggested the dispatcher—and his hand reached out and touched the sender. "The key, for instance?"

"But I don't know anything about it," said Toddles, still helplessly.

"That's just it," returned Donkin smoothly. "You never tried to learn."

Toddles's eyes widened, and into Toddles's heart leaped a sudden joy. A new world seemed to open out before him in which aspirations, ambitions, longings, all were a reality. A key! That *was* real railroading, the top notch of railroading, too. First an operator, and then a dispatcher, and—and— And then his face fell, and the vision faded.

"How'd I get a chance to learn?" he said miserably. "Who'd teach me?"

The smile was back on Donkin's face as he pushed his chair from the table, stood up, and held out his hand—man-to-man fashion.

"I will," he said. "I liked your grit last night, Hoogan. And if you want to be a railroad man, I'll make you one—before I'm through. I've some old instruments you can have to practice with, and I've nothing to do in my spare time. What do you say?"

Toddles didn't say anything. For the first time since Toddles's advent to the Hill Division, there were tears in Toddles's eyes for someone else to see.

Donkin laughed.

"All right, old man, you're on. See that you don't throw me down. And keep your mouth shut; you'll need all your wind. It's work that counts, and nothing else. Now chase yourself! I'll dig up the things you'll need, and you can drop in here and get them when you come off your run tonight."

Spare time! Bob Donkin didn't have any spare time those days! But that was Donkin's way. Spence sick, and two men handling the dispatching where three had handled it before, didn't leave Bob Donkin much spare time—not much. But a boost for the kid was worth a sacrifice. Donkin went at it as earnestly as Toddles did—and Toddles was in deadly earnest.

When Toddles left the dispatcher's office that morning with Donkin's promise to teach him the key, Toddles had a hazy idea that Donkin had wings concealed somewhere under his coat and was an angel in disguise; and at the end of two weeks he was sure of it. But at the end of a month Bob Donkin was a god! Throw Bob Donkin down! Toddles would have sold his soul for the dispatcher.

It wasn't easy, though; and Bob Donkin wasn't an easygoing taskmaster, not by long odds. Donkin had a tongue, and on occasions could use it. Short and quick in his explanations, he expected his pupil to get it short and quick; either that, or Donkin's opinion of him. But Toddles stuck. He'd have crawled on his knees for Donkin anywhere, and he worked like a major—not only for his own advancement, but for what he came to prize quite as much, if not more: Donkin's approval.

Toddles, mindful of Donkin's words, didn't fight so much as the days went by, though he found it difficult to swear off all at once; and on his runs he studied his Morse code, and he had the "calls" of every station on the division off by heart right from the start. Toddles mastered the "sending" by leaps and bounds; but the "taking" came slower, as it does for everybody—but even at that, at the end of six weeks, if it wasn't thrown at him too fast and hard, Toddles could get it after a fashion.

Taken all around, Toddles felt like whistling most of the time; and, pleased with his own progress, looked forward to starting in presently as a full-fledged operator. He mentioned the matter to Bob Donkin—once. Donkin picked his words and spoke fervently. Toddles never brought the subject up again.

And so things went on. Late summer turned to early fall, and early fall to still sharper weather, until there came the night that the operator at Blind River muddled his orders and gave Number Seventy-three, the westbound fast freight, her clearance against the second section of the eastbound Limited that doomed them to meet somewhere head-on in the Glacier Canyon; the night that Toddles— But there's just a word or two that comes before.

When it was all over, it was up to Sam Beale, the Blind River operator, straight enough. Beale blundered. That's all there was to it; that covers it all—he blundered. It would have finished Beale's railroad career forever and a day—only Beale played the man, and the instant he realized what he had done, even while the taillights of the freight were disappearing down the track and he couldn't stop her, he was stammering the tale of his mistake over the wire, the sweat beads dripping from his wrist, his face gray with horror, to Bob Donkin under the green-shaded lamp in the dispatchers' room at Big Cloud, miles away.

Donkin got the miserable story over the chattering wire—got it before it was half told—cut Beale out and began to pound the Gap call. And, as though it were before him in reality, that stretch of track, fifteen miles of it, from Blind River to the Gap, unfolded itself like a grisly panorama before his mind. There wasn't a half mile of tangent at a single stretch in the whole of it. It swung like the writhings of a snake, through cuts and tunnels, hugging the canyon walls, twisting this way and that. Anywhere else there might be a chance, one in a thousand even, that they would see each other's headlights in time—here it was disaster quick and absolute.

Donkin's lips were set in a thin, straight line. The Gap answered him; and the answer was like the knell of doom. He had not expected anything else; he had only hoped against hope. The second section of the Limited had pulled out of the Gap, eastbound, two minutes before. The two trains were in the open against each other's orders.

In the next room, Carleton and Regan, over their pipes, were at their nightly game of pedro. Donkin called them—and his voice sounded strange to himself. Chairs scraped and crashed to the floor, and an instant later the super and the master mechanic were in the room.

What's wrong, Bob?" Carleton flung the words from him in a single breath.

Donkin told them. But his fingers were on the key again as he talked. There was still one chance, worse than the thousand-to-one shot; but it was the only one. Between the Gap and Blind River, eight miles from the Gap, seven miles from Blind River, was Cassil's Siding. But there was no night man at Cassil's, and the little town lay a mile from the station. It was ten o'clock—Donkin's watch lay face-up on the table before him—the day man at Cassil's went off at seven; the chance was that the day man *might* have come back to the station for something or other!

Not much of a chance? No—not much! It was a possibility, that was all; and Donkin's fingers worked—the seventeen, the life-and-death—calling, calling on the night trick to the day man at Cassil's Siding.

Carleton came and stood at Donkin's elbow, and Regan stood at the other; and there was silence now, save only for the key that, under Donkin's fingers, seemed to echo its stammering appeal about the room like the sobbing of a human soul.

"C.S.—C.S.—C.S.," Donkin called; and then, the "seventeen," and then, "hold second Number Two." And then the same thing over and over again.

And there was no answer.

It had turned cold that night and there was a fire in the little heater. Donkin had opened the draft a little while before, and the sheet-iron sides now began to purr red-hot. Nobody noticed it. Regan's kindly, good-humored face had the stamp of horror in it, and he pulled at his scraggly brown mustache, his eyes seemingly fascinated by Donkin's fingers. Everybody's eyes, the three of them, were on Donkin's fingers and the key. Carleton was like a man of stone, motionless, his face set harder than face was ever carved in marble.

It grew hot in the room; but Donkin's fingers were like ice on the key, and, strong man though he was, he faltered.

"Oh, my God!" he whispered—and never a prayer rose more fervently from lips than those three broken words.

Again he called, and again, and again. The minutes slipped away. Still he called—with the life-and-death, the "seventeen"—called and called. And there was no answer save that echo in the room that brought the perspiration streaming now from Regan's face, a harder light into Carleton's eyes, and a chill like death into Donkin's heart.

Suddenly Donkin pushed back his chair; and his fingers, from the key, touched the crystal of his watch.

"The second section will have passed Cassil's now," he said in a curious, unnatural, matter-of-fact tone. "It'll bring them together about a mile east of there—in another minute."

And then Carleton spoke—master railroader, "Royal" Carleton, it was up to him then, all the pity of it, the ruin, the disaster, the lives out, all the bitterness to cope with as he could. And it was in his eyes, all of it. But his voice was quiet. It rang quick, peremptory, his voice—but quiet.

"Clear the line, Bob," he said. "Plug in the roundhouse for the wrecker—and tell them to send uptown for the crew."

TODDLES? What did Toddles have to do with this? Well, a good deal, in one way and another. We're coming to Toddles now. You see, Toddles, since his fracas with Hawkeye, had been put on the Elk River local run that left Big Cloud at 9:45 in the morning for the run west, and scheduled Big Cloud again on the return trip at 10:10 in the evening.

It had turned cold that night, after a day of rain. Pretty cold—the thermometer can drop on occasion in the late fall in the mountains—and by eight o'clock, where there had been rain before, there was now a thin sheeting of ice over everything—very thin, you know the kind—rails and telegraph wires glistening like the decorations on a Christmas tree—very pretty—and also very nasty running on a mountain grade. Likewise, the rain, in the way rain has, had dripped from the car roofs to the platforms—the local did not boast any closed vestibules—and had also been blown upon the car steps with the sweep of the wind, and, having frozen, it stayed there. Not a very serious matter; annoying, perhaps, but not serious, demanding a little extra caution, that was all.

Toddles was in high fettle that night. He had been getting on famously of late; even Bob Donkin had admitted it. Toddles, with his stack of books and magazines, an unusually big one, for a number of the new periodicals were out that day, was dreaming rosy dreams to himself as he started from the door of the first-class smoker to the door of the first-class coach. In another hour now he'd be up in the dispatcher's room at Big Cloud for his nightly sitting with Bob Donkin. He could see Bob Donkin there now; and he could hear the big dispatcher growl at him in his bluff way: "Use your head—use your head—*Hoogan*!" It was always "Hoogan," never "Toddles." "Use your head"—Donkin was everlastingly drumming that into him; for the dispatcher used to confront him suddenly with imaginary and hair-raising emergencies, and demand Toddles's instant solution. Toddles realized that Donkin was getting to the heart of things, and that someday he, Toddles, would be a great dispatcher—like Donkin. "Use your head, Hoogan"—that's the way Donkin talked—"anybody can learn a key, but that doesn't make a railroad man out of him. It's the man when trouble comes who can think quick and think *right*. Use your—"

Toddles stepped out on the platform—and walked on ice. But that wasn't Toddles's undoing. The trouble with Toddles was that he was walking on air at the same time. It was treacherous running, they were nosing a curve, and in the cab, Kinneard, at the throttle, checked with a little jerk at the "air." And with the jerk, Toddles slipped; and with the slip, the center of gravity of the stack of periodicals shifted, and they bulged ominously from the middle. Toddles grabbed at them—and his heels went out from under him. He ricocheted down the steps, snatched desperately at the handrail, missed it, shot out from the train, and head, heels, arms, and body going every which way at once, rolled over and over down the embankment. And, starting from the point of Toddles's departure from the train, the right-of-way for a hundred yards was strewn with "the latest magazines" and "new books just out today."

Toddles lay there, a little, curled, huddled heap, motionless in the darkness. The taillights of the local disappeared. No one aboard would miss Toddles until they got into Big Cloud—and found him gone. Which is Irish for saying that no one would attempt to keep track of a newsboy's idiosyncrasies on a train; it would be asking too much of any train crew; and, besides, there was no mention of it in the rules.

It was a long while before Toddles stirred; a very long while before consciousness crept slowly back to him. Then he moved, tried to get up—and fell back with a quick, sharp cry of pain. He lay still then, for a moment. His ankle hurt him frightfully, and his back, and his shoulder, too. He put his hand to his face where something seemed to be trickling warm—and brought it away wet. Toddles, grim little warrior, tried to think. They hadn't been going very fast when he fell off. If they had, he would have been killed. As it was, he was hurt, badly hurt, and his head swam, nauseating him.

Where was he? Was he near any help? He'd have to get help somewhere, or—or with the cold and—and everything, he'd probably die out here before morning. Toddles shouted out—again and again. Perhaps his voice was too weak to carry very far; anyway, there was no reply.

He looked up at the top of the embankment, clamped his teeth, and started to crawl. If he got up there, perhaps he could tell where he was. It had taken Toddles a matter of seconds to roll down; it took him ten minutes of untold agony to get up. Then he dashed his hand across his eyes where the blood was, and cried a little with the surge of relief. East, down the track, only a few yards away, the green eye of a switch lamp winked at him.

Where there was a switch lamp there was a siding, and where there was a siding there was promise of a station. Toddles, with the sudden uplift upon him, got to his feet and started along the track—two steps—and went down again. He couldn't walk, the pain was more than he could bear—his right ankle, his left shoulder, and his back—hopping only made it worse—it was easier to crawl.

And so Toddles crawled.

It took him a long time even to pass the switch light. The pain made him weak, his senses seemed to trail off giddily every now and then, and he'd find himself lying flat and still beside the track. It was a white, drawn face that Toddles lifted up each time he started on again—miserably white, except where the blood kept trickling from his forehead.

And then Toddles's heart, stout as it was, seemed to snap. He had reached the station platform, wondering vaguely why the little building that loomed ahead was dark—and now it came to him in a flash, as he recognized the station. It was Cassil's Siding—*and there was no night man at Cassil's Siding!* The switch lights were lit before the day man left, of course. Everything swam before Toddles's eyes. There—there was no help here. And yet—yet perhaps—desperate hope came again—perhaps there might be. The pain was terrible—all over him. And—and he'd got so weak now—but it wasn't far to the door.

Toddles squirmed along the platform, and reached the door finally—only to find it shut and fastened. And then Toddles fainted on the threshold.

When Toddles came to himself again, he thought at first that he was up in the dispatcher's room at Big Cloud with Bob Donkin pounding away on the battered old key they used to practice with—only there seemed to be something the matter with the key, and it didn't sound as loud as it usually did—it seemed to come from a long way off somehow. And then, besides, Bob was working it faster than he had ever done before when they were practicing. "Hold second"—second something—Toddles couldn't make it out. Then the "seventeen"—yes, he knew that—that was the life-and-death. Bob was going pretty quick, though. Then "C.S.—C.S.—C.S."—Toddles's brain fumbled a bit over that—then it came to him. C.S. was the call for Cassil's Siding. *Cassil's Siding!* Toddles's head came up with a jerk.

A little cry burst from Toddles's lips—and his brain cleared. He wasn't at Big Cloud at all—he was at Cassil's Siding—and he was hurt—and that was the sounder inside calling, calling frantically for Cassil's Siding—where he was.

The life-and-death—*the seventeen*—it sent a thrill through Toddles's pain-twisted spine. He wriggled to the window. It, too, was closed, of course, but he could hear better there. The sounder was babbling madly.

"Hold second—"

He missed it again—and as, on top of it, the seventeen came pleading, frantic, urgent, he wrung his hands.

"Hold second"—he got it this time—"Number Two."

Toddles's first impulse was to smash in the window and reach the key. And then, like a dash of cold water over him, Donkin's words seemed to ring in his ears: "Use your head."

With the seventeen it meant a matter of minutes, perhaps even seconds. Why smash the window? Why waste the moment required to do it simply to answer the call? The order stood for itself—"Hold second Number Two." That was the second section of the Limited, eastbound. Hold her! How? There was nothing—not a thing to stop her with. "Use your head," said Donkin in a faraway voice to Toddles's wobbling brain.

Toddles looked up the track—west—where he had come from—to where the switch light twinkled green at him—and, with a little sob, he started to drag himself back along the platform. If he could throw the switch, it would throw the light from green to red—and the Limited would take the siding. But the switch was a long way off.

Toddles half fell, half bumped, from the end of the platform to the right-of-way. He cried to himself with low moans as he went along. He had the heart of a fighter, and grit to the last tissue; but he needed it all now—needed it all to stand the pain and fight the weakness that kept swirling over him in flashes.

On he went, on his hands and knees, slithering from tie to tie—and from one tie to the next was a great distance. The life-and-death, the dispatcher's call—he seemed to hear it yet—throbbing, throbbing on the wire.

On he went, up the track; and the green eye of the lamp, winking at him, grew nearer. And then suddenly, clear and mellow through the mountains, caught up and echoed far and near, came the notes of a chime whistle ringing down the gorge.

Fear came upon Toddles then, and a great sob shook him. That was the Limited coming now! Toddles's fingers dug into the ballast, and he hurried—that is, in bitter pain, he tried to crawl a little faster. And as he crawled, he kept his eyes strained up the track—she wasn't in sight yet around the curve—not yet, anyway.

Another foot, only another foot, and he would reach the siding switch—in time—in plenty of time. Again the sob—but now in a burst of relief that, for the moment, made him forget his hurts. He was in time!

He flung himself at the switch lever, tugged upon it—and then, trembling, every ounce of remaining strength seeming to ooze from him, he covered his face with his hands. It was *locked*—padlocked.

Came a rumble now—a distant roar, growing louder and louder, reverberating down the canyon walls—louder and louder—nearer and nearer. "Hold second Number Two. Hold second Number Two"—the seventeen, the life-and-death, pleading with him to hold Number Two. And she was coming now, coming—and—and—the switch was locked. The deadly nausea racked Toddles again; there was nothing to do now—nothing. He couldn't stop her—couldn't stop her. He'd—he'd tried—very hard—and—and he couldn't stop her now. He took his hands from his face, and stole a glance up the track, afraid almost, with the horror that was upon him, to look. She hadn't swung the curve yet, but she would in a minute—and come pounding down the stretch at fifty miles an hour, shoot by him like a rocket to where, somewhere ahead, in some form, he did not know what, only knew that it was there, death and ruin and—

"*Use your head!*" snapped Donkin's voice to his consciousness.

Toddles's eyes were on the light above his head. It blinked *red* at him as he stood on the track facing it; the green rays were shooting up and down the line. He couldn't swing the switch—but the *lamp* was there—and there was the red side to show just by turning it. He remembered then that the lamp fitted into a socket at the top of the switch stand, and could be lifted off—if he could reach it!

It wasn't very high—for an ordinary-sized man—for an ordinary-sized man had to get at it to trim and fill it daily—only Toddles wasn't an ordinary-sized man. It was just nine or ten feet above the rails—just a standard siding switch.

Toddles gritted his teeth, and climbed up on the base of the switch—and nearly fainted as his ankle swung against the rod. A foot above the base was a footrest for a man to stand on and reach up for the lamp, and Toddles drew himself up and got his foot on it—and then at his full height the tips of his fingers only just touched the bottom of the lamp. Toddles cried aloud, and the tears streamed down his face now. Oh, if he weren't hurt—if he could only shin up another foot—but—but it was all he could do to hang there where he was.

What was that? He turned his head. Up the track, sweeping in a great circle as it swung the curve, a headlight's glare cut through the night—and Toddles "shinned" the foot. He tugged and tore at the lamp, tugged and tore at it, loosened it, lifted it from its socket, sprawled and wriggled with it to the ground—and turned the red side of the lamp against second Number Two.

The quick, short blasts of a whistle answered, then the crunch and grind and scream of biting brake shoes—and the big mountain racer, the 1012, pulling the second section of the Limited that night, stopped with its pilot nosing a diminutive figure in a torn and silver-buttoned uniform, whose hair was clotted red, and whose face was covered with blood and dirt.

Masters, the engineer, and Pete Leroy, his fireman, swung from the gangways; Kelly, the conductor, came running up from the forward coach.

Kelly shoved his lamp into Toddles's face—and whistled low under his breath.

"Toddles!" he gasped; and then, quick as a steel trap: "What's wrong?"

"I don't know," said Toddles weakly. "There's—there's something wrong. Get into the clear—on the siding."

"Something wrong," repeated Kelly, "and you don't—"

But Masters cut the conductor short with a grab at the other's arm that was like the shutting of a vise—and then bolted for his engine like a gopher for its hole. From down the track came the heavy, grumbling roar of a freight. Everybody flew then, and there was quick work done in the next half minute—and none too quickly done—

the Limited was no more than on the siding when the fast freight rolled her long string of flats, boxes, and gondolas thundering by.

And while she passed, Toddles, on the platform, stammered out his story to Kelly.

Kelly didn't say anything—then. With the express messenger and a brakeman carrying Toddles, Kelly kicked in the station door, and set his lamp down on the operator's table.

"Hold me up," whispered Toddles—and, while they held him, he made the dispatcher's call.

Big Cloud answered him on the instant. Haltingly, Toddles reported the second section "in" and the freight "out"—only he did it very slowly, and he couldn't think very much more, for things were going black. He got an order for the Limited to run to Blind River and told Kelly, and got the "complete"—and then Big Cloud asked who was on the wire, and Toddles answered that in a mechanical sort of a way without quite knowing what he was doing—and went limp in Kelly's arms.

And as Toddles answered, back in Big Cloud, Regan, the sweat still standing out in great beads on his forehead, fierce now in the revulsion of relief, glared over Donkin's left shoulder, as Donkin's left hand scribbled on a pad what was coming over the wire.

Regan glared fiercely—then he spluttered: "Who in hell's Christopher Hyslop Hoogan—hm?"

Donkin's lips had a queer smile on them.

"Toddles," he said.

Regan sat down heavily in his chair.

"*What?*" demanded the super.

"Toddles," said Donkin. "I've been trying to drum a little railroading into him—on the key."

Regan wiped his face. He looked helplessly from Donkin to the super, and then back again at Donkin.

"But—but what's he doing at Cassil's Siding? How'd he get there—hm? Hm? How'd he get there?"

"I don't know," said Donkin, his fingers rattling the Cassil's Siding call again. "He doesn't answer anymore. We'll have to wait for the story till they make Blind River, I guess."

And so they waited. And presently, at Blind River, Kelly, dictating to the operator—not Beale, Beale's day man—told the story. It lost

"Oh, if he weren't hurt—if he could only shin up another foot—but it was all he could do to hang there where he was."

nothing in the telling—Kelly wasn't that kind of a man—he told them what Toddles had done, and he left nothing out; and he added that they had Toddles on a mattress in the baggage car, with a doctor they had discovered amongst the passengers looking after him.

At the end, Carleton tamped down the dottle in the bowl of his pipe thoughtfully with his forefinger—and glanced at Donkin.

"Got along far enough to take a station key somewhere?" he inquired casually. "He's made a pretty good job of it as the night operator at Cassil's."

Donkin was smiling.

"Not yet," he said.

"No?" Carleton's eyebrows went up. "Well, let him come in here with you, then, till he has; and when you say he's ready, we'll see what we can do. I guess it's coming to him; and I guess"—he shifted his glance to the master mechanic—"I guess we'll go down and meet Number Two when she comes in, Tommy."

Regan grinned.

"With our hats in our hands," said the bighearted master mechanic.

Donkin shook his head.

"Don't you do it," he said. "I don't want him to get a swelled head."

Carleton stared; and Regan's hand, reaching into his back pocket for his chewing, stopped midway.

Donkin was still smiling.

"I'm going to make a railroad man out of Toddles," he said.

—1919

.007

RUDYARD KIPLING

A LOCOMOTIVE IS, next to a marine engine, the most sensitive thing man ever made; and Number .007, besides being sensitive, was new. The red paint was hardly dry on his spotless bumper-bar, his headlight shone like a fireman's helmet, and his cab might have been a hardwood-finish parlor. They had run him into the roundhouse after his trial—he had said good-bye to his best friend in the shops, the overhead traveling-crane—the big world was just outside; and the other locos were taking stock of him. He looked at the semicircle of bold, unwinking headlights, heard the low purr and mutter of the steam mounting in the gauges—scornful hisses of contempt as a slack valve lifted a little—and would have given a month's oil for leave to crawl through his own driving-wheels into the brick ash-pit beneath him. .007 was an eight-wheeled "American" loco, slightly different from others of his type, and as he stood he was worth ten thousand dollars on the Company's books. But if you had bought him at his own valuation, after half an hour's waiting in the darkish, echoing roundhouse, you would have saved exactly nine thousand nine hundred and ninety-nine dollars and ninety-eight cents.

A heavy Mogul freight, with a short cowcatcher and a firebox that came down within three inches of the rail, began the impolite game, speaking to a Pittsburgh Consolidation, who was visiting.

"Where did this thing blow in from?" he asked, with a dreamy puff of light steam.

"It's all I can do to keep track of our own makes," was the answer, "without lookin' after *your* back-numbers. Guess it's something Peter Cooper left over when he died."

.007 quivered; his steam was getting up, but he held his tongue. Even a hand-car knows what sort of locomotive it was that Peter Cooper experimented upon in the faraway thirties. It carried its coal and water in two apple-barrels, and was not much bigger than a bicycle.

Then up and spoke a small, newish switching-engine, with a little step in front of his bumper-timber, and his wheels so close together that he looked like a bronco getting ready to buck.

"Something's wrong with the road when a Pennsylvania gravel-pusher tells us anything about our stock, *I* think. That kid's all right. Eustis designed him, and Eustis designed me. Ain't that good enough?"

.007 could have carried the switching-loco round the yard in his tender, but he felt grateful for even this little word of consolation.

"We don't use hand-cars on the Pennsylvania," said the Consolidation. "That—er—peanut stand's old enough and ugly enough to speak for himself."

"He hasn't bin spoken to yet. He's bin spoken *at.* Hain't ye any manners on the Pennsylvania?" said the switching-loco.

"You ought to be in the yard, Pony," said the Mogul severely. "We're all long-haulers here."

"That's what you think," the little fellow replied. "You'll know more 'fore the night's out. I've been down to Track 17, and the freight there—oh, Christmas!"

"I've trouble enough in my own division," said a lean, light suburban loco with very shiny brake shoes. "My commuters wouldn't rest till they got a parlor car. They've hitched her back of all, and she hauls wors'n a snowplow. I'll snap her off someday sure, and then they'll blame everyone except their fool selves. They'll be askin' me to haul a vestibuled next!"

"They made you in New Jersey, didn't they?" said Pony. "Thought so. Commuters and truck wagons ain't any sweet haulin', but I tell *you* they're a heap better'n cuttin' out refrigerator cars or oil tanks. Why, I've hauled—"

"Haul! You?" said the Mogul contemptuously. "It's all you can do to bunt a cold-storage car up the yard. Now, I—"he paused a little to let the words sink in— "I handle the Flying Freight—eleven cars worth just anything you please to mention. On the stroke of eleven I pull out; and I'm timed for thirty-five the hour. Costly—perishable—fragile—immediate—that's me! Suburban traffic's only one degree better than switching. Express freight's what pays."

"Well, I ain't given to blowing, as a rule," began the Pittsburgh Consolidation.

"No? You was sent in here because you grunted on the grade," Pony interrupted.

"Where I grunt, you'd lie down, Pony; but, as I was saying, I don't blow much. Notwithstandin', *if* you want to see freight that *is* freight, moved lively, you should see me warbling through the Alleghenies with thirty-seven ore cars behind me, and my brakemen fightin' tramps so's they can't attend to my tooter. *I* have to do all the holdin' back then, and, though I say it, I've never had a load get away from me yet. *No*, sir. Haulin's one thing, but judgment and discretion's another. You want judgment in my business."

"Ah! But—but are you not paralyzed by a sense of your overwhelming responsibilities?" said a curious, husky voice from a corner.

"Who's that?" .007 whispered to the Jersey commuter.

"Compound—experiment—N.G. She's bin switchin' in the B. & A. yards for six months, when she wasn't in the shops. She's economical (*I* call it mean) in her coal, but she takes it out in repairs. Ahem! I presume you found Boston somewhat isolated, madam, after your New York season?"

"I am never so well occupied as when I am alone." The Compound seemed to be talking from halfway up her smokestack.

"Sure," said the irreverent Pony, under his breath. "They don't hanker after her any in the yard."

"But, with my constitution and temperament—my work lies in Boston—I find your *outrecuidance*—"

"Outer which?" said the Mogul freight. "Simple cylinders are good enough for me."

"Perhaps I should have said *faroucherie*," hissed the Compound.

"I don't hold with any make of papier-mâché wheel," the Mogul insisted.

The Compound sighed pityingly, and said no more.

"Git 'em all shapes in this world, don't ye?" said Pony. "That's Mass'chusetts all over. They half start, an' then they stick on a dead center, an' blame it all on other folks' ways o' treatin' them. Talkin' o' Boston, Comanche told me, last night, he had a hotbox just beyond the Newtons, Friday. That was why, *he* says, the Accommodation was held up. Made out no end of a tale, Comanche did."

"If I'd heard that in the shops, with my boiler out for repairs, I'd know 'twas one o' Comanche's lies," the New Jersey commuter snapped. "Hotbox! Him! What happened was they'd put an extra car on, and he just lay down on the grade and squealed. They had to send 127 to help him through. Made it out a hotbox, did he? Time before that he said he was ditched! Looked me square in the headlight and told me that as cool as—as a water-tank in a cold wave. Hotbox! You ask 127 about Comanche's hotbox. Why, Comanche—he was sidetracked, and 127 (*he* was just about as mad as they make 'em on account o' being called out at ten o'clock at night) took hold and whirled her into Boston in seventeen minutes. Hotbox! Hot fraud! That's what Comanche is."

Then .007 put both drivers and his pilot into it, as the saying is, for he asked what sort of thing a hotbox might be.

"Paint my bell sky-blue!" said Pony, the switcher. "Make me a surface-railroad loco with a hardwood skirtin'-board round my wheels! Break me up and cast me into five-cent sidewalk fakirs' mechanical toys! Here's an eight-wheel coupled 'American' don't know what a hotbox is! Never heard of an emergency stop, either, did ye? Don't know what ye carry jackscrews for? You're too innocent to be left alone with your own tender. Oh, you—you flatcar!"

There was a roar of escaping steam before anyone could answer, and .007 nearly blistered his paint off with pure mortification.

"A hotbox," began the Compound, picking and choosing the words as though they were coal, "a hotbox is the penalty exacted from inexperience by haste. Ahem!"

"Hotbox!" said the Jersey Suburban. "It's the price you pay for going on the tear. It's years since I've had one. It's a disease that don't attack shorthaulers, as a rule."

"We never have hotboxes on the Pennsylvania," said the Consolidation. "They get 'em in New York—same as nervous prostration."

"Ah, go home on a ferryboat," said the Mogul. "You think because you use worse grades than our road'd allow, you're a kind of Allegheny angel. Now I'll tell you what you . . . Here's my folk. Well, I can't stop. See you later, perhaps."

He rolled forward majestically to the turntable, and swung like a man-of-war in a tideway, till he picked up his track. "But as for you, you pea-green swivelin' coffeepot [this to .007] you go out and learn something before you associate with those who've made more mileage in a week than you'll roll up in a year. Costly—perishable—fragile—immediate—that's me! S'long."

"Split my tubes if that's actin' polite to a new member o' the Brotherhood," said Pony. "There wasn't any call to trample on ye like that. But manners was left out when Moguls was made. Keep up your fire, kid, an' burn your own smoke. Guess we'll all be wanted in a minute."

Men were talking rather excitedly in the roundhouse. One man, in a dingy jersey, said that he hadn't any locomotives to waste on the yard. Another man, with a piece of crumpled paper in his hand, said that the yardmaster said that he was to say that, if the other man said anything, he (the other man) was to shut his head. Then the other man waved his arms, and wanted to know if he was expected to keep locomotives in his hip pocket. Then a man in a black Prince Albert coat without a collar came up dripping, for it was a hot August night, and said that what *he* said went; and between the three of them the locomotives began to go, too—first the Compound, then the Consolidation, then .007.

Now, deep down in his firebox, .007 had cherished a hope that as soon as his trial was done, he would be led forth with songs and shoutings, and attached to a green-and-chocolate-vestibuled flyer, under charge of a bold and noble engineer, who would pat him on his back, and weep over him, and call him his Arab steed. (The boys in the shops where he was built used to read wonderful stories of railroad life, and .007 expected things to happen as he had heard.) But there did not seem to be many vestibuled flyers in the roaring, rumbling, electric-lighted yards, and his engineer only said:

"Now, what sort of a fool sort of an injector has Eustis loaded onto

"There was a roar of escaping steam before anyone could answer, and .007 nearly blistered his paint off with pure mortification."

this rig this time?" And he put the lever over with an angry snap, crying: "Am I supposed to switch with this thing, hey?"

The collarless man mopped his head, and replied that, in the present state of the yard and freight and a few other things, the engineer would switch and keep on switching till the cows came home. .007 pushed out gingerly, his heart in his headlight, so nervous that the clang of his own bell almost made him jump the track. Lanterns waved, or danced up and down, before and behind him; and on every side, six tracks deep, sliding backward and forward, with clashings of couplers and squeals of hand brakes, were cars—more cars than .007 had dreamed of. There were oil cars, and hay cars, and stock cars full of lowing beasts, and ore cars, and potato cars with stovepipe ends sticking out in the middle; cold-storage and refrigerator cards dripping ice water on the tracks; ventilated fruit and milk cars; flatcars with truck wagons full of market stuff; flatcars loaded with reapers and binders, all red and green and gilt under the sizzling electric lights; flat cars piled high with strong-scented hides, pleasant hemlock plank, or bundles of shingles; flatcars creaking to the weight of thirty-ton castings, angle-irons, and rivet-boxes for some new bridge; and hundreds and hundreds of boxcars loaded, locked, and chalked. Men—hot and angry—crawled among and between and under the thousand wheels; men took flying jumps through his cab, when he halted for a moment; men sat on his pilot as he went forward, and on his tender as he returned; and regiments of men ran along the tops of the boxcars beside him, screwing down brakes, waving their arms, and shouting curious things.

He was pushed forward a foot at a time, whirled backwards, his rear drivers clinking and clanking, a quarter of a mile; jerked into a switch (yard switches are *very* stubby and unaccommodating), bunted into a Red D, or Merchants' Transport car, and, with no hint or knowledge of the weight behind him, started up anew. When his load was fairly on the move, three or four cars would be cut off, and .007 would bound forward, only to be held hiccuping on his brake. Then he would wait a few minutes, watching the whirled lanterns, deafened with the clang of the bells, giddy with the vision of the sliding cars, his brake-pump panting forty to the minute, his front coupler lying sideways on his cowcatcher, like a tired dog's tongue in his mouth, and the whole of him covered with half-burnt coal dust.

" 'Tain't so easy switching with a straight-backed tender," said his little friend of the roundhouse, bustling by at a trot. "But you're comin' on pretty fair. Ever seen a flyin' switch? No? Then watch me."

Pony was in charge of a dozen heavy flatcars. Suddenly he shot away from them with a sharp *whutt!* A switch opened in the shadows ahead; he turned up it like a rabbit, it snapped behind him, and the long line of twelve-foot-high lumber jolted on into the arms of a full-sized road-loco, who acknowledged receipt with a dry howl.

"My man's reckoned the smartest in the yard at that trick," he said, returning. "Gives me cold shivers when another fool tries it, though. That's where my short wheel-base comes in. Like as not you'd have your tender scraped off if *you* tried it."

.007 had no ambitions that way, and said so.

"No? Of course, this ain't your regular business, but say, don't you think it's interestin'? Have you seen the yardmaster? Well, he's the greatest man on earth, an' don't you forget it. When are we through? Why, kid, it's always like this, day *an'* night—Sundays and week-days. See that thirty-car freight slidin' in, four, no, five, tracks off? She's all mixed freight, sent here to be sorted out into straight trains. That's why we're cuttin' out the cars one by one." He gave a vigorous push to a westbound car as he spoke, and started back with a little snort of surprise, for the car was an old friend—an M.K.T. boxcar.

"Jack my drivers, but it's Homeless Kate! Why, Katie, ain't there *no* gettin' you back to your friends? There's forty chasers out for you from your road, if there's one. Who's holdin' you now?"

"Wish I knew," whimpered Homeless Kate. "I belong in Topeka, but I've bin to Cedar Rapids; I've bin to Winnipeg; I've bin to Newport News; I've bin all down the old Atlanta and West Point; an' I've bin to Buffalo. Maybe I'll fetch up at Haverstraw. I've only bin out ten months, but I'm homesick—I'm just achin' homesick."

"Try Chicago, Katie," said the switching-loco; and the battered old car lumbered down the track, jolting: "I want to be in Kansas when the sunflowers bloom."

"Yard's full o' Homeless Kates an' Wanderin' Willies," he explained to .007. "I knew an old Fitchburg flatcar out seventeen months; an' one of ours was gone fifteen 'fore ever we got track of her. Dunno quite how our men fix it. Swap around, I guess. Anyway, I've done *my* duty. She's on her way to Kansas, via Chicago; but I'll lay my next boilerful she'll be held there to wait consignee's convenience, and sent back to us with wheat in the fall."

Just then the Pittsburgh Consolidation passed, at the head of a dozen cars.

"I'm goin' home," he said proudly.

"Can't get all them twelve onto the flat. Break 'em in half, Dutchy!" cried Pony. But it was .007 who was backed down to the last six cars, and he nearly blew up with surprise when he found himself pushing them onto a huge ferryboat. He had never seen deep water before, and shivered as the flat drew away and left his bogies within six inches of the black, shiny tide.

After this he was hurried to the freight-house, where he saw the yardmaster, a smallish, white-faced man in shirt, trousers, and slippers, looking down upon a sea of trucks, a mob of bawling truckmen, and squadrons of backing, turning, sweating, spark-striking horses.

"That's shippers' carts loadin' onto the receivin' trucks," said the small engine reverently. "But *he* don't care. He lets 'em cuss. He's czar—king—boss! He says, 'Please,' and then they kneel down an' pray. There's three or four strings o' today's freight to be pulled before he can attend to *them*. When he waves his hand that way, things happen."

A string of loaded cars slid out down the track, and a string of empties took their place. Bales, crates, boxes, jars, carboys, frails, cases, and packages, flew into them from the freight-house as though the cars had been magnets and they iron filings.

"Ki-yah!" shrieked little Pony. "Ain't it great?"

A purple-faced truckman shouldered his way to the yardmaster, and shook his fist under his nose. The yardmaster never looked up from his bundle of freight receipts. He crooked his forefinger slightly, and a tall young man in a red shirt, lounging carelessly beside him, hit the truckman under the left ear, so that he dropped, quivering and clucking, on a hay bale.

"Eleven, seven, ninety-seven, L. Y. S.; fourteen ought ought three; nineteen thirteen; one one four; seventeen ought twenty-one M.B.; *and* the ten westbound. All straight except the two last. Cut 'em off at the junction. An' *that's* all right. Pull that string." The yardmaster, with mild blue eyes, looked out over the howling truckmen at the waters in the moonlight beyond, and hummed:

"All things bright and beautiful,
All creatures great and small,
All things wise and wonderful,
The Lawd God made them all!"

.007 moved the cars out and delivered them to the regular road-engine. He had never felt quite so limp in his life.

"Curious, ain't it?" said Pony, puffing, on the next track. "You an' me, if we got that man under our bumpers, we'd work him into red waste and not know what we'd done; but—up there—with the steam hummin' in his boiler that awful quiet way . . ."

"*I* know," said .007. "Makes me feel as if I'd dropped my fire an' was getting cold. He *is* the greatest man 'top of earth."

They were at the far north end of the yard now, under a switch tower, looking down on the four-track way of the main traffic. The Boston Compound was to haul .007's string of some faraway Northern junction over an indifferent roadbed, and she mourned aloud for the ninety-six-pound rails of the B. & A.

"You're young; you're young," she coughed. "You don't realize your responsibilities."

"Yes, he does," said Pony sharply; "but he don't lie down under 'em." Then, with a side-spurt of steam, exactly like a tough spitting: "There ain't more than fifteen thousand dollars' worth o' freight behind her anyway, and she carries on as if 'twere a hundred thousand—same as the Mogul's. Excuse me, madam, but you've the track. . . . She's stuck on a dead center again—bein' specially designed not to."

The Compound crawled across the tracks on a long slant, groaning horribly at each switch, and moving like a cow in a snowdrift. There was a little pause along the yard after her taillights had disappeared; switches locked crisply, and everyone seemed to be waiting.

"Now I'll show you something worth," said Pony. "When the Purple Emperor ain't on time, it's about time to amend the constitution. The first stroke of twelve is—"

"Boom!" went the clock in the big yard tower, and far away .007 heard a full vibrating *"Yah! Yah! Yah!"* A headlight twinkled on the horizon like a star, grew to an overpowering blaze, and whooped up the humming track to the roaring music of a happy giant's song:

"With a michnai—ghignai—shtingal! Yah! Yah! Yah!
Ein—zwei—drei, Mutter! Yah! Yah! Yah!
She climb upon der shteeple,
Und she frighten all der people,
Singin' michnai—ghignai—shtingal! Yah! Yah!"

The last defiant *"Yah! Yah!"* was delivered a mile and a half beyond the passenger depot; but .007 had caught one glimpse of the superb six-wheel coupled racing-locomotive, who hauled the pride and glory of the road—the gilt-edged Purple Emperor, the millionaires' southbound express, laying the miles over his shoulder as a man peels shavings from a soft board. The rest was a blur of maroon enamel, a bar of white light from the electrics in the cars, and a flicker of nickel-plated handrail on the rear platform.

"Ooh!" said .007.

"Seventy-five miles an hour these five miles. Baths, I've heard; barber's shop; ticker; and a library and the rest to match. Yes sir; seventy-five an hour! But he'll talk to you in the roundhouse just as democratic as I would. And I—cuss my wheel-base!—I'd kick clean off the track at half his gait. He's the Master of our Lodge. Cleans up at our house. I'll introduce you some day. He's worth knowin'! There ain't many can sing that song, either."

.007 was too full of emotions to answer. He did not hear a raging of telephone bells in the switch tower, nor the man as he leaned out and called to .007's engineer: "Got any steam?"

" 'Nough to run her a hundred mile out o' this, if I could," said the engineer, who belonged on the open road and hated switching.

"Then git! The Flying Freight's ditched forty mile out, with fifty rod o' track ploughed up. No. No one's hurt, but both tracks are blocked. Lucky the wreckin'-car an' derrick are this end of the yard. Crew'll be along in a minute. Hurry! You've the track."

"Well, I could jest kick my little sawed-off self," said Pony, as .007 was backed, with a bang, onto a grim and grimy car like a caboose, but full of tools—a flatcar and a derrick behind it. "Some folks are one thing, an' some are another; but *you're* in luck, kid. They push a wrecking-car. Now, don't get rattled. Your wheel-base will keep you on the track, and there ain't any curves worth mentionin'. Oh, say! Comanche told me there's one section o' saw-edged track that's liable to jounce ye a little. Fifteen an' a half out, *after* the grade at Jackson's crossin'. You'll know it by a farmhouse an' a windmill and five maples in the dooryard. Windmill's west o' the maples. An' there's an eighty-foot iron bridge in the middle o' that section with no guardrails. See you later. Luck!"

Before he knew well what had happened, .007 was flying up the track into the dumb dark world. Then fears of the night beset him. He remembered all he had ever heard of landslides, rain-piled boulders, blown trees, and strayed cattle; all that the Boston Compound had ever said of responsibility; and a great deal more that came out of his own head. With a very quavering voice he whistled for his first grade crossing (an event in the life of a locomotive), and his nerves were in no way restored by the sight of a frantic horse and a white-faced man in a buggy less than a yard from his right shoulder. Then he was sure he would jump the track; felt his flanges mounting the rail at every curve; knew that his first grade would make him lie down even as Comanche had done at the Newtons. He swept down the grade to Jackson's crossing, saw the windmill west of the maples, felt the badly laid rails spring under him, and sweated big drops all over his boiler. At each jarring bump he believed an axle had smashed; and he took the eighty-foot bridge without the guardrail as a hunted cat takes the top of a fence. Then a wet leaf stuck against the glass of his headlight, and threw a flying shadow on the track, so that he thought it was some little dancing animal that would feel soft if he ran over it; and anything soft underfoot frightens a locomotive as it does an elephant. But the men behind seemed quite calm.

The wrecking crew were climbing carelessly from the caboose to the tender—even jesting with the engineer, for he heard a shuffling of feet among the coal, and the snatch of a song, something like this:

"Oh, the Empire State must learn to wait,
And the Cannonball go hang,
When the westbound's ditched, and the toolcar's hitched,
And it's 'way for the Breakdown Gang (Ta-rara!),
'Way for the Breakdown Gang!"

"Say! Eustis knew what he was doin' when he designed this rig. She's a hummer. New, too."

"Snff! Phew! She *is* new. That ain't paint. That's—"

A burning pain shot through .007's right rear driver—a crippling, stinging pain.

"This," said .007 as he flew, "is a hotbox. Now I know what it means. I shall go to pieces, I guess. My first road run, too!"

"Het a bit, ain't she?" the fireman ventured to suggest to the engineer.

"She'll hold for all we want of her. We're there. Guess you chaps back had better climb into your car," said the engineer, his hands on the brake lever. "I've seen men snapped off—"

But the crew fled laughing. They had no wish to be jerked onto the track. The engineer half turned his wrist, and .007 found his drivers pinned firm.

"Now it's come!" said .007, as he yelled aloud and slid like a sleigh. For the moment he fancied that he would jerk bodily from off his underpinnings.

"That must be the emergency stop Pony guyed me about," he gasped, as soon as he could think. "Hotbox—emergency stop. They both hurt. But *now* I can talk back in the roundhouse."

He was halted, all hissing-hot, a few feet in the rear of what doctors would call a compound-comminuted car. His engineer was kneeling down among his drivers, but he did not call .007 his "Arab steed," nor cry over him, as the engineers did in the newspapers. He just bad-worded .007, and pulled yards of charred cotton-waste from about the axles, and hoped he might some day catch the idiot who had packed it. Nobody else attended to him, for Evans, the Mogul's engineer, a little cut about the head, but very angry, was exhibiting, by lantern light, the mangled corpse of a slim blue pig.

" 'Tweren't even a decent-sized hog," he said. " 'Twere a shoat."

"Dangerousest beasts they are," said one of the crew. "Get under the pilot an' sort o' twiddle ye off the track, don't they?"

"Don't they?" roared Evans, who was a redheaded Welshman. "You talk as if I was ditched by a hog every fool day o' the week. *I* ain't friends with all the cussed half-fed shoats in the state o' New York. No, indeed! Yes, this is him—an' look what he's done!"

It was not a bad night's work for one stray piglet. The Flying Freight seemed to have flown in every direction, for the Mogul had mounted the rails and run diagonally a few hundred feet from right to left, taking with him such cars as cared to follow. Some did not. They broke their couplers and lay down, while rear cars frolicked over them. In that game, they had plowed up and removed and twisted a good deal of the left-hand track. The Mogul himself had waddled into a cornfield, and there he knelt—fantastic wreaths of green twisted round his crank-pins; his pilot covered with solid clods of field, on which corn nodded drunkenly; his fire put out with dirt (Evans had done that as soon as he recovered his senses); and his broken headlight half full of half-burnt moths. His tender had thrown coal all over him, and he looked like a disreputable buffalo who had tried to wallow in a general store. For there lay scattered over the landscape, from the burst cars, typewriters, sewing machines, bicycles in crates, a consignment of silver-plated imported harness, French dresses and gloves, a dozen finely molded hardwood mantels, a fifteen-foot naphtha launch with a solid brass bedstead crumpled around her bows, a case of telescopes and microscopes, two coffins, a case of very best candies, some gilt-edged dairy produce, butter and eggs in an omelette, a broken box of expensive toys, and a few hundred other luxuries.

A camp of tramps hurried up from nowhere, and generously volunteered to help the crew. So the brakemen, armed with coupler pins, walked up and down on one side, and the freight conductor and the fireman patrolled the other with their hands in their hip pockets. A long-bearded man came out of a house beyond the cornfield, and told Evans that if the accident had happened a little later in the year, all his corn would have been burned, and accused Evans of carelessness. Then he ran away, for Evans was at his heels shrieking, " 'Twas his hog done it—his hog done it! Let me kill him! Let me kill him!" Then the wrecking crew laughed; and the farmer put his head out of a window and said that Evans was no gentleman.

But .007 was very sober. He had never seen a wreck before, and it frightened him. The crew still laughed, but they worked at the same time; and .007 forgot horror in amazement at the way they handled the Mogul freight. They dug round him with spades; they put ties in front of his wheels and jackscrews under him; they embraced him with the derrick-chain and tickled him with crowbars; while .007 was hitched onto wrecked cars and backed away till the knot broke or the cars rolled clear of the track. By dawn thirty or forty men were at work, replacing and ramming down the ties, gauging the rails and spiking them. By daylight all cars who could move had gone on in charge of another loco; the track was freed for traffic; and .007 had hauled old Mogul over a small pavement of ties, inch by inch, till his flanges bit the rail once more, and he settled down with a clank. But his spirit was broken, and his nerve was gone.

" 'Tweren't even a hog," he repeated dolefully. " 'Twere a shoat; and you—*you* of all of 'em—had to help me on."

"But how in the whole long road did it happen?" asked .007, sizzling with curiosity.

"Happen! It didn't happen! It just come! I sailed right on top of him around that last curve—thought he was a skunk. Yes; he was all as little as that. He hadn't more'n squealed once 'fore I felt my bogies lift (he'd rolled right under the pilot), an' I couldn't catch the track again to save me. Swiveled clean off, I was. Then I felt him sling himself along, all greasy, under my left leadin' driver, and—oh, boilers!—that mounted the rail. I heard my flanges zippin' along the ties, an' the next I knew I was playin' 'Sally, Sally Waters' in the corn, my tender shuckin' coal through my cab, an' Old Man Evans lyin' still an' bleedin' in front o' me. Shook? There ain't a stay or a bolt or a rivet in me that ain't sprung to glory somewhere."

"Umm!" said .007. "What d'you reckon you weigh?"

"Without these lumps o' dirt I'm all of a hundred thousand pound."

"And the shoat?"

"Eighty. Call him a hundred pounds at the outside. He's worth about four'n a half dollars. Ain't it awful? Ain't it enough to give you nervous prostration? Ain't it paralyzin'? Why, I come just around that curve—" And the Mogul told the tale again, for he was very badly shaken.

"Well, it's all in a day's run, I guess," said .007 soothingly; "an'—an' a cornfield's pretty soft fallin'."

"If it had bin a sixty-foot bridge, an' I could'a slid off into deep water, an' blown up an' killed both men, same as others have done, I wouldn't'a cared; but to be ditched by a shoat—an' you to help me out—in a cornfield—an' an old hayseed in his nightgown cussin' me like as if I was a sick truck-horse! . . . Oh, it's awful! Don't call me Mogul! I'm a sewin' machine. They'll guy my sandbox off in the yard."

And .007, his hotbox cooled and his experience vastly enlarged, hauled the Mogul freight slowly to the roundhouse.

"Hello, old man! Bin out all night, hain't ye?" said the irrepressible Pony, who had just come off duty. "Well, I must say you look it. Costly—perishable—fragile—immediate—that's you! Go to the shops, take them vine leaves out o' your hair, an' git 'em to play the hose on you."

"Leave him alone, Pony," said .007 severely, as he was swung onto the turntable, or I'll—"

"Didn't know the old granger was any special friend o' yours, kid. He wasn't overcivil to you last time I saw him."

"I know it; but I've seen a wreck since then, and it has about scared the paint off me. I ain't going to guy anyone as long as I steam—not when they're new to the business an' anxious to learn. And I'm not goin' to guy the old Mogul, either, though I did find him wreathed around with roastin'-ears. 'Twas a little bit of a shoat—not a hog—just a shoat, Pony—no bigger'n a lump of anthracite—I saw it—that made all the mess. Anybody can be ditched, I guess."

"Found that out already, have you? Well, that's a good beginnin'." It was the Purple Emperor, with his high, tight, plate-glass cab and green velvet cushion, waiting to be cleaned for his next day's fly.

"Let me make you two gen'lemen acquainted," said Pony. "This is our Purple Emperor, kid, whom you were admirin' and, I may say, envyin' last night. This is a new brother, Worshipful Sir, with most of his mileage ahead of him, but, so far as a serving-brother can, I'll answer for him."

"Happy to meet you," said the Purple Emperor, with a glance round the crowded roundhouse. "I guess there are enough of us here to form a full meetin'. Ahem! By virtue of the authority vested in me as Head of the Road, I hereby declare and pronounce Number .007 a full and accepted Brother of the Amalgamated Brotherhood of Locomotives, and as such, entitled to all shop, switch, track, tank, and roundhouse privileges throughout my jurisdiction, in the Degree of Superior Flyer, it bein' well known and credibly reported to me that our Brother has covered forty-one miles in thirty-nine minutes and a half on an errand of mercy to the afflicted. At a convenient time, I myself will communicate to you the Song and Signal of this Degree whereby you may be recognized in the darkest night. Take your stall, newly entered Brother among Locomotives!"

NOW, IN THE darkest night, even as the Purple Emperor said, if you will stand on the bridge across the freightyard, looking down upon the four-track way, at 2:30 A.M., neither before nor after, when the White Moth, that takes the overflow from the Purple Emperor, tears south with her seven vestibuled cream-white cars, you will hear, as the yard clock makes the half hour, a faraway sound like the bass of a violoncello, and then, a hundred feet to each word:

"With a michnai—ghignai—shtingal! Yah! Yah! Yah!
Ein—zwei—drei, Mutter! Yah! Yah! Yah!
She climb upon der shteeple,
Und she frighten all der people,
Singin' michnai—ghignai—shtingal! Yah! Yah!"

That is .007 covering his one hundred and fifty-six miles in two hundred and twenty-one minutes.

—1898

WIDE-OPEN THROTTLE

A. W. Somerville

"YOU AIN'T NEVER heard tell of Oil-Can Tommy Wilkins and High-Wheeled Mike Cassidy?" demanded Johnny Griswold, freight conductor.

"Not yet," I admitted.

"Kid, they was runners!" said Johnny. "What I mean, they'd take the bridle off and roll! They ate up bad track like you'd gobble hot beans! An' they hated each other. Ain't I ever told you this yarn?"

"Not yet," I repeated.

Johnny stoked his pipe. We struggled east out of Townley on a four-track artery, tons by the thousand of fresh foodstuffs for the hungry stomachs of the seaboard. Eggs, butter, green stuff, grapes, rolling east to the seaboard. Oranges from the Pacific, melons from the Rio Grande, bananas from the tropics, meat from the Western plains, carload after carload of perishable, Red Ball freight. From North and South and West these reefer cars came rolling into Townley, to be rammed to the cities of the East via the great steel highway through Lucas and Bottle Neck and Washburn.

"This was their stampin' ground"—said Johnny—"from Townley east to Lucas an' Bottle Neck an' Washburn. Double track in those days as far's Bottle Neck, an' then single track. Just dirt ballast, paperweight rails, an' rotten, wormy ties. Lucas was a grade crossing then with the Northern Central, an' it 'uz th' place where Oil-Can an' High-Wheeled fine'ly concluded their arguments an' their races.

"You don't hafta believe it, kid, but those two guys helped put this railroad on the map. They showed th' brass collars sumpin' about freight; in fac', you might say they pretty near give 'em a brand-new idea about freight. Th' first Red Ball cards ever printed come from Townley, an' th' first freezers ever carded Red Ball pulled outta here. Nobody believed that a full-tonnage freight train could be kept on a passenger-train schedule until Tom Wilkins an' Mike Cassidy opened up their eyes.

"They was runners, kid. Nobody, before or since, could keep th' butter spread like those boys. Either of 'em could'a handled fifty cars of eggs on a sixty-mile schedule, an' never bust a one! There'd be lotsa cold-storage plants starvin' to death today if there was more like 'em!"

The row between Wilkins and Cassidy began the first day they laid eyes on each other. Oil-Can came to the system from a dinky little logging outfit. High-Wheeled came from a standard-gauge railroad, immediately following a difference of opinion with an engine-house boss. They—Oil-Can and High-Wheeled—met in the master mechanic's office at Townley; both applied for jobs as engineers.

Cassidy was first to ask for a job, but Wilkins was shrewder and grabbed an application blank and filled it out. The written record was given precedence over the verbal application, and from that day on, Oil-Can Tommy rated one job ahead of High-Wheeled Mike on the call board. It galled the Irishman that a scissorbill from the backwoods, a man who had never handled engines other than wood-burning teakettles, should take precedence over a promoted engineer from a man-size railroad.

"You're a wise guy, ain't you?" sneered big Mike Cassidy as the two men left the office. "Come an' shove your application under my nose when I'm askin' for a job! Who ja think you are, you bloody woodchopper?"

"Listen, you!" replied the thick-chested Wilkins. "You quit your last outfit becuz they wouldn't give you seniority, an' this outfit gives a man seniority an' you crab about it. Run along before I rub your nose in the dirt!"

"Whose nose?" inquired Mr. Cassidy.

"Your nose," advised Mr. Wilkins, and socked him on the snozzle.

Mr. Wilkins and Mr. Cassidy tangled violently and enthusiastically. They knotted. They clouted with vigor. They gouged, they scrouged, they pummeled. Mr. Wilkins described a noble parabola complicated by a swan dive, having been on the receiving end of a roundhouse swing to the button.

He lit in a cloud of dust, but rose as a golf ball bounces and met the charging enemy with a haymaker labeled explosion. The aim of the two combatants appeared to be simultaneous extermination.

The master mechanic noted the disagreement from his window, brought a chair out on the office porch, seated himself comfortably, lit a poisonous stogie and proceeded to enjoy the break in the routine. The trainmaster heard the racket, got another chair, lit an equally evil stogie and also proceeded to enjoy the break in the routine. The two officials spoke amiably to each other for the first and last time in the annals of the railroad. The master mechanic bet on Cassidy, the trainmaster bet on Wilkins.

Mr. Wilkins and Mr. Cassidy extended themselves to the utmost, yet neither could accomplish anything really definite in the way of a victory. The immovable object met the irresistible force so many times that the audience became dizzy. It soon became obvious that even a moral victory for either warrior would be a most impossible arrangement. A long-drawn-out conclusion was well on the way.

"We better put a stop to it," said the master mechanic, "as soon as they get tired enough to be handled. I got two engines waitin' on 'em!"

"I've had two trains waitin' all mornin' on you," said the trainmaster unpleasantly and promptly.

"You better start sortin' cars," from the master mechanic unctuously. "I'd hate to stop a good fight just to prove you're still a liar."

The two officials squabbled raucously until an involuntary truce fell between High-Wheeled and Oil-Can. Flesh and blood had been taxed beyond exhaustion, and unconsciousness was about to merge with disintegration. It was a comparatively safe operation to declare an armistice, which the two officials accomplished by sitting on Mr. Wilkins and Mr. Cassidy. The battered pair were informed regretfully that the railroad had to run. The trainmaster had some cars he wanted moved; the master mechanic had two engines ready for service.

Despite overwhelming ocular evidence that both hogheads were in far better shape for a hospital cot than for service on the road, down they went to the engine house. The nose of High-Wheeled

Mike was not a feature but a pancake; his whole ensemble was indicative of a head-on collision with a large and animated Chinese dragon. The ears of Oil-Can Tommy flapped when the wind blew; he had more bumps than a horned toad; he was a sight to bring tears to the eyes of a wolf. They finally got their engines, after defying everyone in the roundhouse. To each was assigned a pilot, for neither knew the road. The trainmaster, by superhuman effort, only delayed them an hour while he made up the trains. They got their orders, or what were known as orders in those days.

It so happened that Cassidy got away first. He headed out on the south track, as his orders stated.

"We've got forty miles to go to Bottle Neck," the pilot informed the battered engineer. "You'll find the switch against you there."

"Yeah," said Cassidy, not much interested.

"If that man on the north track don't show by then," went on the guide, "we'll run around him. But if he's right on our tail, we'll have to let him go. The north track is the superior track."

"Why didn't they put us on the north track?" Mike asked.

"I dunno," was the answer, "unless that guy back there rates. Was he hired before you was?"

"We jes' talked that over," said Cassidy bitterly, between swollen lips.

The Irishman considered as they rolled along. He'd show this scissorbill, this splinter-pusher, this slob of a Wilkins!

He crabbed at the fireman. Steam, announced Mr. Cassidy, was what he wanted. "Put her on the peg, boy, and keep her on the peg! I like to hear her pop," said High-Wheeled, "and I like to watch her roll!"

The tallow pot bailed in the bituminous. Cassidy beat her out of steam, tried to knock the stack off. The tallow stuffed her full. Cassidy took the coal out of the firebox, through the flues, and up the stack as you'd pour salt from a shaker. The tallow leaned on his scoop and gave vent to short but highly expressive words.

"Do you wanta break my back, you Irish tramp?" beefed the shoveler.

Mr. Cassidy leaned down from his throne, annexed the loose-mouthed party with a hand like a clamshell bucket.

"Ye'll shut yer yap," High-Wheeled recommended. "I want nothin' outta you but work! Wur-r-rk! Jes' lemme hear one more dribble outta you an' I'll pinch you in half!" Mr. Cassidy shoved his lopsided, terrifying phiz up against the fireman's mug, and bawled: "I'm a little tired right now, stoopid, or I'd unravel you!" He pushed the man back toward the middle of the cab deck. "Warm that scoop, boy!"

The tallow warmed the scoop—warmed it vigorously. They went battering east over the dirt-ballasted track, throttle wide open, rolling from side to side giddily, pitching like a flipped nickel.

"You like to wheel 'em, don't you, brother?" contributed the pilot nervously.

"That's my name," said Mike Cassidy. "High-Wheeled—that's my name, friend."

The tallow bailed in the coal. Mr. Cassidy tried to knock the stack off. The pilot hung on as best he could.

"There's a crossing at Lucas!" finally shouted the guide. "You gotta approach under control, prepared to stop!" To put the matter lightly—very lightly indeed—the pilot was sore. Blankety-blank hoghead, didn't know the track, didn't know the road, didn't know a bloody thing except to widen out and roll. If he didn't break the train in half on a sag, he'd probably leave the rail on a bad joint. Blankety-blank hoghead! "You gotta cross Lucas under control! Ten miles an hour!"

"I'll watch for it," said Cassidy generously.

"You'll cross at ten miles an hour!" commanded the pilot.

"Zatso?" inquired Mike.

"Yeah, zatso!"

Mr. Cassidy annexed the pilot, using the same effective method employed previously on the tallow pot. And Mr. Cassidy regarded the pilot coldly from very close range, using his best eye.

"My delicate friend," quoth Mr. Cassidy, "you're the pilot on this mill, an' it's your job to tell me about the road. But don't start givin' me orders, becuz I don't like orders, an' I might—I don't say I would, ye understand—but I might beat the compound hell out of you. Becuz you don't look wide enough across the seat to be givin' me orders! What I want outta you," said Mr. Cassidy with great emphasis, "is advice!"

The pilot, without any hesitation, let it be known that he preferred to give advice to any other form of endeavor. Was it possible that Mr. Cassidy could have misunderstood him? Mr. Cassidy was laboring under a delusion. Undoubtedly Mr. Cassidy must be laboring under a delusion. Why, the pilot testified, he would no more think of giving orders to such a capable engineer than he would substitute soft coal for his favorite chewing tobacco.

They came roaring down on Lucas Crossover, thirty miles out of Townley, with the engine knocking her frame bolts loose and the butter spread behind them. "I advise," said the pilot carefully, "that you shut off and find out if your brakes will work."

"I'll take your advice," said High-Wheeled agreeably, and shut off and applied the straight air.

"They work," said the pilot, after moments of doubt.

"I figgered they would," said the engineer calmly.

They rumbled over the crossing. High-Wheeled climbed on top the coal bunker and looked behind. Far to the rear he made out the engine of one Oil-Can Tommy, and there was evidence to the effect that Mr. Wilkins's fireman was doing very little resting.

"He's a good stretch back," Cassidy informed his advisor. Mr. Cassidy beamed; he radiated good fellowship. "Now, as I understand this, if he don't show at Bottle Neck, we bend the rail and run around him."

"That's right," agreed the pilot. "The tower will either give you a highball or a stop signal. It's up to the towerman."

"If I get there in time to clear this guy behind," said the engineer, "I get the board, don't I?"

"Sure," said the pilot.

"Well, watch Mike leave that slob!"

Bottle Neck–bound, wide open, the fireman attaining perpetual motion. Bouncing like a pair of dice, wabbling like a drunken bum, ripping off the miles. Mr. Cassidy liked to wheel 'em.

They had a few miles left to go when the pilot screwed up sufficient courage to unclamp himself from a grab iron and look behind. What he saw caused his eyes to bulge; either of his blinkers could have been knocked off with a stick. Little more than a quarter mile behind was the engine of Oil-Can Tommy, smoking like a forest fire, weaving like a wiggle worm, creeping up behind them! The pilot cautiously advised the emperor of the situation. The emperor checked up personally. So did the fireman.

"That guy must like to wheel 'em, too!" said the tallow, grinning a very sweaty grin.

Cassidy boiled over. He raved. He took the spare scoop and did his best to empty the coal bunker.

Wilkins couldn't pass Cassidy, and Cassidy couldn't run around Wilkins. Another draw. High-Wheeled finally slapped on the air with a red board looking him in the eye, and Oil-Can Tommy rocketed past at sixty miles an hour. And as he passed the gentle Mr. Cassidy, Mr. Wilkins had the indelicacy to thumb his nose! Tut, tut! This gesture, strangely enough, upset Mr. Cassidy frightfully.

The feud between Oil-Can and High-Wheeled, instead of subsiding, grew with the years. It was probably the most cumulative feud that ever came down the railroad. Occasionally they had an opportunity to put on a dizzy race between Townley and Bottle Neck, and when this happened, half the railroad bet on the outcome. Once in a great while Cassidy, handicapped though he was by having the inferior track, made Bottle Neck in time to get a clear board, swing onto the main line, and run around his enemy. Maybe you think the Cassidy cohorts didn't toss a celebration! Once in a great while, also, Oil-Can would leave his rival tied to a post, would take the lead and hold the lead all the way to Bottle Neck, leaving the Irishman to waste good coal and further insult his overworked fireman. Maybe you think the Wilkins adherents didn't tear up lampposts and annoy the peace-loving taxpayers!

Usually, however, when they raced, it ended a draw. Just a dizzy race, twin engines, equal tonnage; two freight trains roaring down the double track, side by side, begging for trouble. It was a long-standing, dog-eared chestnut on the railroad that once Cassidy crossed over into the other's cab, that Wilkins knocked him back into his own gangway, that they fought till neither knew what the score was—and that Cassidy brought Wilkins's train in, and Wilkins herded Cassidy's! Chestnuts to the left-hand side, however, it is a fact that Oil-Can and High-Wheeled made the sport of kings about as interesting as a bruising game of bean bag.

Cassidy kept a record of all his runs; every time he crossed the division he would write down his time, his delays, every incident of the trip. In self-defense Wilkins adopted the same scheme, for High-Wheeled was forever bragging of his performances and belittling the runs made by Oil-Can. Competition, so to speak, was razor-edged. Thus, year after year, the records of these two runners accumulated—these two small black books—as much as any other single item, convinced the brass collars that freight could be handled, day in and day out, year in and year out, on passenger-train schedules. Once this fact became known and acknowledged, then shipments of perishables began to be sought rather than sidestepped.

Now, while Wilkins and Cassidy were conducting their little frolics, marring each other's beauty and running off various heats in their effort to make a bum out of Old Man Time, the necessity for providing for the transportation of perishables was slowly seeping into the brains of the railroad brass collars. In these long-ago years, when the Civil War was still fresh in the minds of everyone, such items as fruits and vegetables from afar were luxuries. Lemons, for instance, came all the way from Italy, and only the wealthy could afford them. Oranges, few in number, came by express from Florida to such cities as New York or Boston, and were worth their weight in gold. No perishable was ever shipped more than fifty or one hundred miles. The green stuff the cities consumed came from strictly neighboring truck farms; local slaughterhouses furnished all meats for any given community.

Interesting to note, one of the first commodities to utilize refrigeration in transit was beer. A car would be insulated with hair, the beer loaded in kegs, the ice shoveled over the tops of the kegs, the car locked. Crude, certainly, but a thousand miles meant nothing to a shipment of amber brew. About the time St. Louis beer began to undermine the state of Kansas, strawberries were successfully transported by means of reefer cars in the East. Coincident with the above, someone came to the conclusion that if heat could be kept out in the summertime, a car could be kept warm in the wintertime. Thus, by means of insulated cars, potatoes were brought over mountains and plains in zero weather.

The railroads began to wake up. Perishables, it appeared, could not only be shipped but a great deal of money could be made from the operation. Obviously there were two elements to contend with—proper refrigeration and fast movement. The refrigeration was simply a matter of insulated, well-built cars and facilities for icing. The fast movement of tonnage trains was a problem of operation.

The city of Townley was the focus of a tremendous, fertile valley. Townley Valley could produce a multitude of perishables—grapes, green stuff, dairy products—but there was no market. The cities of the East lay over the mountains.

"Look here," said the traffic department to the operating department; "suppose we make a stab at this perishable business. If it works out we can load the reefers East with grapes and green stuff and dairy products. We may have to haul a lot of empties back, but even at that the revenue on one carload of perishables is equal to two carloads of grain. Who knows, we might some day be making westbound shipments of these fancy lemons, or oranges, or even bananas!"

One day the trainmaster at Townley sought out Wilkins.

"Tom," he said, "I'd like to borrow your little black book. The one you keep your records in."

"Yeah," said Oil-Can. "What for?"

The trainmaster explained. The brass collars had asked that Mr. Wilkins and Mr. Cassidy allow them to see the record of their runs for the past several years. There was talk of shipping grapes from Townley East. Wilkins handed over his book; later that day Cassidy turned his in.

Two weeks later the trainmaster again approached Wilkins.

"Tom," he said, "we're gonna have a crack at this grape business. They're loading eight refrigerator cars now; you get four cars and your Irish sidekick gets four cars. Tonight."

"I been waitin' for this," said Oil-Can Tommy.

Mr. Cassidy and Mr. Wilkins met just prior to leaving time. They had words.

"Keep outta my way, you scissorbill," said High-Wheeled.

"When they see me pass you," sneered Oil-Can, "they'll think you're backin' up."

They were standing beside one of the new reefers, and on the side of this car was a card bearing the legend *Red Ball Fruit Express.*

"See that, Mister Woodchopper," said Cassidy, pointing. "Th' idee for that come outta my little book, see? I'm th' guy what showed 'em. Five hours from here to Washburn means twenty hours from here to the big onion. Don't you wish you had th' guts to wheel 'em like me?"

Wilkins laughed in his face.

"You shanty louse," he replied. "I'm th' guy they got th' dope from, not you! Say, I been waitin' years for this chance to show you up. Five hours, says you? You'll never smell my smoke."

They pulled out together on the double, but some ten miles out, Oil-Can pulled ahead, and from there all the way to Washburn, Cassidy never so much as glimpsed the markers on the caboose ahead. Oil-Can was a runner; he streaked across the division in four hours and forty minutes—twenty minutes less than the best time his rival had ever produced. High-Wheeled had trouble; he had to stop and set out a car with a bad brass. He made an astonishing run, however—two minutes more than a flat five hours.

Three nights later the two rivals faced east on the double track again with two tonnage trains, and eight cars behind each engine bore the Red Ball tag. They were three miles this side of Lucas with honors even, when a flue opened up on Oil-Can and he couldn't hold the pace. Cassidy ran around his enemy and burnt up the rail all the way to Washburn. His time that night, according to the train sheet, was four hours and forty-one minutes. He explained to all who would listen that he would have clipped another thirty minutes off had he not stopped to give Wilkins a tow!

The runs made by these two men carved eight hours from the temporary schedule. A tonnage freight train on a passenger-train schedule! Delivery of perishables guaranteed in New York the second morning out of Townley! And came that eventful night when two long drags, solid reefers, solid Red Ball cars, pointed out of Townley yard toward the eastern mountains.

"Let 'em race," the brass collars passed the word down the line. "The shippers get a kick out of it. Let 'em race as far as Bottle Neck, and the first man to the distant signal gets the main line. Arrange with the Northern Central to clear Lucas Crossover for us."

The traffic men sold the idea of the race to the brass collars. "Publicity," said the traffic department, "will put this perishable business over like a tent. Cash in on this chance! There isn't a taxpayer in Townley Valley who hasn't heard of Oil-Can Tommy and High-Wheeled Mike. Let the people of the big city in on this; let them know that the grapes, the tomatoes, the green stuff—every perishable out of Townley—was a stake in the greatest race ever staged by man! Twin bolts of smoky lightning! Wide-open throttle! Cash in—cash in!" So they did.

Just before leaving time Wilkins met Cassidy.

"I'm sick of your blab," said Oil-Can. "You've been shootin' off your mouth about me havin' th' north track, an' you've talked once too many times! I'll swap tracks with you, an' I'll throw mud in your eye from here to Bottle Neck!"

"Th' hell you will," said High-Wheeled Mike.

"Th' hell you won't," said Oil-Can Tommy.

They sought out the trainmaster.

"It don't make no dif'rence to me," declared that worthy, when informed of Wilkins's magnanimous offer. "You got about an hour. I don't care what you do."

So they swapped tracks. Oil-Can wanted the world to know just how matters stood.

"He can have th' best track." Mr. Wilkins, speaking very loudly. "Whadda I care for track? I can beat that fathead with no track at all!"

"Aw, shut up!" bawled High-Wheeled from his cab.

Mr. Cassidy was invited to descend and make Mr. Wilkins shut up. Mr. Cassidy descended with that intention foremost in his mind.

"An' were you speakin' to me?" inquired Mike politely.

"I wasn't speakin' to you," corrected Tom, "I was beggin' you."

"Now listen, boys," spoke up the master mechanic indignantly. "There's been enough of this foolishness. Upstairs, both of you!"

"Ye scissorbill," said Mike, closing in slowly, carefully, ponderously, "ye never had nothin' to eat before you come here but pine cones. Ye never knew there was such things as grapes. I'll give ye a lesson in manners."

"You lousy mick!" said Tom, circling, watching for an opening. "I was eatin' grapes before I could walk. I wasn't born in no shanty."

They came together, mauling. The master mechanic narrowly missed being sandwiched; he bawled for succor like a lost calf. Help arrived in the person of the trainmaster and half the population of Townley. It was something of a problem to separate Mr. Wilkins and Mr. Cassidy. They seemed to have an affinity for each other. Quite a few pounds of steam were used, several square yards of hide were mangled, not to mention the loss of a quart or so of blood, before the two warriors were pried apart and subdued.

"Neither of you," said the master mechanic bitterly, tenderly caressing a cracked shin, "has the brains of a jackass! Get on the job or get off the railroad!"

Upstairs went Oil-Can Tommy, shouting pleasant little reminders to his playmate. Upstairs went High-Wheeled Mike, shouting very consistent answers. And three minutes later two whistles screamed, two stacks retched, two trains lunged eastward toward the barrier mountains.

They had equal tonnage, twin engines, and both men were runners. Cassidy had the better track, but Oil-Can didn't give a hoot—a very weak hoot—for rough track. The best way to get over a bad stretch, said Mr. Wilkins, was to get over it fast. Thus were the bumps ironed out.

They left Townley even; five miles out, in open country, they were still neck and neck. Pilots even, gangways even, walking down the double, throttles wide open! Twin bolts of smoky lightning! The greatest race yet staged by man!

Each could see the other plainly in the glare from open fire-doors; at times the cab roofs all but scraped as the engines rolled on the rotten track. Cassidy saw Oil-Can pull on the throttle to make sure the cylinders were swallowing every ounce of steam he could cram into them, saw him wrestle the reverse bar back a notch, saw him step down to the deck to swing a scoop in unison with his fireman. Double shovel; let her pop, boy—let her pop! Let her roll, boy—let her roll! Come on, boy, we'll show this slob!

Cassidy yanked on his throttle, set the reverse bar back with one hand, joined his fireman. Double shovel; let her pop, boy—let her pop! Fill her belly and let her roll! Come on, boy, we'll show this scissorbill!

Thirty miles to Lucas Crossover—thirty long, rough miles. Thirty miles in thirty minutes by two battered, broken watches! Thirty minutes, thirty miles; they were on the crossing, rolling like two avalanches; they struck like two mammoth, uncontrolled projectiles!

The trainmaster might have prevented the accident. But he, like the two engine crews, had definite assurance from the Northern Central that the crossing would be clear. How was the trainmaster to guess that a Northern Central freight would pull a drawbar, break in two, and thus block the eastbound reefers?

Wilkins and Cassidy were on the decks of their respective engines,

"Double shovel; let her pop, boy—let her pop! Fill her belly and let her roll! Come on, boy, we'll show this scissorbill."

bailing in coal. Were they afraid of a fast crossing? Not this pair.

Neither looked. Neither of the firemen looked. The trainmaster was five cars back, working his way forward on High-Wheeled's train, fighting a tornado. He saw the boxcars block the crossing, he tried to reach the cab in time. He failed.

The two engines struck simultaneously, tremendously, awesomely. Cassidy's mill clung to the rail, shredding a boxcar like kindling, breaking timbers like matches. Wilkins's engine ripped through a car, rode up over a four-wheeled truck, slithered as though on skids, smashed into the side of the other engine, bounced crazily, and swapped end for end in midair. She was headed due west when she lit, and no less than nine freezers buried her. Cassidy's engine derailed when struck, but her drawbar broke and she rolled clear of the main pileup. She stripped herself clean as a varnished pole and the fountain and steam pipes broke in the cab.

The mess the reefers made is indescribable. They were everywhere. Out in open fields, rammed one within the other, smashed beyond recognition or repair. The crossover was ripped up by the roots; the two big pileups were at the crossover and at Wilkins's engine.

What few men there were for rescue work—mostly from the Northern Central—found Cassidy first. He was wandering around, dazed, his face wrecked, his clothing in ribbons. Cassidy's fireman had jumped as the engine derailed, and though badly hurt, was judged to be in luck. Cassidy had not jumped, and, though none knew at the time, was most decidedly out of luck.

With crowbars and axes the little gang of men went to work to get Wilkins out. He was alive, somewhere beneath them. They cut and pried, finally got to him. The tank was on his lap; there was no human way to get him out alive without the aid of a wrecker. His fireman was somewhere under the barrel of the engine; they couldn't even get to him. Wilkins had only a few moments of life left, and knew it.

"Hello, Tom," said Mike Cassidy.

"Why, hello, Mike," said Tom Wilkins.

They stared at each other in the gloom.

"I guess I oughta tell you," said Oil-Can after a moment. "I don't blame you, Mike, for bein' sore about me gettin' hired. I don't blame you for bein' sore." He stopped, summoned his waning strength. "It was a lousy trick. You should'a rated me on th' call board."

"Don't feel that way about it, Tom," croaked Mike dismally. "I was a rotten loser, see. That's all. I knowed all along you really rated me."

Neither spoke for a moment.

"Say, Mike, we've been knowin' each other eight years. We ain't never shook hands yet."

High-Wheeled fumbled about, found the one free hand of his old enemy—a big, knotty hand. They shook.

"I'm sorry." Wilkins's voice was very weak. " 'Twas a dirty Irish trick I played you, Mike."

"Hey?" demanded Mike.

"A shanty-Irish trick," said Oil-Can, and cashed in his chips.

Cassidy made sure that Wilkins was gone, then laboriously climbed out of the wreckage. He was growing weaker; he found it all but impossible to breathe. He stumbled away from the pileup, lay down in a clear space. The trainmaster found him.

"What's the matter, Mike?"

"They got my number," said Cassidy with difficulty.

"There'll be a relief train here in fifteen minutes," promised the official. "Stick it out."

"I swallered half the steam in the boiler," said High-Wheeled. "I got jammed up agin the fountain. I'm cooked."

The trainmaster knew what live steam does to a man's lungs.

"Anything I can do for you?"

"Naw," said High-Wheeled Mike. He grinned a wretched, tortured grin. "Dammit," he said, "I never could get ahead of that scissorbill Wilkins. Jes' now he had th' gall to up an' die first!"

JOHNNY GRISWOLD regarded his pipe intently. He lit a match very deliberately, puffed carefully.

"I never could get very sentimental over them two roughnecks gettin' bumped off, kid," he finally said. "Th' railroads in them days, you see, was man-killers. If you didn't want to take th' chances, you didn't have no right bein' in th' game." He puffed and puffed. "Some of them old-timers was tough," he concluded lamely.

We ripped past the tall tower at Bottle Neck, an eastbound avalanche of food. Through the open door at the end of the swaying caboose shone the dazzling, blue-white eye of a locomotive.

Slowly she overhauled us, came alongside on the parallel track. Her rods were blurred, her crosshead a streak of reflected light. Up she came, an inch at a time; I felt my scalp tingle, and there was a feeling like to bursting under my ribs. She was a sight to see.

"Who?" I shouted to Johnny.

"Oranges," from Johnny. "Oranges and melons."

We stood in the side door of the caboose, a few feet below the level of her cab deck. The roar of her passage was like a bombardment. The engineer was grinning, the fireman was standing in the gangway, watching us. We could have shaken hands by leaning out and stretching.

"Howdy, Mike!" shouted Johnny.

"Howdy, John!" I could read the engineer's lips.

Inch by inch the high-wheeled engine forged past us, then the tank, then the cars tagged Red Ball. A foot at a time, a car at a time. Johnny and I went back and sat on the locker.

"He may pass us," said Johnny, "an' again, he may not. Tom Wilkins's boy is pullin' us. That was Mike Cassidy's son that just went by. They're old men. Believe it or not," said Johnny flatly.

He smoked enthusiastically.

"Didja ever stop to think, kid," he spoke abruptly, "that it cost sixteen million bucks to put these four tracks down? Sixteen million iron men. An' all th' good it does is to save about thirty minutes' time on, f'rinstance, an orange from California. Sixteen million dollars, kid, to save thirty lousy minutes on an orange travelin' three thousand miles! Whatcha think about that?"

"What are you talking about?" I demanded.

"Whatcha think I'm talkin' about?" came back the skipper belligerently.

"You were talking about Oil-Can and High-Wheeled," I reminded him.

"I still am," announced Johnny loudly.

"What?" I inquired incredulously.

"Aw, hell!" exploded the skipper, rising angrily. "You couldn't see in front of the end of your nose!"

—1930

STANWICK'S BUSINESS

OWEN WISTER

I. AT THE BUREAU OF INFORMATION

I had, that hot afternoon, after all the preliminaries of ticket and baggage were serenely accomplished, a luxurious little margin of minutes before my train's departure to the New Jersey coast; so that amid the press and gasp of obviously desperate travelers in front of me at the Bureau of Information (where I merely wanted the new summer timetable) I stood reflecting how great among our lesser blessings it is to have enough time at a railway station—especially when the whole world, apparently, is (as I saw it put in a newspaper headline) "Rushing to Neptune's arms." I was making this comfortable reflection when Stanwick came up behind me and, in his inveterate way, apprised me of his imminence by giving me a slap on the back at which even the bystanders turned round. I never knew him to fail in this demonstration. Of course, I turned round myself; and my greeting to him was, I cannot choose but suspect, moderate. I've nothing against Stanwick; his good humor is sleepless, he is always eager to back his opinion with a bet, or to beat you at golf, tennis, billiards, and dominoes, or to swallow more food or drink than you can; his railroad stories command a thrilled and enormous public, and there is an egregious go to them—as there is to him. For he walks with an egregious go, and he sits down with an egregious go, and there's an egregious go about his shirt linen; and when I see him coming—though I've absolutely nothing against Stanwick—I am apt to speed from his approach. I hoped we weren't taking the same train this afternoon. But, as it immediately turned out, we were.

"Going to the shore?" he resounded at me, and told me, without waiting, that Salamis Grove was his point. "Best place in Jersey!" he declared heartily. "Best surf, best hotels, best sport. I've tried all the others—Charlemagne Beach, Sorrento Park, Sneak-box River, Squankawan, Shakespeare-by-the-Sea—the whole bunch of 'em, and give me Salamis. Where have you been lately?" he now asked, and again saved me the effort of speech by informing me that he had been to Scranton. "Yes. Been to Scranton. Getting material for big railroad wreck story—hot stuff!" Stanwick too frequently employs the distressing idiom of the hour. "Are you going to the shore? Salamis Park, in my opinion—"; but you need not hear Stanwick's further opinion of this spot. Indeed, I did not hear it myself. Stanwick (as you will doubtless have noticed) has the jovial monologue habit. Every fifty or sixty words he drops you a question, and goes immediately on with the monologue. Thus is created for him the illusion that he is hearing all your news, while at the same time he is spared the wear and tear of listening to you. But the jovial monologue habit spares you, also; I didn't learn Stanwick's opinions any more than he learned my destination; I merely said, "Ah-ha" and "Um-um" at him now and then, and thought of something else. He would soon ask me if I had read his new story, and I would say yes, because he would never stop long enough to find out the truth.

Still, my previous serenity was growing troubled. We were approaching the window of the Information Bureau at the usual speed of three inches a minute. A piebald cluster of us pressed forward together. Most of us carried chattels, and all of us glared with mournful, unanimous eyes at the young man in the Information window. A white lady with a basket of plums was asking him the best way to go to Skaneateles; next her a black clergyman from time to time very sadly inquired if the Tuskegee Convention special car started from this station; behind him a stumpy woman with emigrant hair poked a scrawl of paper up at everybody in general, and hoarsely ejaculated the word "*Smork*"; two Italians with shifting feet paid no heed to my freshly polished, defenseless shoes, while a stolid agriculturist pressed a live rooster against my heart. There were more of us; but now my body from neck to heels was latticed with trickling streams of sweat, and my endurance gave forth a sigh. I said: "All I want is a timetable to Shakespeare-by-the-Sea."

The young man in the window lifted his eye from the volume whence he was gradually extracting the route to Skaneateles. "Then you want Long Branch Division," he remarked, and he reached me the timetable.

Stanwick broke his monologue. "Long Branch? That's my train. Going pretty soon, isn't it?"

I told him, in nine minutes.

The young man lifted his eyes again and spoke in the cold voice of supremacy. "Four o'clock just gone. Next train 5:58 tomorrow morning."

"The dickens!" Stanwick cried out.

"It's nothing of the sort!" I proclaimed emphatically, for I don't like the cold voice of supremacy. "It goes at 4:09 by the Delaware Bridge, and I'm taking it myself."

The young man got a timetable and saw he was in error; then, with the chronic self-justification that distinguishes the inaccurate, he growled: "Well, she wasn't running *last* Monday. It's only 468's second trip this season."

"And they call this an Information Bureau!" exclaimed Stanwick.

"Certainly," I said. "Information for the young man. Thus the Pennsylvania road causes its patrons to educate its recruits."

"Does the Tuskegee Convention—?" began the clergyman mildly.

"Wait for your turn!" barked the young man.

"Smork," said the emigrant again; and on this we left the group.

We moved toward the newsstand, for I wished an afternoon paper. I was, however, not destined to read this.

"Seen my new story?" Stanwick inquired. "Out yesterday." He did not hear my hasty assent.

It would have been hard to escape seeing that such a tale existed; the magazine announced it flamboyantly all over the newsstand, with the author's name, and a red-and-blue locomotive upside down in a river. "Buy it for you," the author continued. "You can read it in the train and tell me how you like it." And he employed another idiom. "It's a peach!" he stated, while I murmured words of gratitude and anticipation not listened to by him. I now made out, in front of the books and periodicals which he was studying sourly, another literary acquaintance, a critic, whom Stanwick saw at the same time and instantly hailed with one of his claps on the back.

"Hello, Ortley! Going to the shore? I'm bound for Salamis Park. Best surf on the Jersey coast. Guess you've read my new story. You critic chaps have to keep up with—"

But Ortley, with acid imprudence, cut in: "I've had no time for your new story, and I'm taking the 4:09 to Plantagenet Harbor."

Stanwick clapped him again. "My train! Buy it for you. You'll read it on the way, and I'll get your expert testimony. Ha, ha! Expert testimony!" and he beckoned the news agent, shouting, "Two copies of the July *Colossus*."

Ortley made his favorite conservative gesture; he stroked the silken cord of his eyeglasses. But he and I and all quiet people are no match for Stanwick. I rather wondered at Ortley's attempting to cope with the author as he returned upon us, a *Colossus* in each hand, saying: "There you are—cost you nothing. Cost the public ten cents."

"And what, pray, does it cost the magazine?" inquired Ortley—a most foolish method of attack.

Stanwick did not even see it *was* an attack. "Oh, it's expensive for them. I don't know how much they pay for the illustrations, but they have to pay me fifty cents a word."

Ortley winced as the *Colossus* was thrust into his limp fingers, but he still attempted to cope. "I'm surprised you don't get more."

"Oh, I'm going to on the new series that the editor of Pan-America has arranged for. Let's get to the parlor car or there'll be no seats."

He forged onward through the crowd, through the gate; and Ortley, following helpless in his powerful wake, held my arm tight and hissed incessantly: "Fifty cents a word! Fifty cents! He shall have expert testimony."

II. EXPERT TESTIMONY

I always like to see what kind of locomotive is going to draw my train; especially on the Pennsylvania Railroad, where, in their struggle for motive power as efficient as the New York Central's, they have indefinitely multiplied their types of engine. I, accordingly, in the few minutes that remained after we had secured our seats, strolled along our short train from the parlor car in the rear to our locomotive. She was Number 853, class P, with a Belpaire boiler and medium drivers—sixty-eight inches at most—not much of a locomotive; the railroad has better than that, though I naturally abstained from any such tactless comment to the engineer. Evidently, before my arrival he had given them the air, the brake testing was over, and he was down now, out of the cab with his oil can.

"So they don't run an E on this train," I began to him.

Even in this his engineer's pride felt an inferential slight upon 853. "We get all the speed we want."

With that, spoken very quietly in a capable, independent voice, he continued his last preparations before the start.

I watched him drop some oil on the guides, and I put conciliation in my next attempt at talk. "Of course you do! Only they seem to be running E's on all their fast expresses: E's and L's."

To this, which called for no answer, he gave none. He was thirty-three, I suppose, with a face of marked seriousness, and he wore spectacles, something that I never before happened to notice an engineer wearing. But for a certain hammered, weather-beaten courage in his features, he might have passed for some Greek or History professor wearing inappropriate overalls.

Still I didn't give it up. "I suppose with this light train through a country like Jersey you can make any time you please?"

He finished oiling a crank-pin, and looked at me quietly and without encouragement. "We can generally get there," he remarked; and then his eye fell on the *Colossus* in my hand. He made a brushing gesture at it with his knuckles, and said: "They've hired a prize liar to write for them." And on my inquiring who, he explained: "There's a railroad story in that thing. The call boy had it in the roundhouse, and we took it away from him."

"You don't say so!" I exclaimed.

"Yes. We took last month's away from him, too. That one had an engineer putting on full speed to cross a weak bridge. The boy is intending to be a railroad man, and we don't care to have him grow up on matinée-girl trash like that."

He actually showed no interest in why I laughed so; he dropped some final drops of oil upon his locomotive. "The author," I now told him, "gets fifty cents a word for it."

And this did at last awake symptoms of some emotion in him. His eyes flashed through the spectacles, though I don't know what with. Anger, it may have been, but never amusement; at any rate, I had seen that his expression could change, which I had begun to doubt. Once more I was to have a proof of it, but that came later in our little journey. He now had much interest for me, while I—alas!—had none for him; he climbed actively into his cab without more notice of me, and made it impossible to ask him how an engineer should cross a weak bridge. I decidedly wished to know!—and how extremely Ortley would wish to know! When you are a boy, I reasoned, and you go skating, you always skate as fast as possible over those thin spots, denoted "tickly-benders." You break through if you don't. Why, then, should not a weak bridge . . . well, speculation couldn't help me; but what a close miss—and close misses are always the hardest to bear! I fairly grieved to think how near I had grazed possessing knowledge with which not merely to cope with Stanwick, but to slay him outright.

These thoughts had brought me back along the platform to the cars, and were broken by the voice of the newsboy coming to me out of the open windows.

His was a wandering voice, carrying its chant slowly through the train: "Nothing sold after leaving. Buy your reading matter now. *Colossus* for July, just out. Nothing sold after leaving."

I saw the conductor with his watch at the rear steps of the Pullman, his hand waved a sign, the air-whistle sounded forward in the cab, and our train got into faint motion. I mounted the steps nearest me, and passed on my way to the Pullman between the thick, luxuriant rows of hot passengers, the pink, damp foreheads, the shirt-sleeves, the bare necks, the fans. A sudden leaning motion of our train on one of the yard switches tilted me down upon the stout breast of a lady who was reading the *Colossus;* but after this I steered a straight course to my car and seat. My seat was not at all the kind that I wished to stay in; this forward half of the car was a sleeping-car (a singular arrangement for an afternoon journey of less than three hours, and a too-plain symptom of an economical use of old rolling stock designed for long Western runs); ladies, nurses, and children filled the sections, and I was glad to escape to the observation half of the car, where you could sit in a wicker chair, smoke, order a drink, and be out on the rear platform with a camp-stool, if you desired. Stanwick had the defenseless Ortley there already, with his *Colossus*, and he vigorously beckoned me to come and occupy the stool he had kept for me. I beckoned back through the big, clear window that I would stay where I was; upon which Stanwick came for me and jovially took me out.

"Ever so much better out here," he declared. "Fresh air, good view; bring the story along."

So there sat Ortley and myself on two camp-stools, each with a *Colossus*, and Stanwick owning both of us. We were now slowly leaving the West Philadelphia Station. For fresh air, in that gigantic railroad yard, we swallowed the smoke of generations of locomotives, and for view we saw these same locomotives, old and young, freight and passenger, and beyond them the flat, mediocre city. William Penn and his tower were blotted out in thick, black, Pennsylvania Railroad smoke.

"When you've finished that story," said Stanwick, "I'll tell you about my next one."

Words quite suddenly came from me: "At what speed should an engineer take his train over a weak bridge?"

"As slow as he can, of course. Why?"

The tunnel stopped me—the tunnel where the New York tracks go under those of the main line—and when we were out of its sulphurous fumes Stanwick was off with his monologue.

"Want to know the technical explanation? Well, it's simple. What kills a bridge is first, vibration, shaking, and then the drag on it—the drag, you see, of the engine's drivers catching the rails as they haul the train—and, of course, the parallelogram of forces is to be reckoned with most. Queer thing—you'd never think it—but you combine the gravity pull with the horizontal pull, and it's a worse strain than just the gravity alone, in spite of the diminished angle. Now, as your gravity pull is a fixed quantity, your point is to have as light a horizontal pull as you can. See? So the engineer shuts off for his bridge, slows down, and gets over it, if he can, on momentum alone."

I was happy to murmur that I "saw"; and, as Stanwick galloped forward with more monologue, I dimly did see; the parallelogram of forces waked in me college memories of freshman physics, intricate, chilling memories, which I hastened to banish in a more immediate wonder: Which was the barefaced one, Stanwick or the engineer? What possible motive had the engineer for making up for my benefit a story about a bridge which Stanwick had never told? Or could Stanwick be so brazen as to fabricate a whole false and impossible technical procedure when he knew the truth?

The sudden, wide vista from the Delaware Bridge roused me to the fact that we had left the Schuylkill and North Philadelphia behind us. I saw Ortley crossly reading the *Colossus,* I heard Stanwick still copiously discoursing about himself to me. "You see, I know about these things," he was saying. "I wasn't a railroad man ten years for nothing. Well, I won't keep you from my story any longer."

We had now swung off from the double-track Atlantic City road, and come into that seashore branch which passes through Mount Holly and Whitings on its way to Bay Head. I read Stanwick's title: "Old Irongrip's Last Signal."

"Got the material in California," Stanwick put in. "Happened in the tules during the '94 strike. But I don't want to interrupt you."

What did interrupt me was Jersey's fecund yellow loam, rising, as we swept through West Moorestown, in cloaking clouds, blinding my eyes, turning gritty the pages of my magazine.

"There's no use out here!" I said.

"It's better after this," said Stanwick; "but the sun's hot." And all three of us came in from the platform.

Stanwick's story began:

> "Let them dare," said Old Irongrip, as he turned his steel-gray eyes from the time board, and rested them with proud affection upon the blooming slip of a girl who had addressed him.

Yes, it was once more the egregious go, right in the first line; and I counted the pages to see how much of it there was going to be. I presently found that I had read nothing more, but was gazing emptily at the illustrations, which were plentiful, and just like photographs. To be just like photographs is the triumph of magazine art.

"Glad to see you, sir," said the conductor, an acquaintance of several summers in the train. He handed my return coupon back. "You got that, too?" he commented; then his hand made a brushing gesture at the *Colossus*. "Only one thing wrong with that story," and he laughed gaily.

Hope, at these words, stirred in my heart. "What's wrong?"

At his next words my heart leaped. "The printed matter. The illustrations are all right." He again laughed gaily.

His ticket duties took him away from me, but I sat happy; I would get things out of that conductor. We were only at Hainesport, the train was just picking up speed again after the bad S-curve and the drawbridge, Jersey corn and farm fields were not yet merging into Jersey sand and pines; oh, yes! there was plenty of time for that conductor to help me cope with Stanwick.

I now sped with haste through Old Irongrip's adventure, and by the time I had read the last words we were just reaching Whitings. At this melancholy junction a passenger got into our car and bellowed at everybody who would look at him, "I've waited an hour and nineteen minutes!" until somebody fiercely said: "That's nothing for Whitings," which rendered him silent. But I was grateful to him; the conductor had to return to our car for his ticket, and this produced a better arrangement than I had planned for Stanwick. Instead of seeking the conductor in one of the forward cars where he kept himself, I had him and his expert information comfortably in our midst.

Ortley had not finished Irongrip, Stanwick was sipping something with cracked ice that the porter had brought him, when I began on the conductor. We had seven or eight minutes before the stop at Tom's River would take him away from me, and I started my stratagem well. "Do you know, I rather like this story?" I frankly handed him the *Colossus*, open.

He held it, looking in it. "Well, the public seems to." His laugh interrupted him. "We railroad men—look here: now I suppose this caught you." He began to read aloud the final sentences, and at the words, and his skillfully blighting tone, all things happened as I wished; Ortley laid down his *Colossus* and Stanwick took the cracked-ice beverage from his lips. " 'Though he well knew what must come [read the conductor], he never stirred from his seat, never took his steady hand from the throttle as the locomotive made its fatal plunge through the trestles. And so they found faithful Old Irongrip, still holding that throttle, in the mud and slime. No; it was only his crushed, mortal clay that they found. Heaven had given the white signal to him, and his soul had an open track.' There!" said the conductor. "And the newsboy sells out his stock of that magazine, and a fat lady up front is crying over it right now. She don't know why they happened to find old what's-his-name—Eagletooth—"

"Irongrip," said Stanwick.

"Dead in his cab at the bottom of the river."

The train slowed, the conductor broke off abruptly; it was Tom's River.

"Oh, come back!" Ortley wailed.

"I'll get a chance," said the conductor, "after we leave Seaside Park."

Ortley elaborately congratulated Stanwick. "What luxury," he murmured, "to have one's tales appreciated by those they so accurately describe!"

Stanwick was all good humor: "That's all right! Do me the favor, when he comes, not to tell my name." He rose. "I want to see that lady cry. Come on, Ortley."

But the critic sat. "Thank you, I'll take the conductor's word for it."

"Nothing the matter with Ortley," Stanwick remarked to me as I went forward with him, "except that he doesn't get fifty cents a word. Now, where's that old lady?" We traversed two cars, and caught up with the conductor.

"I know her," I told Stanwick, and I took him toward the matron upon whose breast I had fallen.

"Yes, that's her," said the conductor. "Lord, lord, why the men are fooled by it, too!"

"You don't take these stories as hard as your engineer does," I said. And I related my experience.

"Well, he's taking all life with some emphasis just now," the conductor explained. "He had two hundred dollars in a building association, and it busted."

"That lady," said Stanwick, "has a strong, intelligent countenance."

I looked, and I could not contradict him. She was lending her *Colossus* to a neighbor, and a fragment of her words reached me. ". . . teach an ideal of duty. So much healthier than most fiction."

Something public in her voice struck me, and I touched the conductor's elbow. "Do you remember where she's going?"

"Temperance Heights," he replied. "Midsummer meeting is on."

I informed Stanwick of this as we turned back. "She will very likely lecture on your story," I said.

Ortley met us here. He hadn't been able to sit alone with his curiosity. "I have counted them," he bitterly said to me. "Seventeen passengers are reading that thing." And we returned to our wicker chairs at the rear.

"Well, I don't want to spoil your enjoyment," said the conductor—we were now running along the narrow sea-sand between the Atlantic surf and the great smooth blue inlet—"but the reason they found Old Eaglegrip in his cab was because he *hadn't time* to jump. That's the reason whenever you find an engineer dead in his cab. It ain't like a captain going down with his vessel. *He* stays to control his crew and get the passengers off. Engineers have nothing like that. When a smash is unavoidable the engineer has only one duty, and that's to save his life if he can, and so be ready to help the injured instead of adding to their number. When he has sounded his whistle, and shut off steam, and put on the emergency brake, he can do no more for his train, and his place is on firm ground if he can get there. Of course, if the cab happens to be the *safest* place, he stays there. Why," pursued the conductor, becoming humorous again, "if the Brotherhood was to catch an engineer with a sense of duty like Old Irontooth they'd suspend him till he got common sense! Why, to employ such a fool would be a *crime;* he'd be dangerous! He belongs in a lunatic asylum! But the newsboy sold his stock out, and I guess the writer of that story knows his business. He's not writing for us railroad folks." The train was slowing for the flag stop at Mantoloking, and the conductor left us.

It had not come out with a handsomeness equal to my hopes, equal to what the engineer, I felt, would have made of it if he, with his more emphatic view of life, could have given us his opinion of the story and its writer. The lighter-minded conductor had, with a sophistication that denoted his higher development, praised Stanwick's knowledge of the emotional public. Still, Stanwick might feel a trifle stung by the blast which laid bare his total perversion of railroad life, and knocked clean away the underpinning of his hero.

Ortley, I could see plainly, expected to triumph, and addressed the author with: "And what have you to say now?"

But Stanwick had by no means been stung; his good humor

gushed. "Say? Why, the conductor has said it all, and said it straight. I could have told him the duties of an engineer: I've been one myself. But I'm an author now, and I write for the sentimental million who don't want realism, but the unreal realistically described. Where's your melodrama in an engineer who jumps? Why, don't you know that the heroic engineer who dies with his engine is one of our biggest popular delusions? He's an ideal with all boys and women, and most men; and if I can make fifty cents a word out of him why should I go and bust him? I couldn't get five cents a word for an engineer who jumped."

"No matter," said Ortley; "the truth before everything."

"But why, Ortley?" I cried, for I was beginning to enjoy the critic. "Why destroy their ideal?"

Stanwick added: "Where's the harm for them to believe an engineer sticks to the throttle—so long as they're not going to be engineers?"

Ortley couldn't see it. "No good ever comes from fraud," he snarled.

Stanwick's good humor fairly bathed the critic. "Ortley, you are simply immense! Well, I must go get a look at those seventeen passengers reading about poor Old Irongrip."

This, however, was a feast not destined for his eyes.

III. AT THE Y-SWITCH

You must know that north of Bay Head Station the single track goes immediately upon a trestle across a brown Jersey pond, and then for a few curving yards to a crossroad where a flagman is. A little grove—a Jersey grove of little oaks, little pines, and thick, short foliage in general—hides from the engineer what's ahead until he has finished the curve and reached the grove, and he may be going pretty fast; for now he has a straight mile or so of double track to Point Pleasant. The grove lasts for perhaps two hundred yards to another road-crossing and a Y-switch. The engines of both the Pennsylvania and Jersey Central trains from New York, which end their run at Point Pleasant, come down to use this Y-switch, and any engine backing from it to the main track is invisible until too late; hence an engineer leaving Bay Head watches the flagman. This afternoon there happened to be the combination of one careless man and one imbecile.

We had left Bay Head, crossed the trestle, come to the grove, and Stanwick was on his feet to go watch his seventeen passengers, when three, four, five—I don't know how many—hoarse, horrible whistles screamed from our locomotive. I saw us all staring at each other, Stanwick shooting forward and catching something; then came a dead, heavy shock. It tipped my wicker chair, objects rattled on the floor, and next we were all stone-still, silent, with the little quiet, green Jersey grove outside, a rear vista of track, and a flagman staring, joined hurriedly by two more starers, and up front, somewhere, a crazy roar of steam in the silence. A voice outside said, "They're killed"; other voices added variously: "You can't see him. He's underneath. Did the fireman jump? No. The other one's all smashed, too. You can't see anything for the steam."

Somehow we inside were all saying: "You hurt? No. I just fell against the buffet. We're all right. This car's all right." On the track behind the observation platform, the conductor, with a very white face, was speaking: "What time do you make it, gentlemen? I make it fifty-six now." "Yes; fifty-six by mine," said a passenger. "We're due here at fifty-five," went on the conductor, still looking at his watch, and writing notes at the same time. "The responsibility for this must be fixed. He has no right to be here with me due. I must have some of your names, gentlemen." He got our names. "How did it occur?" somebody asked. "That Central engineer. Backing on our track and never sent a flag in front of him. So that man down at the road gives us a white flag. So we come right on and into it."

I had begun to live again. It is curious how one can stop living while the mere mechanical part—the heart, the lungs, the circulation—goes on. I don't think it is fright. I think it's surprise; but thoughts, will, attention, all cease, and one is no more than a vegetable. But now all parts of me were going again, and I was curious and anxious. I hoped we should find no awful disaster up ahead. Stanwick and Ortley and I were walking slowly along together, quite silent, by the empty, open windows of the train. All the passengers were down, grouping, dispersing, stopping; and each man and woman seemed to be relating aloud eagerly their sensations to everybody, and nobody listened to them. It was not bad, no passenger was hurt, we were not wrecked; yet even coming so near was sinister and numbing for the moment; that roar of steam seemed like a spout from the world of death that we had just not entered; the terrible, invisible forces around us were hissing at us in that steam.

And now rustic Jersey was scantily gathering to the show. Our crash had happened at the end of the grove, where the second road crossed and the Y-switch came in. Here stood a man with a string of fish, talking to a man with a wagon of vegetables. "I knowed what was comin' when I heard them whistles." And the vegetable man said, "I could'a told 'em it would happen with him backin' that way"; while two little girls, who had evidently been wading somewhere, beckoned wildly to three little boys running to us across a field. Other natives arrived, and all expressed the sentiment that they "could have told you so."

Meanwhile, here was the show, not very terrific to see. On the Y-switch, a few yards off, where we had knocked it, stood the delinquent Jersey Central locomotive. She was not hurt; only one corner of her tank was mashed in, and lifted a trifle from its frame. We had evidently struck that corner only, just as it was getting clear of us; if we had struck it full and square—well, never mind, that had not happened. Our locomotive was worse punished on this side—the engineer's side. Her firebox was ripped open, tank and cab somewhat crunched together in a kind of splintered hill of broken wood and bent metal, one feed pipe twisted to a corkscrew. From the gash in the firebox the dying steam was ebbing. Poor old 853 would not haul us any farther this day; and any human life that had been caught between cab and tender when they crushed together would now be crushed like them.

My eye fell on two very grimy men to whom the conductor was intimately talking, while the baggage master was offering to sponge the wrist of one from a bucket somebody had just hastily given him. He—why, he was the fireman, and the other grimy man was our serious engineer! The brakeman had just picked his unbroken spectacles from a bush.

"I remember throwing them before I jumped," said the engineer.

"I'm very glad you got out of it," I said to him.

"If we had jumped half a second later—" said the fireman.

"Yes," said the engineer. "I hadn't much time to lose."

The fireman's wrist was the single hurt between them, nor was it broken, but merely hard-struck by something. Washing would almost cure everything that was the matter with them. The engineer looked the worse. In jumping he had been thrown on the cinder ballast, and from numerous digs in his face and forehead blood trickled between a rich plaster of dust and ashes. His appearance was quite shocking, but it was mostly appearance.

I heard exclamations of pity and admiration behind me, and, turning, I beheld the Temperance Heights lady with clasped hands, gazing with passionate benevolence at the engineer. She then hastened away, and some new person offered a bucket to the unknowing object of her solicitude. He plunged his head in the water, after handing his spectacles to the conductor. I saw now that there was a tie of strong fellowship between these two, and that the conductor had been really somewhat unnerved by the narrow escape of his mate. I stood by and witnessed as thorough a ceremony of getting clean as ever I saw under conditions so limiting. Buckets were brought, one after the other, fresh and full, soap had appeared, and a second sponge, and from his plastered grime the engineer was beginning to emerge as does the dawn from night. The concern for him manifested by the conductor, the deference paid him plainly by the other train hands, his acceptance of it as a matter due his position—all this glimpse of disturbed railroad life held me on the spot, although I could plainly discern the Temperance Heights lady standing by the grove, and surrounded by a crowd of passengers whom she was addressing with vehemence. But one cannot be in two places at once, and I remained near the engineer.

"Is it hard to jump?" I presently ventured to ask him.

He gave me his quiet, expressionless look. "It comes easy when you have to."

I found myself desirous of expressing sympathy about the building association; but what business of mine was that? Stanwick was examining the locomotive's injuries with a technical eye. Ortley was looking at his watch.

"When shall we reach Plantagenet Harbor?" he inquired.

"Dear knows," said the conductor. "I've asked Point Pleasant for an engine, but the division ends there, and red tape may keep us any length of time."

"Why, they can *see* us!" protested Ortley, waving petulantly at Point Pleasant. "I can count three locomotives up there now."

"So can we all," replied the conductor; "but counting won't bring them."

"Good gracious!" Ortley snapped. "What a way to do things!" And he stepped about in a peppery manner.

I saw the conductor wink at the engineer, but this less frivolous person merely continued to wash, remarking, "That Central man will be out of a job."

"He'll claim it's only our second run," said the baggage master.

"Nothing excuses his sending no flag back," said the conductor. "And we ran all last season."

"The flagman down at the road could have stopped us, anyhow," I suggested.

"He's a Jersey flagman," observed the conductor.

Stanwick came from inspecting our wounded engine. "Pity she's so light," he said. "An E would have pounded them and stood the shock herself."

"No E could have acted better than she did," retorted the engineer promptly.

I thought I would go and listen to the Temperance Heights lady, but her exhortation must have been brief. She was approaching us, a little in advance of her recent audience, who seemed to recognize their leader in her. Well, their curiosity was going to be disappointed if they had come to stare at the engineer. His sensational grime and blood were gone, and there was nothing to see now but a recently-washed person with some scratches. He had, moreover, put on his spectacles, which still further removed from him the suggestion of disaster.

"I always think of them now," he said to the conductor. "Once I jumped with them on, and I thought the oculist would never get through with me."

The Temperance Heights lady here burst in upon our small group. "Old Irongrip is not dead," she began with trained but sincere rhapsody; "he is here with us. Sir"—she now directly addressed the engineer—"your deed has spoken to our hearts, and our hearts go out to you. Defying destruction, you sat at duty's post with your faithful hand on the throttle, and shed your blood to save us. Earth has no fitting reward for such deeds, but"—here she failed to keep her eloquence quite up—"accept these one hundred and ninety-seven dollars and fifty cents from the men and women who thank you for keeping your faithful hand on the throttle."

Amid general cheers from the passengers I heard explosive noises beside me. It was Stanwick enjoying himself. His story had splashed like a stone into our pool of humanity, and he was delightedly watching each widening ring of result. Ortley was purple with protest. He was incoherently yelping, "But he jumped, I tell you. He did. They all do," when I clapped my hand upon his mouth. "Don't you dare to destroy their ideal!" I fiercely commanded. Then, as the cheers ceased, I also addressed the engineer. "Here are two dollars and a half more, making two hundred—your loss in the building association is covered."

I have already mentioned that a second time came this afternoon when I saw that the engineer's features could express emotion. It was now. His spectacles stared; stupefaction dumbly opened his mouth.

"Do not try to speak," the Temperance Heights lady urged in romantic tones. "We know how weak you must feel. Good-bye." And she departed, taking with her the passengers, happy every one. Their ideal had been preserved.

"Oh, he ain't weak, but I am," observed the conductor. He retired to a fence and leaned against it.

The engineer now spoke. "What does all this mean?"

But from the fence the conductor said: "Put the money in your pants, and don't ask questions."

Well, the engineer obeyed the first part of that at once. I can't but think it was later made clear to him how Stanwick's story, already expensive for the *Colossus*, cost the passengers two extra hundred dollars.

It was two hours before help came to us, but I regret to chronicle that Ortley's outraged feelings had not calmed when he left us at Plantagenet Harbor. His last observation was, "Fifty cents a word!" in a voice of despair for the literature of his country.

As I got off at Shakespeare-by-the-Sea I asked Stanwick why this was not material for him, and his reply was convincing:

"This? Why, where's the melodrama? This would be satire, and the millions don't appreciate satire. Come see me at Salamis Grove."

I suppose he does know his business, as the conductor said.

—1904

NOTES ON THE AUTHORS

Harry Bedwell (1888–1955) has been called by railroad historian Frank Donovan "the last of the great railroad storytellers." Bedwell worked on the Pacific Electric Railway for many years and later, during World War II, for Southern Pacific. As a writer, he achieved national prominence in the early 1940s with his Eddie Sand stories published in *The Saturday Evening Post.* "Smart Boomer" is based on an experience Bedwell had at the age of nineteen, when, as a telegraph operator, he helped avert an impending collision. Bedwell mourned the passing of "boomers" such as his hero Eddie Sand. "They were a restless breed," he wrote, "and their lives were high adventure. They were the glory of railroading. They'd split their last dime with you, or bust your nose if they thought you needed it." Bedwell also published one novel, *The Boomer* (1942).

The short stories of **O. Henry**, born William Sydney Porter (1862–1910), are among the most popular in all of American literature. The genesis of "Holding Up a Train" is noteworthy. As a young man, Porter was accused of embezzling funds from the Austin, Texas, bank where he worked. He spent the next several years as a fugitive, eventually fleeing to Honduras, which had no extradition treaty with the United States. While in Honduras he met another American fugitive, the train robber Al Jennings. "Holding Up a Train" was a story Jennings told Porter. Jennings's and Porter's escapades in South America are fictionalized in Porter's *Cabbages and Kings* (1904).

Thomas Wolfe (1900–1938) is well-known as the author of the classic novels *Look Homeward Angel* (1929) and *You Can't Go Home Again* (1941), among others. "The Far and the Near" appeared in *From Death to Morning* (1935), a collection of stories which were originally part of his sprawling novel *Of Time and the River* (1935). Wolfe said of the pieces in *From Death to Morning* that they were "as good writing as I have ever done."

Douglass Welch's "Mrs. Union Station" was the most popular railroad story of the 1930s. Welch (1906–1968), a self-described "old time table reader from way back," is best-known as a journalist who twice received the Hearst Newspapers Award for humorous news reporting. His daily King Features Syndicate column, "The Squirrel Cage," ran for many years.

In 1899, **Frank Norris** (1870–1902) told his friends that his proposed Trilogy of the Wheat was "a big idea, the biggest I ever had." In three volumes, Norris hoped to dramatize the production, distribution, and consumption of an essential commodity. *The Octopus* (1901), the first volume of the trilogy, is often cited as America's greatest railroad novel. Norris based the story's climax on the Mussell Slough Affair of May 1880, an infamous gun battle between wheat growers in the San Joaquin Valley and agents hired by the Southern Pacific Railroad. Norris completed only one other volume of the trilogy, *The Pit* (1903). His 1899 novel *McTeague* ranks as a masterpiece of American naturalism.

Octavus Roy Cohen's Epic Peters was at one time the South's most famous porter—albeit unofficially. During the 1920s, Peters's adventures were immensely popular with the readers of the *Saturday Evening Post.* These stories survive as one of the few portraits of the life of a black railroad porter. Cohen was born in Charleston, South Carolina, in 1891, and is best-known for his mystery novels and stories. He died in 1959, the author of more than fifty books and plays.

Frank H. Spearman (b. 1859) was the most popular writer of the American Railroad School and is generally considered the best of those writers. Unlike Frank Packard and Cy Warman, Spearman never worked for a railroad. Spearman was a banker in western Nebraska with a gift for listening and near-perfect recall. His first stories were based on conversations with the railroad men who were his clients. He started writing railroad stories in 1895 and published the classic collection *Held for Orders* in 1901. His 1906 novel *Whispering Smith* was made into a film in 1915 and 1926. His other story collections include *The Daughter of the Magnate* (1903) and *The Nerve of Foley* (1901). Spearman received honorary doctorates from Notre Dame, Santa Clara, and Loyola. He died in Los Angeles in 1936.

Cy Warman (b. 1855) was a locomotive fireman and engineer on the Denver and Rio Grande Railroad. Warman's collections of stories, all closely based on his real-life Western experiences, include *Tales of an Engineer* (1895), *The Express Messenger* (1897), and *The Last Spike* (1906). Warman died in 1914 after years of service as the confidential assistant to Edson J. Chamberlin, president of the Grand Trunk, the Grand Trunk Pacific, and Central Vermont Railways. Railroad enthusiasts rank his stories with those of Frank H. Spearman and Frank L. Packard.

Jack London (1876–1916) believed that his success as a writer was largely due to the "training of my tramp days." Oddly, his fiction based on his hoboing years is not as successful as the autobiographical sketches found in *The Road* (1907), from which "Hoboes That Pass in the Night" is excerpted. He is best known as the author of *The Call of the Wild* (1903), *White Fang* (1906), and *Martin Eden* (1909).

As a novelist, poet, and essayist, **Christopher Morley** (1890–1957) was an important member of the American literati from the 1920s to the 1950s. His well-known novels include *The Haunted Bookshop* (1919) and *Kitty Foyle* (1939). Morley's personal collection of railroad literature, housed at The University of Texas's Harry Ransom Center, testifies to his fascination with the rails.

Frank L. Packard (1877–1942) was one of America's preeminent writers of railroad fiction. Born of American parents in Montreal, Packard was educated at McGill University and at the University of Liège. His work in the Canadian Pacific shops provided the background for his three excellent books of short stories—*On the Iron at Big Cloud* (1911), *Running Special* (1925), and *The Night Operator* (1919). His son, L. H. Packard, says that his father thought "The Night Operator" was his best story—a "corker" as he put it.

Rudyard Kipling (1865–1936) wrote ".007" during his four-year stay in Brattleboro, Vermont, from 1893 to 1896. Many railroad buffs consider ".007" the best railroad story ever written. While researching Kipling's life, biographer Angus Wilson said he heard the story praised by railway men and that he "received a letter from a train driver stressing the value of this part of Kipling's work."

A. W. Somerville was a prolific and popular writer of railroad fiction in the late 1920s and early 1930s. He published seventeen railroad stories in the *Saturday Evening Post* between 1927 and 1931, and when he stopped contributing to the *Post*, his readers demanded more stories. Somerville was born into a railroad family in 1900 (his father worked for the Burlington); Somerville himself began his railroad career in Marshall, Texas, on the Texas and Pacific. Throughout his career he was classed as a machinist.

Owen Wister (1860–1938), author of *The Virginian: A Horseman of the Plains* (1902), is often credited with having written the first western. Raised in a prosperous Pennsylvania family and educated in Europe and at Harvard Law School, Wister probably would have never come to know the West had he not been sent there in 1885 for health reasons. He became enchanted by America's remaining frontier and soon aspired to be a "Kipling saving the sage-brush for American literature." Wister wrote more than sixty short stories, almost all set out west; "Stanwick's Business" is one of his few "Easterns."